MW00877516

Knight of the Empress

Book 2 in the
Anarchy Series
By
Griff Hosker

Contents

Knight of the Empress

Published by Sword Books Ltd 2015
Copyright © Griff Hosker First Edition

A CIP catalogue record for this title is available from the British Library.

Cover by Design for Writers

Part 1 Matilda

Chapter 1

Caen 1122

We barely had time to tend to our wounds when the King sent for me. He had only raised the siege the previous day and already the energetic monarch was busy planning his next moves. I was with Edward, a knight who now served me. Harold, my squire, was also there, repairing my armour which had been damaged by Richard, a traitorous knight who had left my service and tried to kill me. When you served King Henry you had little time to reflect on life. I had almost been killed and now I was summoned to serve him once more. The King's messenger stood anxiously watching as I left instructions for my conroi.

"I do not know when we will have to be ready to move, Edward. Let us assume it is to be soon. Have the weapons sharpened and the horses groomed. It would be better to be prepared."

"My lord, the King awaits you!"

I glared at the servant who quailed before my stare. I had served Emperors. He backed away from me. I needed to give my instructions to Edward.

"What of Sir Richard, my lord? Do you wish me to send Dick to find his trail?"

"We will deal with that snake in due course." I doubted that even Dick, one of the archers we had found in the forests of England, would find one knight amongst the hundreds who had fled before the King. "Oh, and make sure the saddles and bridles are in working order. They have a smith here. It would be as well to use him." I turned to the messenger, smiling. "And now we can leave."

I was led to the large hall in this fortress of Caen. King Henry had arrived just in time. The forces of Count Fulk of Anjou had been about to pour over the walls when the King had reached us. The castle was now filled with knights such as myself. Each of us had fulfilled our obligations and brought a conroi to fight for our lord. I wondered why I alone had been summoned.

When I reached the hall, there was just King Henry and his illegitimate son, Robert of Caen, Earl of Gloucester. The King gave me a thin smile as I entered. "You were right about de Mamers. His son confessed to all." I looked at the King expectantly. I had killed his father and brought Geoffrey de Mamers to Normandy so that he could be questioned. "Oh, he is still alive. He is to be a guest of ours for a while. He may be a useful trade; if not then we will drop him into the sea." King Henry had not achieved what he had by being merciful. His brother still languished in the Tower. "My son here has told me of your skill in battle. Many of my knights are fine warriors but they cannot think. You, apparently, can do both."

"I was trained by the best knights in Constantinople."

"Hmm. Now I asked you, when I arrived, to protect my daughter, the Empress. You must have thought me a foolish, doting father for she would be safe within these walls." I said nothing for any answer could have resulted in a punishment. "The fact is that she is to return to her husband, the Emperor. He is at the castle of Regensburg on the Rhine. When she leaves here then you and your men will escort her safely back to her husband, to her home in Germany."

My heart soared at the thought of being with that lovely creature but, at the same time, I was afraid of the responsibility. I had travelled from Genoa to Caen and knew how dangerous travel could be. She was not just the daughter of a King; she was the wife of an Emperor! "My liege, what of her own escort? Surely locals would be better suited to such a task."

"Are you refusing a request from your King?"

"No, your majesty. I am not certain that I am up to the task."

He relaxed a little. "That is for me to decide. My son here assures me that you are. Your problem will be finding a route which does not bring my daughter into danger from my enemies." He drank some of the wine he had been nursing. "It is not just Count Fulk who regards me as an enemy. Charles, the Count of Flanders is an implacable foe, too, and Louis of France would love to have a hostage whom he could use to wrest lands from me." This was getting better and better. I not only had to escort her I had to do so while negotiating a maze!

"The Empress has two knights assigned to her by the Emperor and they each have five men at arms. With your men, she should be well protected." The Earl of Gloucester was trying to be helpful but this also made things worse.

"When we are on the road, who makes the decisions?"

King Henry looked up. "Why you do, of course! They are just bodyguards after all!"

I sighed; this was not going to be easy. "And when will we be leaving?"

"Not for some days. We have a treaty to negotiate with Count Fulk and I do not wish to give him the chance to kidnap her and use her as a means to manipulate me. Get to know her. She is young and you are her age. She is most dear to me. I have lost my son and heir and until my wife gives birth then she is the only one to whom I can leave England."

I began to see politics at work here. This was the woman who shared the throne of the Emperor. If she was Henry's heiress then she would be able to inherit England, Normandy and part of Wales. I could almost feel the weight on my shoulders already. "And when I have safely delivered her, do I return here?"

"No, when our business with Fulk is concluded I will release my knights. You may return to Norton. You will have fulfilled your obligations." He looked up at Robert. "And now we had better make arrangements to meet with Fulk and discuss terms."

I was dismissed. Poor Robert gave me an apologetic shrug as I departed. Edward and Harold, my squire, awaited me. I knew that they must have been aware of my moods lately. They saw my black look and remained silent. After I had quaffed a beaker of wine I snapped, "We are to escort the Empress back to the Emperor." It was not them I was angry with it was the situation. How could a handful of men escort an Empress through such danger?

"When?"

"After the negotiations with Fulk. The good news is that we get to go home after that. We return to England."

Edward shook his head, "That is not good news my lord. I was a hired warrior for many years. You become richer in such wars. We never mind peace but we like to do some fighting first. There is profit in fighting; especially if you are good. We received no ransom from the de Mamers boy and the knights we slew were outside the walls. We need profit from this journey."

I had not thought of that. "Is that the way life works?" They nodded. "And the manors, at home?"

"I am sorry to disillusion you Baron, but Norton and Stockton are poor manors both. They do not produce wheat. You can eke out a living but you cannot live well. If your father had not brought so much gold from Constantinople then you would not have had the coin to pay your masons. I know not how much remains but when that runs out you will have to find another way to subsidise your manors."

"And we will not have the opportunity to do so whilst escorting the Empress."

He shook his head, "No and it will cost us money to do so."

"Cost us? How?"

"We will have to buy food, lodgings and stables to wherever she is going and then back to the coast. Then we will have to pay for a ship to sail home. I hope you have coin with you sir or else we have to sell something."

This was becoming more depressing with every utterance. "Now I see why Richard left me." I shook my head. "Perhaps you made a mistake in joining me, Edward."

He laughed, "Do not worry sir. My men and I have been through hard times before. When we get home, we can make more money."

"By raiding?"

"By raiding. De Brus has been cut off. The King will let you raid his lands whenever you choose."

"But they are poor lands."

"Not the ones south of the river at Guisborough. And then there are the Scots. They are poor warriors but they have cattle and we can always sell those."

He thought to cheer me up but he was making me feel worse. Was I to be a cattle thief? I was a knight. My father had enjoyed a reputation for honour. He would never have been a cattle thief. What would the last of my father's retainers think of me? I shuddered to think of them looking down on me.

A messenger came to the door. "Baron Norton, the Empress wishes to see you. If you would follow me."

He left, expecting me to follow him. This too was becoming tiresome. I did not leave Constantinople to be ordered around like a servant. As much as I wanted to be with the Empress I had the responsibility of her safety in my mind. As I walked the corridors I thought of just abandoning everything and returning to the east. I owed nothing to Norton save that my father's body lay there. There were Crusader kingdoms now and English knights were much sought after. I could take my conroi and enjoy a pampered existence in a warm land with fine food and wine. The thought made me smile so that, as I entered the antechamber of the Empress, I was smiling.

"I am pleased that someone is happy, Baron Norton."

I bowed for I was in the company of an Empress. "I am sorry, Empress Matilda, I was thinking of my life in the east when I was growing up."

She laughed and I looked up to see a beautiful young woman. "Do not apologise for being happy. It is a welcome change in this gloomy castle with such serious-faced men." She pointed to a chair, "Sit!" I felt like a hound but I obeyed anyway. She waved an imperious hand at the hovering servants, "Leave us. I will summon you if I need you."

And then we were alone. I wondered why she had sent the others away. She stood and went to the door. After glancing along the corridor, she returned to her seat. I watched her as she moved. She was a slight woman; I almost thought of her as a girl for she looked so thin and waif-like. In those days, she wore her hair long, hanging down her back. I soon came to realise that the style of her hair reflected her moods. When it was tied back and piled upon her head, as she wore it when with the Emperor, then she was like her hair, tight and unhappy. The hair hanging down was a sign that she felt free and more comfortable.

"You are to be my escort back to my husband in Germany. My father told me."

Something in her voice warned me that this was not going to be straight forward. "He told me it would be Regensburg, Empress, but it matters not to me where in Germany for I do not know the land or the people."

She laughed again. I learned that when she laughed she was showing the real Matilda. I discovered that it was a mark of the trust she had in me. "I asked for you, Alfraed of Norton, as my escort and guard. Did you know that?"

I was genuinely shocked. "No, I did not. May I ask why?" I added, "It is an honour, of course…"

Laughing she stood and went to the table to pour two goblets of wine. "Your honesty is one reason. My half-brother told me that he had never known you lie and that there was neither a dishonest nor a dishonourable bone in your body."

"I like your brother."

She handed me my goblet, "So do I. He is the one I trust the most in this castle and in my homeland." She raised her goblet, "I hope that I can trust you too."

I toasted her back, "I swear that I will not let you down and I will guard you with my life."

"That is the other thing I heard of you. That you are wonderfully old fashioned. Oaths mean something to you."

I knew what she meant for as I had discovered, there were many who broke oaths as easily as bread. "It was the way I was brought up. My father had been a Housecarl of Harold Godwinson." I was beginning to relax, "But you have your own German guards. Why do you need me and my men?"

She leaned forward, "Your name is Alfraed, is it not?" I nodded. "I shall call you Alfraed. The two Teutons who came with me, I do not trust those men. When I know you better I shall explain why but I asked for a knight, Norman or English to protect me because I fear for my life. My brother said your blade was as quick as any and you have the finest archers and men at arms in England. He thinks highly of you." She looked suddenly sad and vulnerable. "It is lonely in my palace. I have a fine castle and beautiful home but I am alone."

"Do you not have women to serve you?" Even as I said it I felt guilty for poor Adela and Faren had none at home.

"I have but they are not Norman. I live amongst Germans and they are like their language, they are harsh. I miss the poetry of Normandy." She ran her finger around the edge of her goblet. "My brother said that it was not only your blade which was quick. You have wit too."

I smiled, "That is kind of him to say so."

"He was not flattering you. He meant it. He said that you and your men were all worthy warriors. That is why I asked for you."

There was a knock at the door. A servant put his head around. "Empress, it is Lothar and Konrad. They are coming here."

Her face fell. "My Teutonic bodyguards." She sighed. "I suppose we will have to meet with them but," she took my hand, "I am now content knowing that you have sworn to protect me."

Her touch sent tingles along my arm and I found myself smiling. It was not the best expression to have upon my face when the two Teutons walked in. Lothar and Konrad were not tall knights but they were broad. They both wore the full-length mail shirt which came below their knees. It contrasted with the fine tunic I wore for we were inside a castle and there was little likelihood of fighting. They had their long swords strapped to their baldrics. Both had the moustache and beards favoured by the knights from further east. One had a scar which ran from below his eye and which seemed to melt into the moustache. It gave a strange permanent half-smile which was ironical as Konrad did not have any humour in his body. They both gave me a contemptuous look as I stood.

"Lothar, Konrad, this is Baron Alfraed of Norton. He and his conroi will be escorting us home when my father allows us to leave."

I saw a look exchanged between them. Their English was crude at best. "We need no Normans!"

"Then it is as well that I am English and not Norman." I smiled broadly. I learned that this just irritated them. Once I discovered that I smiled ever more. The Empress held her hand over her face to disguise her expression. She too was laughing. The King had told me I was in charge. Before I had met them, I had thought to defer to them but now I took the bull by the horns. "When King Henry gives us permission to leave then I will let you know. It has been good to meet you. I daresay we will get to know one another on the road back to Regensburg." I gave a slight bow to the Empress and then, impulsively lifted her hand and kissed the back of it. "It will be an honour to serve you." I stood and looked at the two Germans. "And to protect your life with my own." If Matilda feared her bodyguards then I was letting them know that they would have to go through me to get to her. Their eyes narrowed and, although they said not a word, I saw pure hatred on their faces. I would need my men to keep their eyes upon my back.

Edward saw me smiling as I entered the stables. He and Harold were helping the other men at arms to groom the horses. "From your smile, I take it that we are going home after all."

"No, Edward, I fear that we will have to endure a journey to Regensburg with the Empress. And the Teutons who come with us are as unpleasant a pair as you are ever likely to meet."

He spread his arms in exasperation. "Then why in God's name are you happy, my lord?"

I gestured for the two of them to join me. Once we were away from curious ears I said, "Because this promises to be an interesting journey. The Germans are not to be trusted." Their eyes widened. "Do not tell the men yet but make them aware that they need to keep their eyes and ears open." Edward and Harold nodded. I could trust both of them. "And Edward, I want you and Harold to go into the town later and see if you can get another sumpter or two. With the fighting being over they have come down in price. I fear we may need them."

"Do we have enough coin?"

I nodded. "And I will work out a way to get more."

Considering how depressing the events of the morning had been I felt remarkably happy. Part of it was the Empress; she was hard to refuse but more than that it was the thought that I was doing something of which my father would have approved. That, to me, was more important than anything else.

Chapter 2

We left ten days after the meeting with the Empress. Over those ten days, I discovered, through conversations with Robert and Matilda, the reason for the visit of the Empress. I had to piece it together from the two of them but it seemed that Henry wanted the support of the Emperor. He had his eyes on Flanders. Anjou was too large a mouthful for the son of the Conqueror but he had his father's appetite for land. Anjou would be his but it would take subtlety. It explained why Matilda had arrived without the entourage of an Empress. She was there as Henry's daughter. When I discovered this, I felt much better. I understood such plotting; it was Byzantine. King Henry would use anyone to achieve his ends. He had remarried recently in the hope of fathering another legitimate male heir to the throne.

Edward and Harold had managed to acquire more sumpters. It meant that all of my men at arms could ride and we had four horses for our equipment. The two Germans only had enough horses for six of their men and the two of them cast envious glances at our mounts. I had seen little of them since that first acrimonious meeting. I had still to bring up the thorny issue of command. It was not that I baulked at a confrontation with them but I preferred it to be on the road. There I would have the advantage of all of my men around me. If I had to then I would abandon the Germans; nothing would get in the way of my mission.

I had seen Matilda each day. I was obeying the King's instructions; I was getting to know her. When we were in company she spoke of me as Baron but when alone it was 'Alfraed'. It was as though she was two different people: The Empress and the vulnerable young woman. She had told me why she feared the two Germans. I had thought, at first, that her husband wished her ill as she had yet to conceive but the Germans, it seemed, had another paymaster. She could not determine who but she felt at risk. I would have to find out who wished her harm.

She said farewell to her father while I spoke with Robert, Earl of Gloucester. "Watch over my little sister, Alfraed. We have different mothers but she is as dear to me as though we had the same." He slipped me a purse of gold. "Here is some recompense for you. You may need it on the journey." I nodded, "And watch those Germans. Like my sister I do not trust them."

Once on the road, I set the precedent of riding next to the Empress with Edward and Alan ahead of us and Harold and Wulfric behind. With my archers as scouts, the Germans had little choice but to follow behind. The rest of Edward's men at arms brought up the rear with the horses. The Germans were trapped. They could attempt no treachery in such a position.

We had been on the road but half a day when Matilda said, "Baron, I have to tell you that we are not going to Regensburg as we said in Caen. We are going to Worms."

It did not matter overmuch to me, in fact, Worms was closer but I was curious. "Why the deception? Did you not trust me?"

She had the good grace to blush, "When your father is Henry and you are Empress you give away as little as possible. Forgive me. I could not risk word leaking out of our real destination. I know that we have to travel on the same road but the lands closer to Regensburg are easier for an ambush. We could be waylaid and captured there."

"The Empress of the Holy Roman Empire?"

She nodded, "It is why I came west in disguise."

"I do not understand why you took such a risk. If it is a dangerous road then why come all this way?"

She lowered her voice, "I came with a message from my husband for my father. You need not know the content of the message but I am the only one they can both trust. It is a burden I must bear alone."

"Then why did he not send better guards?" I jerked my head in the direction of the Teutons.

"I had four Swabian knights when I set off. They were loyal to me. When we reached Nancy, they ate some bad fish and we had to leave them there to recover."

Suddenly everything became clear. "You had a larger escort then?"

"We did. These two were the only knights not affected by the bad fish."

"That seems a little suspicious." My voice was also almost a whisper.

"That was when I began to fear for my life."

"And the men at arms?"

She shrugged, "I know not."

I began to plan at that moment. The first thing we needed to do was to change the route we had agreed. Lothar and Konrad had been too agreeable to the idea. I did not like that. "Will your knights still be in Nancy?"

"I know not. Perhaps. Why?" I ignored the question for I was busy trying to remember the maps I had studied with Robert. "You are planning something?" I nodded. "And when are you going to tell me what it is?"

"Empress Matilda, when I have worked out the details then you shall be the first to know." I was acutely aware that I was more than naïve when it came to the politics of Europe. The politics of the east were familiar to me. "Tell me, Empress, do we have enemies on the route we selected?"

"Not enemies as such but Louis of France and my father have had disagreements in the past. The Count of Flanders is an enemy of both my husband and my father."

"We avoid the northern route." She nodded. "I think we will avoid Paris too then."

"Why? We were welcomed there on our way west."

"That was when you were accompanied by your German guards. They may take offence at twenty-five Normans marching through their city. It would be best to avoid confrontation."

"But that will take us close to Flanders."

"Yes, but it is a shorter route." I could hear the doubt in her voice. "Trust me, Empress. We will get you home and I am happier now for I believe I know the problems we face. That is easier than travelling in the dark."

We stayed that night in the castle of Evreux. The lord was with Henry but we were treated with both honour and respect. After we had eaten I took Edward to one side, while the Empress chatted to the lord's lady. I told him of our suspicions.

"I can just slit their throats tonight, my lord. It would be no bother." He grinned, "We have done it before."

"A nice thought but I suspect the ramifications would come back to haunt us. No, we just watch the two of them. Who are the two men we trust to watch them?"

"Any but the best would be Roger and Edgar. They are both bright lads and handy with their weapons."

"Good then ask them to keep an eye on the two knights. Have them ride behind them. And tomorrow watch out for trouble when I take us to Rouen."

"Rouen?"

"I want to stay in Normandy as long as I can. We cross the narrow part of France. We just have Rheims to pass through and then we should be away from the French."

"Are we at war with them?"

"No, but we aren't at peace either."

"That is a pity. If we were at war then we could make a little bit of gold out of this!" Edward was always looking for the pot of gold at the end of a rainbow; even when there was no rainbow!

I slept outside the Empress' chamber. I woke when she opened the door in the small hours of the night. She gave a squeak of surprise when she almost stumbled across me. "Why are you sleeping here? Is there no bed?"

I stood and stretched. "Aye but this way I guarantee your safety."

She took a dagger from the folds of her shift. "I am armed."

"That did not help your Swabians. I will endure this until we reach Nancy. I will be happier when we find those loyal to you."

As I expected Konrad and Lothar questioned my route when I took us northeast towards Rouen."

"This is not the way we agreed."

"No, but it is the way we shall be travelling." I stared at Lothar. He was not willing for a confrontation yet. We outnumbered them but I could see in his eyes that he wanted to pull his sword and kill me there and then.

He shrugged, "It matters not. Once we cross into our homeland there is but one way to go."

That confirmed what I had thought, it would be closer to Lorraine where the danger would come. We had to pass through Nancy in Lorraine and the danger would come before we reached that city. The two of them needed watching and I would not let them anywhere near our food but I did not think there would be an ambush until we were forced to rejoin our original route.

The first five days were relatively easy for we were travelling through Normandy. When we saw Rheims in the distance I began to fear for our safety. We were now in foreign parts. Our shields and livery were unknown but we were marked as Normans by our style of dress. People stared at us as we rode through the narrow streets. Matilda oozed confidence and smiled at those we passed. I admired her strength for I knew that, inside, she was as fearful for her life as we were.

Miraculously we were welcomed. We were accommodated in the Bishop's Palace. At least we four knights and Matilda were. Our men had to camp in the grounds. It was a small price to pay for the security the Bishop afforded.

As we left, the next morning, hope began to soar in my heart that this might not be as hazardous as I had expected. I was heading for La Cheppe. There was a small castle there and I hoped that they would offer us hospitality. We were now in unknown territory. Lorraine and the Empire were friends but that did not mean that we would be welcomed. The Empire was a loose confederation. Every landowner could, potentially, be a prince or a king if events went in their favour. Smiles in these parts meant nothing.

"Harold, take Dick and ride ahead to the castle. Let me know what it is like."

"Do you want us to speak with them?"

"No, but just see if they have a closed gate or an open gate. Do they have banners hanging from their walls?"

He grinned, "Yes my lord, to see if they are friendly!"

"Exactly."

Harold had been an outlaw before he joined me. His father had been the leader of my father's archers after the conquest. He had shown that he had the potential to be something better than an archer and I was training him to be a knight. Although he had much to learn the task I had given him was perfect for him. When I saw the two of them galloping hurriedly back I knew that there was trouble.

"What is it, Harold? Is the castle prepared for war?"

He shook his head, "The castle has been taken and burned. But there is more. There are warriors in the woods ahead and there is an ambush waiting for us."

I did not insult him by asking how he knew. He was as skilled at laying ambushes as any. If he said there was an ambush then there was one. I held up my hand and then waved the two Germans forward along with Edward. "The castle we were heading for has fallen and I think that those who took it have seen us and are waiting in ambush where the road passes through the forest."

The Empress asked, "Think you that they come for me?"

"Possibly but I doubt it. They could not know we were coming this way. I believe this is just a coincidence. Now we cannot go another way so let us spring this trap. Padraig and Geoffrey, you ride on either side of the Empress. Keep her safe." They nodded, "Dick, take the archers in a long sweep to the south of the road. Use your arrows to attack those ambushing us." I turned to Lothar and Konrad. Have your men at arms guard the horses at the rear. We four and our squires will be the vanguard and draw the sting of this ambush."

Konrad looked incredulously at me. "You would ride into an ambush?"

"Unless you have a better idea, then yes. Are you afraid?"

He shook his head, "We are afraid of no one. We will ride with you!"

"My men will take care of those on our right. Our shields should protect us from those on our left. Once we know where they are then we will attack. The four knights and the two squires will charge whoever awaits us. The rest ride through as quickly as you can. It is the forest so we will just use our swords." Everyone nodded. "Dick, ride!"

My archers headed south. I doubted that the ambushers would spot them for we were more than a mile from the woods and there was a slight rise before us. When we crested the rise in the road then they would anticipate our arrival. They would nock arrows and prepare spears.

I said, more for the benefit of the Empress Matilda than anything, "Take it nice and steady. Let us appear as though we do not expect an attack and allow Dick and the archers the time to get behind them. Those on the right, slip your shields to your right arms." I loosened my sword in my sheath. "Steady, Scout." The fact that we had not changed to our warhorses would add to the illusion that we were unprepared for an attack.

Edward was a little nervous, I could tell from his question, "How many do you think there are, my lord?"

"Enough to take a castle. Perhaps too many for us but we will try them anyway."

Lothar sneered, "And risk the Empress?"

I turned and glared at him. "The Empress will be safe. I guarantee that! You have the word of an English knight and I am never foresworn."

My answer made Edward smile. I knew that I had good mail; it had been made in Constantinople by a master craftsman. The helmet too afforded me protection and was still light. However, when you were riding into an ambush you had no idea what Fate had in store for you. My father had always been quite philosophical about death. The problem with Christianity was that it did not allow for accidents such as fate. I would have to trust in my armour and my skills.

15

As we neared the woods I scanned them for the ambushers. They were not very good at this for I saw three of them crouched behind some small bushes. They had spears. I slowed a little. I spoke in English so that my men would understand. "Three men with spears to the right."

"I saw them, my lord." Harold had sharp eyes. "If I had my bow then there would be three dead men!"

Edward laughed loudly, "But you are become a knight and have to wait! Now there is an irony!"

The laugh must have persuaded our ambushers that we were unprepared. As we entered the trap I drew my sword and yelled, "Ride!"

A number of things happened at once. Dick and his archers began to rain arrows down on the attackers to our right. The three spearmen leapt forward to spear us and arrows fell from our left. My reins were long ones and my shield straps equally long. It meant I could reach across with my mailed mittens as the spear came towards Scout's head. I pulled the spearhead towards me as I slashed down with my sword. The soldier should have let go but he did not. My sword smashed through his thin and badly made helmet to split his head in two. Alan and Harold took care of the other two.

I jerked Scout's head around to the left as Edward pulled his own around. "Charge!"

The ambushers to our left were not expecting us to attack. They thought we would be disorientated. Those to our right could do nothing to help for the finest archers in the whole of Europe were slaughtering them with ruthless efficiency. I pulled my shield tighter to me to protect my body and leg and as much of Scout as I could manage. I leaned forward and sought an enemy. I saw a knight on a horse. He had an open helmet and a shield which was slightly smaller than mine. Although he was uphill, he was stationary. It was a mistake. I might not have been on Star, my warhorse, but Scout knew how to fight too. I feinted to my left, which was the side I should have gone; we would have been sword to sword. As he pulled his horse's head around to face me I used my knees and the reins to yank Scout around to the shield side of the knight. As I reached him I stood in my stirrups and brought my sword across from the side. It smashed into his head. He was stunned. His horse was just standing there and so I brought Scout's head around behind him and slashed horizontally with my sword. It severed his mail and ripped into his gambeson. A poorer blade would have stopped there but mine had been made by a weaponsmith who had been trained in Constantinople in the far east. It sliced into his back and came away red.

The combination of the blow to his head and my swipe to his back caused him to fall to the ground and I whipped Scout's head around as I sought another enemy. I saw two men at arms hacking at Harold. He was still learning to be a swordsman on a horse. His natural skills were saving him but it could not last.

Scout bundled into one of the men at arms as I brought my sword down across his back. I severed the strap holding his shield and ripped into his shoulder blade. As the shield fell he pulled his horse's head around to flee. As the second man at arms turned to face me Harold gutted him like a fish. There were no more horsemen but I saw bows being nocked as the men on foot tried to bring us down. They did not know us and we charged at them. It takes a brave archer to stand against a mounted, armoured knight and they fled. We pursued them until our horses tired. As we returned to the road I counted ten dead archers and spearmen.

"Harold and Alan finish off any who are wounded and bring anything of value."

Edward lifted his helmet. "That went easier than I thought."

I nodded as I lifted my mask. "Aye, but where were our German friends?"

Edward pointed to the road where they both stood; their swords still sheathed. I would deal with them later. My men and the German men at arms had obeyed me. The two German knights were nowhere to be seen. I halted beside the wounded knight. Dismounting I rolled him over. He was not wounded, he was dead. He must have bled out. I took his sword, for it was a good one and searched him. He had a few coins and a signet ring with the mark of a wild boar. I took them both and his horse. Edward gathered the other four horses.

Dick and the archers were on the road and they held up their own treasures. "They had little enough but we took it."

"Good, watch our backs and we will find the Empress."

Geoffrey and Padraig had halted a short way from the burnt-out motte and bailey castle. "We thought you might want us to wait here. There is no one ahead."

"We will wait for Harold and Alan." Our two squires reached us. "Anyone behind us?"

"Just the archers."

"Ride to the castle and see if anyone still lives there. We will camp there if we can."

As they rode away I turned and, drawing my sword, held it to Lothar's cheek. "Take out your sword and show me the blade."

Edward had his blade at Konrad's neck whilst Padraig and Geoffrey levelled their spears at the men at arms. Lothar had anger on his face and I pushed a little harder until blood trickled down his cheek. "Unless you want a scar-like your friend there then do as I say. I care not if I rip a hole in your face."

He pulled the sword out and I saw that it was clean. I nodded and took it from him. "Now either you are a piss poor knight or you are a coward. You did not fight. Which was it?"

He remained silent and I pushed the sword into his cheek to make a large hole. He winced. I withdrew the blade. He spat blood to the ground and snarled, "You had those bandits under control. We are here to protect the Empress and not you!"

"You did neither. As far as I am concerned you are useless baggage and I am tempted to end your worthless lives here and now."

"Stay your hand, Baron!" I turned and saw that the Empress had closed with us. "Do not kill him. Give them another chance."

I was ready to end his life but I nodded. "The Empress has just saved your life. Next time we meet trouble then you two, the scar-faced twins, will go first." Lothar and Konrad exchanged a look between them. They knew that I meant what I was saying. I had not enjoyed what I had done but these two were merciless killers. I knew that I should have killed them there and then but the Empress had stayed my hand. "From now on we watch you!"

My archers appeared at the same time as Harold and Alan descended from the castle. "Anyone left alive?"

Dick shook his head, "No, my lord."

"Harold, the castle?"

"We will have to get rid of the bodies of the defenders but we can shelter there."

"Good then let us go." As we led our horses up the hill I nodded to Wulfric. I watched as he took two more men at arms and followed the two Germans up the hill. The German men at arms had not understood one word of what had gone on and I wondered what they made of my scarring of the German knight. German was one language with which I was not familiar. As we ascended I said, "There is another warhorse for you Harold. It is slightly better than the one you have."

"Thank you, Baron, but I am happy with the one I have."

"If you are to be a knight then you will need a warhorse. Take it."

When we reached the burned-out castle, I saw that it had been devastated in the attack. It would need rebuilding when it was reoccupied. Luckily for us the ditch still stood and that would deter any who tried to sneak up on us. I helped the Empress to dismount. "My lady, I think that you need to speak with your men at arms. They understood none of the words I spoke to the knights."

She nodded, "Thank you, Alfraed. You did the right thing."

While she went to speak to the men at arms I had Dick and the others begin a fire for food. Edward joined me. "They are an unpleasant pair of bastards although I have to say you have done nothing to improve their looks."

"Would you have done things differently?"

He nodded, "I would have run both of them through. They deliberately held back, hoping that we would be killed. If you weren't such a wild man we would have been." Shaking his head, he added, "Charging uphill on a palfrey takes some nerve Baron Alfraed. You scared me, I will say that!"

I went to Scout to see if he had suffered any injuries in my wild charge but he appeared to be whole. I found an apple and gave it to him. He munched contentedly. I should have been riding Star for battle but in my haste, I had forgotten to do so. And now my mind was filled with the problems of the Germans. I could do as Edward suggested and execute them out of hand. They had behaved dishonourably. On the other hand, I needed the German Men at Arms. We still had over three hundred miles to go and who knew what enemies we might face?

My archers had been used to fending for themselves in the forests of Sherwood and it was they who organised the food. I glanced over at Matilda who was still speaking with the Germans. Lothar and Konrad were sharpening their swords. That was ominous. Wulfric and his men were still watching every move the Germans made. I would not have to worry about them launching an attack.

Harold joined me. "What do we do about the Germans, lord?"

"Edward says to kill them. What would you do?"

"I do not know. I think I would find it hard to kill a man in cold blood. Their only crime was that they did not fight. Do we kill a man for cowardice?"

"If that gets another killed then yes but it is not cowardice which prevented them from fighting today; it was treachery. That is the real reason I do not kill them. There are too many unanswered questions. Whom do they work for? Are there others waiting for us? Warn the others to keep their eyes on those two."

I took out my sword and handed it to my squire. "You had better put a sharp edge on this. It looks like I may need it."

The Empress joined me and I saw a frown upon her face. Amongst the mail, shields and weapons she seemed so fragile. I cursed her father for putting her in so much danger. Politics!

"They are not happy, Baron."

"With me?"

"They did not understand your actions although they all admired your courage. I have now explained what you have done and they understand but they are unhappy with Lothar and Konrad. They were angry that their knights did not help."

I was relieved. I had worried that I had turned them against me too. "Edward wants me to kill the two knights."

She was her father's daughter. She nodded. "It would make sense. My husband and my father would have slain them already." She gave a sad smile. She had wished them kept alive but her husband was like Edward. He would have eliminated the threat.

"And you think I am weak for not doing so?"

"No, I was the one who told you not to kill them."

I led her over to the crude bench my men had made from some unburned timbers. We sat down. Grant brought us some of the food they had cooked. It was not the sort of food an Empress was used to but she smiled graciously anyway. When we were alone I began and told her what I had told Harold. "I am keen to speak with your Swabian knights in Nancy. There must have been a reason they were poisoned. If the two Teutons are still with us by then we may get answers."

"You think they will flee?"

"Possibly or they may try to harm you and then we would kill them." I ate for a while without tasting the food. "They do not want you dead! They just want you. Someone wishes you to be taken. Perhaps for ransom? A hostage? Leverage?"

"Both my father and my husband have many enemies. That would make sense." She smiled, "You see I knew there would be a good reason for your actions. You are right, Alfraed. We need to find out who is paying them."

"And they will not just give us that information."

We kept a good watch that night both for enemies without and enemies within. I used the German Men at Arms as well as my own. I had to show the Germans that I trusted them. We would need them before too long.

Chapter 3

The next morning, we continued our journey east. This was all new territory and we crossed an uncertain land. The Lords of Lorraine owed fealty to the Emperor but they were not as committed as the Emperor might like. The Emperor's disagreements with the Pope had not helped. These malcontents who wished to rule themselves had a good excuse now. They could be seen to be siding with the church. There was much political manoeuvring as they each sought a throne.

We had left as soon as dawn had broken. I had the two Teutons just in front of me and Edward with the Empress between us. With the German men at arms behind us, I was able to use my archers to range far ahead as scouts. I knew that Harold was itching to be with them but he was taking his new role seriously. He was a squire now but he would be a knight one day.

We saw occasional castles on the hillsides as we passed but they looked as small as the one at La Cheppe and no-one investigated us. Their gates remained closed as they watched our banners moving ever east. We were a large conroi and the sun shone from our armour and our mail. We looked intimidating. I wished now that we had questioned one of those who had attacked us. The presence of a knight did not suggest bandits but why would they risk attacking such a force as ours? Perhaps I was seeking plots where there were none. They could have been opportunists or they could have been after the Empress.

Dick galloped up to us. "My lord there is a castle ahead. It is next to the road."

I looked at Matilda, "Empress, do you know who is the castellan?"

She looked at Dick. "What banner flies from the walls?"

"Two fish and three flowers."

She looked relieved and she smiled. "Then it is the County and Castle of Bar and the Count of Bar is a supporter of my husband. He is an old fashioned loyal knight. You will like him. We will be safe there."

I wondered at that but I had to trust someone and if I could not trust the Empress then we were in trouble.

As we approached the castle the gates were opened and armed men came out. There were eight knights and the leader rode a magnificent destrier. They had lances with pennants showing their nobility and were supported by crossbowmen on the walls. I hoped that the Empress was right. The leader took off his helmet. I was intrigued by the design for it was made in one piece so that nothing of his features could be discerned. I saw that he had a grey flecked beard and looked to be of an age with Wulfstan. More importantly, was his smile which made me relax.

"Empress! We wondered who came with such a conroi of knights. What brings you here?"

"I have been visiting my father and now I return home, to Worms."

"Then tonight, you and your men will stay with me for there are bandits abroad."

She nodded, "We know. They wasted La Cheppe and tried to ambush us."

The Count was an old-fashioned knight. His wife, the Countess, had died giving birth to his youngest son. Having no daughters, I think he enjoyed being a genial host to the Empress. It certainly explained the warm welcome. It was a large castle but, even so, the archers and the men at arms had to camp outside the walls of the castle. I left Wulfric in charge of them. I did not think the two Germans would try anything whilst we were under the protection of the Count du Bar but we would need to confide in him our suspicions at the earliest opportunity. It would not do to have the Count or any of his people suffer because of us.

The Count took the Empress to her quarters while we stabled the horses. As I fed Star and Scout I said quietly to Edward. "You three keep an eye on our Teutonic friends and I will try to find out the lie of the land ahead of us." Edward fingered his dagger and I shook my head, "Not yet. We have much to discover and many leagues to travel yet."

We took only our swords to the hall and left our armour, helmets, mail and shields in the stables. It would have been rude to go to the meal prepared for battle. The two Germans had to, reluctantly, follow suit.

When we reached the hall the Count and the Empress were seated before the fire. I saw that there were retainers on the doors and I wondered why. As soon as we had entered the Count gave a command and the two Germans were seized before they could draw their weapons. "Take these two Teutons away for questioning!" It was an imperious command and the guards were not dainty as they hauled the two Germans from our sight. He smiled and gestured forward three knights who looked like younger versions of the Count. "My sons and my nephew will give your knights and squires a tour of the castle, Baron

Alfraed, and you can join us here." This was a ruler. He gave commands as though he was born to it. He reminded me of my father.

The others left the three of us alone. He poured me some of the red, heavy wine of the region. He saluted me with his goblet as I drank, "The Empress has told me of your little problem. For one so young and with so few knights you have done well. The raiders you slew are a band of men from Flanders. Their Count has sent them across to our lands to cause mischief. So far he has avoided annoying me; he knows that my vengeance would be swift but he has preyed upon some of the smaller demesne." He waved his servant forward to pour us all some more wine. "Abelard, leave us and see how the food for this evening's feast progresses. We have important guests and I wish everything to be done well." The servant bobbed his head and then left us alone.

"I trust my servants but sometimes they gossip and I believe I have information which you might find useful."

"Anything would help my lord, for we have a long way yet to travel. And I still have little idea who is behind these Germans."

Matilda put her hand on mine, "I think, Alfraed, that it is the same man who is causing this land so much trouble."

The Count du Bar nodded, "It is Charles Count of Flanders. His land is poor and prone to flooding. He has been casting his covetous eyes south, to King Henry's domain and east to the lands of the Emperor." He shook his head. "I am afraid, my dear, that the Pope has much to answer for. He has weakened the position of your husband and thereby encouraged those who seek to take lands from the Empire."

"But surely the Emperor is Emperor of the Holy Roman Empire!"

The Count laughed, "You are naïve, young man. The Pope is as political an animal as any. Come let me show you something."

He led us to a cupboard in the corner. He opened it and took out a map. It was beautifully decorated and looked expensive. He pointed with his dagger which was adorned with well-cut jewels. "Here we are. My lands are on the borders of the Empire. Here is the County of Champagne and Blois. And here are the lands of the County of Flanders. We are like the nut which can be cracked from two sides. It is only the strength of my arm which holds them back."

Matilda said, "My cousin Stephen is from Blois."

"And your father's mother was from Flanders. Count Charles fears that your father will claim Flanders and Stephen's family, well they just want more land." He smiled. "It is lucky you came this route to return home. I can provide an additional escort. It will not be many for I needs must protect the borders of my lands but it will be enough to discourage any attempts to take you captive." There was a knock on the door. "Come!"

A servant appeared, "The food is almost ready my lord, can we prepare the table for the food?"

He waved them in, "Come we will go and see these Germans. It would be useful to find out what they know."

We descended by a spiral staircase into what must have been a stable at one time. It reminded me of the lower level of my castle in Stockton. This one now had a door and I could see that it was being used as a cell of some sort. The Count's sons, Edward and the squires were there and, manacled to the walls, were the two German knights.

"I am sorry, I was rude not to introduce you, this is my elder son Geoffrey, my younger son Raymond and my nephew Guy of Dijon." They nodded. "Did you find anything when you searched them?"

Geoffrey held out his hand and there were a number of gold coins in his palm. "We found much gold and it all bears the mark of Charles of Flanders. It was hidden beneath their saddles and was cunningly concealed."

I could see from their bloodied faces that the two Germans had been struck. Konrad spat out a tooth and snarled, "We came by that money honestly!"

The Count put his face close to the Teuton and asked, "How?" The hesitation proved it was a lie and this was confirmed by the downcast looks of Lothar. The Count turned to me, "This knight thwarted your attempt to harm the Empress and I have been told that you did not try to defend the Empress against her attackers. Your animals, weapons and gold are forfeit. I will send a ransom demand to your families. Until then you shall enjoy my hospitality." He smiled, "I could of course make your stay more comfortable were you to tell me who hired you and what the Empress can expect on her way home." The two remained sullenly silent. "Bread and water only!"

On that sobering note, we returned to the hall and the feast. I discovered that the Count's sons and nephew not only looked like him but they took after him too. They were most interested in life in England and found my story of our journey from Constantinople to England fascinating.

"I will take a crusade one day. When this land is settled and quiet then I shall visit the Holy Land and make a pilgrimage."

The Count shook his head, "Raymond, my son, it is unlikely that this land will ever enjoy peace and as for the Holy Land, it seems to me that men go there for profit and an idle life."

I added a word of caution. "We suffered in Constantinople when the Crusaders passed through following Pope Urban's call to arms. We did not see much Christian fellowship. The knights who passed through looked to be looking out for themselves rather than Christ."

The Count nodded, "I heard that. And I have also heard of counts going there just so that they can become king. There are greedy knights without any honour. A throne thus gained is not worth sitting upon."

It was a pleasant interlude. In the middle of our long journey, we found safety and sanctuary with the Count of Lorraine. The Count and his family were both courteous and entertaining. The whole evening was illuminating.

When we left the next day, the Count insisted that I take the Germans' warhorses but I refused the gold. "It is blood money, Count, and not earned honestly. Do not fear we will make from this journey. You keep it for your hospitality and for your nephew's lance and men at arms." The eight men at arms with Sir Guy looked as though they knew their business.

Empress Matilda looked happier too now that the spectre of Konrad and Lothar was gone. Guy proved to be a lively companion. He told us how his father had been dispossessed of his lands by a rival Baron. He had been the only survivor of a savage midnight raid and now, thanks to his uncle's generosity, was building up his own conroi. "I know what my uncle said about the Holy Land. For me, it may be my only recourse. I do not mind serving my uncle and learning from him but it would be a different matter to serve my cousin. How about England? Is there any way a knight can make his fortune there?"

I smiled, "The northern borders are lively. If you are good enough then you can carve out a demesne for yourself but it is a never-ending struggle. I left almost as many men at home as I have brought with me. The Scots will be trying to steal my cattle and my people and then there are neighbours who seek to take what is mine."

The Empress said, "And it is thanks to me that you cannot be with them. I am sorry."

I was appalled to think that I had upset her. "No, my lady, I was bound to serve your father and this is a much more pleasurable task I can assure you."

Guy laughed, "Why, we have the perfect knight here. Not only is he skilled with weapons and tongues, but he is also a troubadour too!"

"Tell me, Sir Guy, where did your uncle get the helmet I saw him wearing? I have never seen the like."

"It is from Italy. I am surprised you did not see them in Byzantium."

"When we left England, the helmet I have was the latest design."

"My uncle's was made especially for him. It gives him all-round protection. It is called a great helm. I like yours. Your neck is well protected. The aventail is light but it is mail and will stop a blow. I shall buy myself one when we have the next tourney."

"I will have to get myself a great helm. I can see the advantage of them."

"The vision is not the best but it gives the wearer an advantage in a mêlée."

Once again, we had my archers scouting far ahead of us. They were woodsmen and rode comfortably through the trees and fields which lined the road. If they did not wish to be seen then they would not be. They warned of us of castles and Guy was able to tell us if they represented danger or not. His presence was invaluable. We slept safely in the manors of friends of his uncle. We were just a day or so from Nancy when they brought us news of danger. Only half of them returned. "My lord there is a party of armed knights and men at arms waiting on a small hill about two miles up the road."

"Did they see you?"

Dick smiled, "No my lord! We left Grant and the others to watch them."

"You have done well." I turned to Sir Guy. "What do you make of it?"

"I vaguely remember the hill your archer speaks of. It gives a good view of this road and the advantage of a hill down which to charge."

"Can we avoid it?"

"No, for it has a good view of the smaller roads too. It is why a watcher would choose it."

"Then this is deliberate."

"I would think so."

"Dick, how many men are there?"

27

"Altogether I would say twenty. From their standards and their shields then I would say, eight knights."

They all looked to me. I was now the leader. "We have three knights and two squires. They have more knights than we do. They will be charging downhill and their horses will give them an advantage."

The Empress looked worried, "Perhaps we can talk with them."

I shook my head. "We are close to Nancy and these knights are waiting. If we had the Germans here we could question them. I am certain that they would have known of this." They looked at me still. "Arm for war. Use the warhorses and break out the lances. Dick, I want you to ride back to Grant and the others. When they charge us, I want you to use your arrows on their flanks. It may be our only advantage."

"Yes, my lord."

There were only eight archers with me but they were good. As we changed horses and gathered our lances I sought out Edgar. "I am leaving you to watch over the Empress. I will also leave the Germans. They are sound fellows, I think. You have a few words of their language do you not?"

"Aye sir and I will watch her like she was my own."

"I know you will. I want you close enough to see if it goes ill with us. If it does then ride back to the Count."

The Empress shook her head, "Do not think that way."

"We have to be prepared for the worst, my lady. There are three of us with experience and we do not know the mettle of these enemies yet. I hope to be successful but we cannot guarantee anything in this life. Would you tell the Germans that I leave Edgar in command?"

While she went I summoned Brian. He was the youngest of my men at arms and the least experienced. "I leave the horses to you, Brian. If you have to flee then you may have to let them go."

"My lord I cannot do that."

I put steel in my voice, "It if is a choice between the horses or the Empress then there is no choice. Save the Empress." I saw that we were ready and Empress Matilda nodded. "We will attack, if it comes to that, in an arrow formation. I will ride in the centre, Edward to my right and Guy to my left. Harold and Alan tuck in behind me. The men at arms will be in two lines. Until we see them we will ride in a column. Do you all understand?"

They all shouted, "Aye, my lord!" And we rode to war.

28

This would be the first time I had led my own men against a superior enemy using lances. I just hoped I was good enough. The lances we used were well made with an eight feet long ash haft and a well-made iron head. Alf had done a good job manufacturing them. I was confident that we had good shields but I worried about Alan and Harold. Both of them had yet to be trained with a long spear. This was no place to learn.

We passed my archers in the woods. As soon as they saw us pass they disappeared. I could rely on them. As soon as we emerged from the gloom of the forest I saw the conroi on the hill. They were half a mile away. All of them had the long shield which had been used at Hastings and the conical helmet. That gave me hope. Perhaps their mail was not as good as ours. They had their horses in a line. I saw that the leader had a quarter design on his shield and that the top right-hand quadrant had a yellow sun with a white flower in the middle. Guy said. "These are from Flanders. Their leader is Guillaume of Ghent the illegitimate half brother of Count Charles."

We had halted to watch their intentions. "And the others?"

"Most look to be from Flanders but the knight on the end has a plain red shield and I know not him. He may be a mercenary come to try to gain fame and fortune. There are many like him in the borderlands."

I saw their lances lowered as they began to trot down the hill. There had been no chance to talk. It could be they wanted us for ransom and the presence of the Empress was an accident but I did not believe that. The Count of Flanders had been ever-present since we had landed in Normandy. I would have to discover why later but first we had to battle them.

"Stay tight together. Do not worry about their speed. We stay as one."

I turned Star and headed towards them. They were now cantering down the slope and I spied hope for the first time. They were no longer knee to knee. We started to trot and I resisted the temptation to glance behind me. It would not give my men any confidence. I had to make them believe that we could win and that I was confident. I was not. I watched the charging knights lean forward and pull back their lances. I spurred Star to make him go ahead of the other two so that our line would become the arrow. Out of the corner of my eye, I saw the spears of Harold and Alan. They were riding as close to me as they dared. The slope meant we could not go very fast but it increased the speed of the eight knights who were now galloping full tilt towards us. As they did so they lost the valuable cohesion they needed for an effective charge.

I suddenly spied a gap big enough for Star emerge between Guillaume of Ghent and the knight next to him. We were just thirty paces apart and I yelled, "Charge!" I put my spurs to Star. He leapt forward and I pulled back my right arm. I had my shield as tight to my left side as I could get it. I knew that this knight would aim for my head and expect me to do the same. I readied my arm and at the right moment, I punched forward. As I had expected his shield was held high and the head of my lance slid over the cantle of the saddle and tore into the mail and gambeson. His lancehead clattered into my shield and slid up to my helmet. The angled cap took the blade away. The force of my blow and the weight of the knight and horse broke my lance and I threw the useless haft away.

As I drew my sword I saw the mortally wounded knight slipping backwards and holding on to the lance which had struck his vital organs. Our formation had taken them by surprise. Half of their knights had not had to face an enemy for my men at arms, like their own were some thirty paces behind. I saw that the men at arms had lances and I risked a glance over my shoulder. We had felled three knights and, as far as I could see lost none.

"Mêlée!"

Even Harold and Alan knew what to do. It was every man for himself and you tried to do as much damage as you could to those around you. The men at arms coming towards us were not in a single line and their speed meant that it would be possible to avoid their lances if you were agile enough. The first Sergeant at Arms who tried to kill me also made the mistake of hitting my head but he forgot to punch and the blow was weak. I jabbed at him with my shield and slashed down with my sword at the same time. The combination made him fall from his mount and I was through their line. As I turned to attack their rear I saw two men at arms with arrows sticking from them. My archers were doing what they did best. The men at arms did not have full mail and the arrows were deadly.

I ignored the men at arms and rode for the knight who was fighting with Harold. Both their lances had broken but the knight was having the better of it. Now I had the slope and Star galloped hard. This was what he had been bred for, fighting. I came behind the knight and brought my sword above his cantle and across his back. The heavy sword, the force of Star and the slope shattered his spine and almost tore him in two. His lifeless body fell to the ground. I know not if it was the archers or my sudden attack from behind but the others took flight and headed back up the hill, running the gauntlet of Dick and his archers.

I could see that we had taken casualties. Alan was lying on the ground and did not appear to be moving. Two of Guy's men at arms were also down while Padraig and Geoffrey were not on their horses. I heard Edward shout, "Secure the horses."

I rode to Alan. Harold had lifted his helmet. I could see a huge dent in the side. His shield also showed where a lance had scored a mark along it. He grinned at me. "Well sir, that was lucky!"

I dismounted and handed him my reins. "Aye, but Alan was not so lucky." His face fell. The two were good friends. I waved my arm and Brian led the Empress and the Germans towards us. I rolled Alan over. His left arm looked to have been damaged for it lay at an awkward angle. More seriously I saw that the mail covering his stomach had been scored and he was bleeding. "Wulfric!"

Wulfric was our healer. A huge man he could be incredibly gentle when he needed to be. He dismounted and handed his reins to Roger. He smiled. "Looks worse than is it is. If it was a serious one he would be gushing blood. I'll get his shirt off and have a look."

I nodded and joined Edward with the prone Padraig. I rolled him over and saw that he was dead. The head of the lance was still embedded in his chest. I had lost one of my men and I felt sick. There was some relief when I saw Geoffrey stagger to his feet.

Guy joined us. "That could have been worse. We beat them!" He sounded almost happy.

"I have lost one man and another is wounded."

He pointed up the hill, "And two of my men lie dead. It happens. It is war." He put his arm around my shoulder, "Your plan worked Baron. I never would have believed that three knights and two squires could clear the field of eight knights but we did! This was a great victory. Come we will see what we have."

The three knights were all dead. Guillaume of Ghent had died almost immediately. One of the others had fallen and broken his neck whilst the last had been speared by Guy. An impressive blow, he had sunk his lance into his neck. The mail of two of them was usable but my spear had rendered Guillaume's useless. We took their swords, their horses and their shields. Each also had gold about them and they bore the face of Charles of Flanders.

Empress Matilda joined us. She looked pale when she saw the three bodies of our men. "They died for me!"

Guy shrugged, "Empress, I said to the Baron here that this was a great victory. Three knights have fallen." He pointed up the hill. "And there are five dead men at arms."

Edward nodded, "He is right, my lord. Come let us head east. I am keen to reach safety. I would not wish to push our luck."

"What about Alan. He has been wounded. It looks like a broken arm and he has a wounded side."

Wulfric looked up. "He'll be all right my lord. I will stitch him up. Roger, get some of that aqua vita." I saw that Alan's eyes were open and he was smiling although he was very pale. "Now then, my son, this will hurt but you fought well today and will have a nice scar to impress the women with." He suddenly realised that the Empress was still standing there, "Begging your pardon ma'am."

She laughed, "Do not worry about my sensibilities. Care for him."

Wulfric poured some of the spirit we had bought on the road over the wound. I saw Alan wince but he did not cry out. He took a long draught of it and then, closing his eyes nodded. Wulfric took out a bone needle and some catgut from his leather pouch. He soaked both in the spirit and, after taking a drink himself, he began to sew. It was a huge needle. The physicians in Constantinople had much finer, delicate instruments. I wished we had brought some with us. I could see this happening regularly.

While he was being sewn we buried our dead. I said a few quiet words over Padraig's grave; I was just pleased that all of my men were single. None had left families behind. Harold and Wulfric helped Alan to his horse and Harold agreed to watch his friend. We now had three more warhorses. Guy would take two back with him but we now had a spare. That was the harsh reality of life in a conroi. Men's lives were balanced against the profit that we made. It was sad really.

Chapter 4

Nancy had a fine castle and the Empress was loudly welcomed by the burghers of the town. Although we were not recognised she was. I was impressed that her first thoughts were for the four Swabian knights she had left there. As soon as the castellan greeted us she asked after them. We all breathed a sigh of relief when we discovered that there were Swabian knights in a small inn in the centre of the walled town. I left Guy and Edward to arrange our lodgings and Harold and I escorted the Empress to the inn. We heard the clash of arms from the enclosed courtyard. As no one was hurrying to see what the problem was then we kept our weapons sheathed. There were three knights in their gambesons and two were practising with their swords.

As soon as the Empress entered they dropped to their knees. "Empress Matilda! You are safe. We waited here for you as we were not certain of your route home."

"Rise Rolf, Carl, Gottfried," she looked around, "where is Gurt?"

The eldest of the three shook his head. "He died of the poison. We have only been up for two days. Carl here was close to death." He glanced at me suspiciously.

"This is Baron Alfraed of Norton and he and his men were charged with escorting me from Caen."

The three of them came closer. "And the Teutonic knights?"

The Empress glanced at me, "I suspected that they were plotting against my life and Alfraed here was suspicious too. He stopped them before they could do us more harm. They are in Lorraine with the Count of Bar."

Rolf suddenly looked angry. "Then when we have returned you to Worms we will visit Bar and end the lives of these treacherous murderers." He paused, "We discovered it was they who paid for our food to be poisoned. They owe us a life!" He put his hand out to me and smiled for the first time. "I am sorry I was suspicious of you, friend. You have saved the life of the Empress. They had an ambush planned but we could not find out where."

33

I pointed west. "Eight knights and their men at arms ambushed us. We escaped."

"I am pleased that you had many knights to protect you, Empress."

She shook her head, "No, Rolf, we had but three knights and two squires."

He laughed and put his arm around my shoulders. "You look like a strong wind would blow you over but you have a warrior within you Englishman. Three knights against eight show you have the skill as well as God on your side."

I felt much happier the next day, as we left Nancy with the escort of three Swabian knights. These were experienced warriors. No wonder the Teutonic knights had had them poisoned. I would not have liked to face them sword to sword. They immediately took charge of the German men at arms. As we headed north and east I noticed that the sergeant at arms sported a black eye. At our noon stop, I asked Rolf about that. He shrugged, "I wanted him to know that I was less than happy with the way they had served us. If they knew nothing of the Teutons plans they should have been suspicious of their behaviour."

"What I do not understand, Rolf, is why they did not kidnap or harm the Empress after they left Nancy."

"Did you not think it strange that they had no squires with them?"

"Now you come to mention I did but as the Empress had not mentioned them..."

"That is because they were the ones who poisoned us and they left to take a message to the Count of Flanders, their master. We had been watching the four of them since we had left Worms. Gurt was certain that he had seen Lothar with an agent of the King of France."

"The King of France? I thought you said that it was the Count of Flanders to whom they fled."

He laughed as we mounted our horses, "Politics, my naïve English friend. The King of France uses the Count of Flanders to undermine your King and his position. He would dearly love to add Normandy to his lands. You know whom he keeps in his court do you not?"

"No, who?"

"The son of King Henry's brother, William of Clito. While William's father is a prisoner in your Tower in London, his son is being courted by the King of France. It is a devious pond into which you have stepped. The King of France is pulling the strings while others do his deeds. It is said that he even has the Pope under his spell. Do not cross the King of France, my friend, it would be fatal."

"And the squires?"

"They may have been with the ambush," he shrugged, "if I see them again then they will die. Gurt was a good friend and I had served with him these ten years."

As we rode I pointed to his surcoat. It covered his mail. I had seen them in the east but, until we had entered the Empire I had not seen them in Europe. "Why do you wear these, Rolf?"

"We became used to wearing them in the Holy Land. There they keep warriors cooler. They are useful for that in parts of the southern Empire. Mainly, though, they identify us in battle. If a knight has his back to you then you know not if he is friend or foe."

I nodded, "It makes sense. You can tell that you three are in the same Conroi."

Carl added, "They also protect our mail from the elements."

I turned to Edward, "We will have some made when time allows."

"Do not forget your shields too, Englishman. Your plain blue shield tells the world that you do not wish to be identified. That normally means you have something to hide."

"Like the knight with the red shield." I had told them of the mysterious knight in the hope that they could identify him but they knew him not.

"Exactly."

"We could have a blue background and a star. Guillaume of Ghent's star was effective."

I shook my head, "One star suggests a target! We could have two for the two knights in our conroi."

We spent the next half a day discussing the design with our Swabian friends. I had noticed that my archers and men at arms looked martial but they also looked a little like brigands for all wore their own clothes. The archers, in particular, looked like bandits. We had a little coin we had gathered and I still had the purse given to me by Robert of Gloucester. Thanks to Sir Guy we had not had to use much on the road. It would be worth the investment to have blue padded tunics made for my men. We could have a pair of blue stars sewn on to them. Surcoats would make my men at arms look the same.

We had almost reached Worms when we had our last run with those who wished harm to the Empress. We had begun to relax. Alan's stitches had begun to itch which Wulfric assured us was a good sign that he was recovering and we had had no attacks for seven days. We headed for an island on the River Lauter. There was a hunting lodge upon it used by the Holy Roman Emperors. Although it was uninhabited unless the Emperor was there it had a roof, beds and wood for the fires. The Empress was keen to use it. She knew it well. Rolf thought it safe as it was on an island and the river would protect us from danger. He was proved wrong.

The lodge was just big enough for the knights. The squires and the men at arms slept outside under quickly erected shelters. Our archers were at home in the huge forests and brought back food for us to cook. Perhaps we relaxed too much. We had good food and we had a river to protect our island. The men at arms stood guard but we, as knights, did not supervise the watches and we left them to it. Whatever the reason, we were surprised by attackers in the middle of the night.

It was a shout which woke me. I opened my eyes and saw nothing for the room was in darkness. I began to doubt that I had heard anything at all. Perhaps it had been a bad dream. Then I heard the clash of arms. I grabbed my sword and ran for the door. As I opened it a huge axe came in my direction. It was wielded by a bearded giant. I threw myself back to avoid having my head split open. I landed on the floor and felt myself winded. Behind the giant, I saw a battle was going on outside our doors. I had to roll to the side as the axe came down again. I had to take charge and end this. I dived forward and my sword ripped into his kneecap, just below his leather byrnie. As he stepped back on his good leg I jumped to my feet and thrust the sword into his throat. He had no metal there and he collapsed in a heap.

"Edward! Watch the Empress!"

Guy was behind me. He had his sword in his hand but, like me, he was just in his gambeson. "I hoped they might have given up."

"No such luck. Ready?"

"Aye ready."

We leapt from the door. As far as I could see the men who were attacking us had no mail. That did not help us for neither did we. However, they were not skilled swordsmen and I hoped that we could take advantage of that. It was a large band which had invaded our camp and sheer weight of numbers meant that some had got through our men at arms. A huddle of seven came hurtling towards the two of us. Three were thrown to the ground by arrows sent into their backs. I stepped forward and swung my sword in a wide sweep. I held my hand before me and, as my sword ripped into the shoulder of one warrior I managed to grab hold of the shaft of the spear which was heading for my eye. I continued to bring the sword around and it sliced through the top of the skull of the spearman. I retained hold of the spear and, flipping it the air, used it defensively in my left hand as some protection from that side.

More men had broken through and, although my archers were felling as many as they could we were in danger of being overwhelmed. I heard a roar of anger behind as I threw the spear left handed at an advancing man wield an axe. At the same time, I swung my sword at head height to keep the others at bay. Guy and I were back to back. Suddenly the three Swabians came hurtling from the door of the hunting lodge. They had their mighty swords in two hands and they charged so quickly that we were in danger of being knocked over by our allies. As the axe man looked in terror at the three Swabians I darted forward beneath his axe and gutted him.

Guy and I followed the three swordsmen as they drove the terrified assassins down the hill towards the river. Our task was easy. We swung our swords and hacked at any who were wounded by the wild charge of the Empress' protectors. By the time we reached the river the hillside was cleared. It took the Swabians some time to return by which time we had made sure that there was no further danger to the Empress. Seven of the German men at arms had paid the price of defending the Empress with their lives. I had lost two more men. Wilfred, the man at arms, and Grant, the archer, were gone. Both had died in the first assault. We had one prisoner. He would not last until morning. Guy's sword had ripped across his stomach and those wounds were always fatal.

"Wulfric, see to our wounded. Brian, make sure the island is secure."

When the Swabians returned we had them question the man. They were not gentle. They spoke in German and I understood not a word. Finally, Rolf nodded, took his sword and took the man's head.

"He asked for a quick death in return for information." He pointed to the dead, "They were hired by a Frenchman. He did not know who paid but I am guessing Louis. They were sent for on the same day you reached Nancy. There must be a spy or agent in the town."

When Wulfric and Brian returned they had a puzzled look on their faces. "There are no wounded and the German Sergeant is missing."

Rolf nodded, "I thought there was something suspicious about him. He must have been Lothar and Konrad's man."

I wiped my sword on the tunic of one of the dead. "The sooner we reach Worms the better. We cannot afford to lose any more of our men."

There were few coins on the men. I suspect they would have been given half first and would receive the balance on fulfilment of their contract. This was a harsh world of politics into which we had stumbled.

I went down to the river to wash the blood from me and my sword. I heard a noise behind me and I whipped my sword around. It was Empress Matilda. Her eyes widened when she saw the sword. I lowered the blade, "I am sorry, my lady. You should not be out alone. It is not safe."

She walked close to me and put her hands on mine. She reached up and kissed me gently on the lips, "I am safe when I am with you, Baron Alfraed of Norton. You have saved my life over and over on this journey. When you raced out to fight these wild animals I thought I had lost you and I would have no protector. Keep yourself safe, my English knight. I know now that our destinies are intertwined."

Guy suddenly appeared with his sword in his hand, "Thank God! I thought one of them had managed to return and abduct her."

She turned and smiled at him as though no words had passed between us. "I needed to bathe my face and cool it down. Thank you for your concern, Sir Guy. I am lucky to have such noble knights to protect me."

When we finally saw the towers of Worms, in the distance, I was relieved beyond words. We became more relaxed once we knew we were close to this centre of Imperial power and took off our mail. Our horses were beginning to suffer. We had travelled hundreds of miles and even a good horse like Scout could not continue to travel each day with a mailed warrior on his back. It also felt good to be riding without helmets and let the fresh air blow through our hair. The journey had been fraught. I had known it would be a hard task but I had had no concept of the twists and turns the road would take. What I did know, as we rode through the huge gates of the town, was that Matilda, Empress of the Holy Roman Empire, was someone for whom I would lay down my life. When I had raced from the hunting lodge on the Lauter, half dressed and barely armed, I had expected to die. That told me much about my feelings for Matilda for I would have done so gladly.

Gottfried spurred his horse on to warn the Emperor that his wife was coming. We saw the crowds gathering in the distance. Guy was quite amusing and, now that the journey was almost done, he entertained us with some stories of his cousins when they were younger. The three of us were laughing as we approached the first of the crowds. Matilda waved cheerfully to them.

As she did so I spoke to Guy on her other side. "I envy you, Sir Guy. You grew up with young cousins. I had old warriors to play with. They were good tutors and stalwart warriors but there was little laughing and joking."

Matilda turned to me and, putting her hand on mine said, "And no mother too. You had a hard upbringing."

I laughed, "And yet, like Sir Guy, I appear to have survived." She laughed too but, as I looked up I saw her husband, the Emperor for the first time and his face was dark with anger. I wondered what he had read into the Empress' harmless gesture. The anger was replaced by a smile as we neared them. We waited outside the gates whilst they were reunited and then the Emperor, on his white charger, led her into the palace. We were left to our own devices. I felt a little lost. Did we just turn around and head back to Caen? I did not understand the protocol involved. Rolf laughed when he saw my puzzled expression. "Come, Englishman, we have our own quarters here for you and your men. This may not be Paris, London or Caen but we will be comfortable here. We rode through the gates. The Swabians appeared to be well known but we were the focus of attention and all stared at us.

The stables were enormous, clean and well equipped and I knew that our mounts would be well looked after. Due to the deaths and our success we now had plenty of spare mounts. The squires would be kept busy. I made sure the men at arms were taken care of in the old warrior hall. It looked like it had not changed since the time of Charlemagne. Then Rolf led us by a back door into the palace. Compared with the Emperor's palace in Constantinople, this was just a large castle and it was barely bigger than Caen. The six of us would share a room whilst our squires would have to make do with the servant's quarters. Harold was still impressed. He shrugged when he saw where he would sleep, "When you have slept for most of your life in the green sward then a roof is a luxury. I am content, Baron."

Once we had washed and changed into more comfortable clothes I asked Guy and Rolf for they seemed to know more than I did, "What happens now? Do we eat and then return to Caen tomorrow? We have done as we were asked."

Rolf said, "We are based here anyway but I would imagine that there will be a feast and then the Emperor will want to reward you."

"Are you certain?"

He shrugged, "It is normal and he sometimes likes cavalry games."

"Cavalry games?"

"Aye, knights fight with blunted weapons watched by the King's heralds. The victor normally gets a prize." He held up a beautifully decorated dagger. "I won one and received this. These are precious stones upon the hilt."

Edward and Guy nodded, "I have heard of these. My uncle, the Count, has spoken of holding one when more peaceful times descend upon us."

"When I served in the borders some of the Normans there liked them. They are good for training." Rolf was a well-travelled knight.

"How do they work then?"

"You fight in conroi. There might be six or seven different conroi. When the herald thinks you would have been wounded then you leave the mêlée. The last man standing normally wins although if you fight bravely enough then you are rewarded too."

I shook my head, "It sounds like the gladiatorial games from ancient Rome."

"No, my friend, they were to the death. You receive bruises only and damage to your reputation; that is all. I will try to discover what is happening. If there is nothing then we will explore the town. There are some interesting sights."

While he was away Edward and I sought our men. We left Guy polishing his sword. He hoped to catch the eye of the Emperor. He was a landless knight who could not even afford a squire. He had to impress where he could. "Keep yourselves amused and out of trouble."

Wulfric laughed, "Easier said than done, Baron."

Edward nodded, "If idle hands need something to do then paint your shields blue. The Baron and I have decided we shall all look the same. People will know, on the field, that we are Norton!"

They liked the idea and we left them discussing how to make the paint that they would need. Edward chuckled, "That is better than having them spending their coins in the taverns and getting into fights with the locals."

"Would they do that, Edward?"

"They would not mean to but they are Englishmen and, as such, think they are worth ten of any foreigner." He suddenly realised what he had said, "Sorry, Baron, I meant no offence."

It was my turn to laugh, "I wouldn't worry. I think of myself as English rather than Greek. We had better take some coins with us in case we have the chance to buy a surcoat or two."

"Is that likely, my lord?"

"It depends if there is a tailor here who wishes to earn money. But we will wait until we discover what Rolf has to say. It may be that we leave the day after tomorrow."

Even as I said it I knew that I did not want to leave. Empress Matilda held a fascination for me. I suddenly felt guilty as I thought of Adela, back in Stockton. She had given me a lucky charm and obviously thought much of me and I had not even thought about her once. This was the first time and that was only because I thought of my castle.

While we waited for Rolf's return we explored the public areas of the castle. There were many rooms forbidden to us. Stern faced guards moved poleaxes across the doors. We were guests, just about, but I suspected that, in the Emperor's eyes, we were not welcome guests. By the time we had explored what we could Rolf was back and we met him in our room where Guy had finished his polishing.

He looked at me askance before saying, "There is to be a feast tomorrow and then three days later a tourney to celebrate the return of the Empress. He wishes you three to participate as a conroi."

"But I have never even seen one."

Rolf laughed, "Do not worry, my English friend, I have seen you fight. You and your companions are more than up to it. Now let me show you Worms. It is an interesting place."

As he led us through the ancient town he regaled us with stories. He had been a mercenary; indeed, he was still one for the Emperor used the three Swabians as his most trusted bodyguards. He had travelled and fought throughout Europe. No wonder poison had been the method the Teutonic Knights had chosen. When we were in the market place I asked, "Are there tailors here who could make us surcoats such as the ones you wear?"

"Of course! There is a man just down one of the alleys here. He is expensive but they are fine garments."

"So long as they fit then I am happy."

Guy said, "I will go with Gottfried and Carl. They have promised to take me to taste some of the finest beer in the world." He shrugged, "Why drink beer when you can have wine? Still, I will go with them. It would be rude not to."

The tailor proved most accommodating. He apologised for his lack of variety. "I only have two blues, my lord. I can send for more if you wish."

"I am afraid we are only here for a short time. Will you be able to make them in such a short time?"

"I can put aside my other work for the knight who saved the Empress but it will cost you, Baron."

"If they are ready in time and fit then you will be paid their worth."

"A man can ask no more. How many would you require?"

I took a deep breath. "At least five and, if you could manage it then ten."

He almost took a step back. "Sir, I could do that but I would have no more stock left in that blue." I took out one of the gold pieces with the face of Count Charles of Flanders. I said nothing but I twirled it before him. "I will have five ready for tomorrow and the rest three days later."

"One more thing. I wish two blue stars over the heart. They need not be the same blue."

"That can be arranged, sir. I shall hire two seamstresses."

I flipped him the coin. "Then we have a deal."

"Yes sir. Shall I measure you or your other knight first?"

I shrugged, "It matters not but let Edward go first. The others are his size."

When they disappeared into the back room Rolf said, "It is good we are alone. What I have to say to you is for your ears only."

"You sound serious."

"I am. I like you Englishman. You are honest, forthright and brave. More than that I can see that your men would follow you to hell and back. You are a leader." He lowered his voice, "The Emperor suspects that you and the Empress have, how should I say, become close."

"You mean..." He nodded, "But that is ridiculous!"

"I know but he is the Emperor. All that I am saying is be more circumspect around her and watch your back in the tourney."

"That is easy. I will not participate."

"I am afraid that would make matters even worse. It would be considered an insult to the Emperor." He saw my crestfallen face. "I am sorry, my friend. My brothers and I will be in the tourney and we will do all that we can to protect you."

"It is not me I worry about but Guy and Edward. They have done nothing wrong."

"And that is another reason I like you; you are honest and protect those who serve you."

"That is the way I was brought up. My father's men were oathsworn."

Rolf smiled, "Oathsworn. I have not heard that word for many years. I like the idea."

Edward came out, "He's ready for you, sir!"

Rolf just nodded to me as I entered the tiring booth. He was on our side. He would say no more and it would be up to me to speak to my men.

Chapter 5

Although I had decided to tell my men of the dangers we might face that night they were in no condition to hear my words. Even Harold and Alan had been into the town to sample some of their beer. They were reeling as they fell into their beds. I had spoken with Edward on the way back to the castle and told him.

"That's the trouble with women sir, they don't mix with war. And don't worry. You did nothing wrong. It must have been good for her to have someone she could speak to in her own language. The sooner we are out of here the better."

I nodded and added, gloomily, "You realise we shall have to go back the way we came. We cannot go north; we would have to pass through Flanders."

He laughed, "Yes Baron but, to be honest, we can get back a lot quicker. We have spare horses and we don't need to go sedately. We can cut the journey in half and we know where to avoid now, don't we?"

He was right and his positive attitude made me feel better. I prepared for this feast I would have to attend. I was not looking forward to it. I had made sure that I had one decent tunic. It was from Constantinople. Not only was it beautifully made, but it was also extremely light. I could not get used to the lack of bathing here in the west. I had Harold fetch me a large bowl of hot water and I bathed from head to foot. I still had some of the oils I had brought from the east and I oiled my body with them. I could, at least, smell civilised for a while.

We were told to be on time for the feast. The two squires were invited. Poor Guy felt bad about not having one. "I could never afford one Baron but seeing Harold and Alan makes me envious."

"Surely you can afford one now, Sir Guy. You have some of the coins we took from the dead Flemings."

"Not enough. I would have to equip him with armour and horses."

"But we have spare horses we captured."

He brightened, "True, and if we can win the tourney then I may be even richer."

I did not want him under any illusions about the tourney. We would be the target from all but the Swabians. I took him to one side and explained the Emperor's attitude.

He did not seem put out. "If they all come for us so much the better. We can show them how brave and skilled we are. Do not worry Alfraed, we are good. I know that sounds like boasting but that charge up the hill showed me how good we are." He put his arm around me. "And do not worry; tonight I drink only wine and I will be less boisterous than I was last night!"

I saw my companions look at each other as we entered the Great Hall. Apart from me they appeared to be shabbily dressed compared with the fine gowns and clothes on display. It looked like a deliberate attempt to put us in our place. To me, it seemed like a statement of our status; we were good enough to be hired swords only. The tables were set out in a large hollow square and we were directly opposite from the Emperor and Empress. Matilda did not look happy although she smiled when anyone addressed her. The food and the drink were brought to us continuously. It was the first time I had eaten German cuisine and there seem to be a lot of heavy pork dishes and sausages. There was wine on offer and, like Guy, I stuck to that.

I chatted with Rolf, on one side of me, and Sir Guy on the opposite. I would miss both of them when I returned west. Sir Guy would be with us as far as Bar but it was unlikely that I would ever see my Swabian comrades again. Rolf surreptitiously pointed out some of the more important people. "The man seated next to the Empress is Count Stephan of Stuttgart. He fancies himself as a swordsman. He and his conroi usually win the tourney. I expect he thinks they will win this one too. On the other side of the Emperor is Count Charles of Aachen. He is the most untrustworthy man in this whole room. I would steer clear of him. He is keen for power. If I were the Emperor I would keep both eyes on him. He smiles but it is a false smile."

I swallowed the wine that was left in my goblet. "I have already had enough of this intrigue. We leave as soon as the tourney is over. If the King does not need me then I return to the Northern Marches."

"You wish for a dull life then?"

Edward had heard the comment, "Dull? I think not, my friend. We have had less fighting on this journey than we see in a month at home."

"Whom do you fight?"

I held up my goblet to be refilled, "There are Scots. We still have occasional Viking raids and then there are traitors like the De Brus clan who are a Norman version of the Count of Aachen. They would get on well together." Edward and Guy laughed.

The Emperor's Chamberlain banged his staff on the floor. We all fell silent. The Emperor stood. He looked a little thin and pasty to me. He was no warrior. He smiled and spread his arms as though to embrace the room. "We are here to celebrate our dear wife, the Empress' safe return. Thanks to our brave knights she came to no harm. In honour of these knights, we are holding a tourney so that they can demonstrate the skills which kept Empress Matilda safe." Everyone cheered and banged the table. The volume of each cheer was an indication of the amount of beer and wine they had consumed.

He held up his hands for silence. "We have decided to reward them for their services to the Empire." He waved his arms and three servants appeared behind us. They had three of the great helms similar to the one worn by the Count du Bar. They were magnificent. "To my brave Swabian knights, Sir Rolf, Sir Gottfried and Sir Carl I present these helmets."

The three Swabians took them and lifted them up. The whole room cheered. As he sat down Rolf said, "I bet the damned thing doesn't fit. I have an enormous head you know!"

When silence fell once more he waved his arm again and a servant came behind us with a purple cushion. "I know that Sir Guy of Dijon has worked tirelessly in my borderlands. To Sir Guy I give the demesne of La Cheppe. Since the last owner was so treacherously slain it is good to know that I will have a guardian for my road once more."

Sir Guy stood and, taking the chain of office, put it around his neck. Once more there was cheering. I wondered what our reward would be. I could not see us being given a manor and if it had been a helmet we would have received ours with the Swabians. I was intrigued more than anything else. When the Emperor stood I knew it was not going to be anything good. He had a sly smile playing about the edges of his mouth. "The two English knights have served their king well and I have no doubt that King Henry will reward his men in his own way."

Two servants came behind us and placed a cushion before both Edward and myself. On it was a single coin. It was a gold piece of Flanders. The face of Charles, Count of Flanders, stared up at me. Edward looked at me and I gave a slight shake of the head. I stood and, smiling, said, "We thank the Emperor for his gift but he is quite correct we need no reward. The Empress Matilda's safe return to her home was reward enough."

As I sat down, this time amid a hubbub of chatter, Rolf said, "This is a disgrace! You and Edward did more than both myself and Sir Guy here. He is insulting you."

I said, calmly, "Of course he is but at least we know where we stand now, don't we Edward?"

Edward laughed, "Aye sir, and this will come in handy! It might not be much to him but it is half a year's earnings for me."

I was only half listening for I was watching the flushed face of the Empress who had obviously not approved of what she had seen and heard. I also saw the sniggers from the two Counts who were seated on the top table. From the animated conversation which was going on between them and the Emperor, they were obviously a party to it.

Sir Guy turned to me, "I feel awful about this, Alfraed. You have nothing and I have my heart's desire."

I smiled, "I am happy for you and for your uncle. La Cheppe is close to his manor and it makes that part of the road safer. I expected nothing. It appears I have upset the Emperor. He has no reason to suspect me and I can do nothing about his thoughts. I will soon be gone from here. Do not let it worry you. I will soon be back in England and I will be far from his influence."

"Thank you for your understanding." He studied the seal of his new manor. I realised that I had obtained my manor in a similar way. One owner died and the king, or in this case, emperor, replaced him as though he had never existed. Such was life. We were pawns to be used in this grand game of chess which emperors, kings and princes played. I remained quiet. Our table was relatively quiet; the others examined the three great helms and discussed how they might affect a knight when fighting.

"We shall discover this at the tourney. I, for one, am looking forward to this." Gottfried was turning the helmet around in his hands.

"It might impair your vision and your hearing. The holes for the eyes have to be small else a blade could get in there and render the whole thing useless." Edward was ever the practical knight. He had been a man at arms for almost fifteen years and what he did not know about fighting was not worth knowing.

"Possibly but it would be very hard to get a lance below the edge and almost impossible to force such a helmet off a head. I have seen it tried before and failed."

Edward pointed a thumb at me, "The Baron here doesn't go for the head. He goes for the middle."

"Surely that is a harder target?"

I had not been paying close attention. I was still watching the top table, "What? Oh, the middle. It is a bigger target than the head. If you miss when you aim at the head you have a good chance that your lance will go above your enemy's head. A middle thrust which misses either hits the chest or the cantle. Both can dismount a rider."

Rolf nodded, "Interesting but perhaps you have given your secret away for the tourney."

I smiled, putting the Emperor and his machinations from my mind, "Perhaps I have others."

"You will bear watching."

The eight of us were the first to retire. I did not fall asleep straight away. Although I had done nothing to justify my treatment by the Emperor I knew that I had in my thoughts. Matilda was an Empress and the daughter of a king. What could she see in a lowly Baron who had a tiny manor at the edge of the world?

I was up early and I resolved that I had sat on my backside long enough. I sought Wulfric and Dick. "Today we become warriors again. I want every weapon sharpened. We need more arrows manufacturing. I want every shield painted blue."

"Already done, Baron and Sir Edward mentioned the gambesons for the archers. We bought some dye yesterday and they are drying now. We found a washerwoman who made them blue for a few copper coins. She said if we get some blue stars she will sew them on for us too.

Dick nudged Wulfric in the ribs. "Of course, old Wulfric here sweet-talked her too, eh?"

Wulfric sniffed, "There's more than one way to skin a cat, my friend."

I clapped them both on the back. "Excellent. We have a tourney coming up and as soon as it is over we will be heading back with Sir Guy and his men. He now has a manor."

"Good, I like him, sir. He is approachable. Not like that Sir Richard. I never liked him!" My men were honest to the point of bluntness.

We went to the tailor and picked up our surcoats. He promised me that the others would be ready by the tourney. I was about to leave and he said, "Baron, I hope you don't mind but someone heard I was making your surcoats and asked which one was yours. I told him the one with the blue flower in the middle of the upper star. I hope I did right."

I nodded, "It matters not but could you tell me who it was?"

"It was the steward of the Count of Aachen."

"Thank you."

I did not bother Rolf or the Swabians with that information but I did tell Edward, Sir Guy and my men at arms.

"That means they will be looking for you on the field."

I smiled, "Better me than one of you two. It seems I have made myself a target. When this tourney is over we will revert to plain blue stars."

The tourney was to be held on the site of an old Roman fort. There was a circular ring which the Roman Cavalry had used when they had trained. I had seen them in the east and when we had travelled from Genoa to Caen. In the time of Charlemagne, they had begun to use it again to practise formations. The Emperor had extended its use. He entertained his people. It now afforded a good view for spectators and was large enough for charges and retreats. We lined up before the dais containing the Emperor and the Empress. Emperor Henry stood. "The prize for the winner today is this chest of silver." It was a small chest but worth winning. "The judgements of my heralds will be final. If you fall from your horse then you are eliminated. If you are knocked to the ground you are eliminated. All other decisions will be made by my heralds. May God be with you."

There were four conroi and each had a table where there were wooden swords and spare lances. I suspected that they would all come for me as soon as it began and I would be eliminated first. It mattered not. I had already sent a message to the Emperor, through Rolf, telling him that we would be leaving immediately after the tourney. An early elimination would not hurt. Apart from the conroi of Swabians, there was the Count of Stuttgart and his team. There was another team who were dressed like Lothar and Konrad. They had black surcoats with a white cross above their hearts. I suspected they were their friends and they would seek to hurt me.

As we waited for the trumpet signalling the start I said, "Our only chance is if we fight as we did the other day. Stay tight on me and listen for orders. Let me know when danger comes." I nodded in the direction of the Teutons. "They will come at us in a wild rush. Rolf and his Swabians will challenge the Count."

"How do you know?"

"Rolf told me!"

The trumpet sounded and, as I expected, the three Teutons hurtled at us. Thankfully they came at us individually and did not keep as tight as we did; it gave us a distinct advantage. We galloped towards them and I pulled my arm back. I punched forward at the middle knight's cantle with the long lance. As I did so I lifted my shield and it deflected his spear up. Mine hit him squarely in the middle. I had used Star to lean in too so that he was thrown from his saddle. I saw Edward do the same to his. The lances of Sir Guy and the last Teuton were broken. We rode back to replace them. I had the opportunity to watch the other battle. Carl was down but Rolf and Gottfried were holding their own.

"Sir Guy, can you take the last German?"

"Having watched you two, yes. Go and help Rolf."

With new lances, Edward and I galloped to the other side of the circle. Rolf had knocked one of the Count's men from his saddle but he was then struck from his by the Count himself. Carl fought bravely but he was outnumbered. He was knocked from his saddle.

The two knights turned and rode back to their table. Protocol determined that we had to let them re arm. We galloped towards them. I intended to take out the Count but he had other ideas and he made directly for Edward. He charged across my front and his horse was fast. His lance thudded into Edward throwing him from his horse. I wheeled around and shattered my lance as I smashed its head into the shield of the other knight. He was not thrown from his horse but I could see that I had hurt him.

I returned to pick up a second lance and saw that Sir Guy had finished off the last of the Teutons. "Two against two eh, Baron? We have a chance."

"Watch out for the Count he is tricky."

Sir Guy had the joy of battle upon him. I had seen it before. He did not wait for me but turned and charged the two last knights. It was a mistake. The Count led with his injured knight protecting his lance side. It meant that they could hit Sir Guy with two lances.

I spurred Star to help my friend. Even as I charged I knew I would be too late. Sir Guy was dumped unceremoniously from his horse and, worse still the two knights, with whole lances, came directly for me. I had, however, seen the fate of my companion and I would not fall into the trap. I knew the Count was the stronger and I decided to take out the man I had injured. As I approached them I made them think I was going to the Count and the two knights closed up. Using my knees, I moved Star right and then jerked the reins around so that I rode directly for the injured knight. Once again, I punched but this time there was anger in my blow. There was a huge crack as my lance broke when it struck the shield. Then there was a cry of pain.

I wheeled my horse around to replace my lance. At any moment I expected a blow from the lance which the Count still held but it never came. When I turned, at the table, I saw that the injured knight was being helped from his horse. He could no longer continue. The Count handed his lance to one of his retainers and was handed another by a sergeant at arms. I grabbed my own and turned Star. It was now the Count, the knight who always won these tourneys, against me, who had never fought in one until that day.

I allowed Star a few moments to recover. He was a powerful horse and he was eager for battle. I needed to control him. I saw the Count move and I spurred Star. I shortened my reins and held my shield tightly to my head. The Count had a great helm upon his head. I relied upon the fact that his vision might be slightly impaired, I raised the tip of my lance so that it was aimed at his head, as his was with me. I pulled back my arm and braced myself. As we closed I ducked behind my shield and punched at his cantle with my own lance. I heard a whinny from Star as his lance struck her on the mane and then punched into my right shoulder. I felt a sharp pain but my knees still gripped Star and my own lance had made the Count and his horse stagger to the right. I threw away the broken haft and drew the wooden sword.

It was now my sword skills which would be tested. I rode after the Count who was trying to control his horse. Star was angry and snorted as he leapt after them. I stood in my stirrups and brought the sword down across the middle of the Count's back. I think he must have thought that I was down for he had not drawn his own sword. He was, however, a good horseman and he wheeled his horse in a tight circle whilst drawing his own sword.

I could not afford to let this superior warrior get the better of me. He had the advantage for he had done this before. I was a novice. I swung the sword, as we closed horizontally. I saw the weakness in the great helm for he only saw that it was coming for his head at the last moment. It clattered into the helmet and his head jerked back. As we passed he smashed his sword across my back. It hurt.

I pulled to the right and headed for his sword side. He, too, turned and, standing in his stirrups brought the sword above his head. I raised my shield above my own head, spurred Star and swept my own sword across his middle. Star's speed, my blow and his unbalanced stance meant that he tumbled backwards over his horse's rump to land in a heap on the floor of the arena.

The cheers from the stands told me I had won and when Edward, Guy and the Swabians rushed to me, it was confirmed. I took off my helmet and felt the cool air around my hot head. Edward patted Star's mane, "That was superb sir. You cut him down to size." Suddenly he stopped and held up his hand. It was bloody. Star had been cut. "Baron, look at this."

The others stopped smiling and looked at the bloody hand. Rolf examined Star's neck. "There is a long cut here."

"Perhaps the lance splintered. See if there is wood within."

Rolf shook his head, "No, Sir Guy, this was made by metal it is sharp." He pointed to my surcoat. "And there is a hole in Baron Alfraed's surcoat. This was a metal tipped spear."

I held up my hand. "I am not hurt and Star will heal. Say nothing. Let them think that we do not know what they have done. Come on, smile and cheer, we have won."

Rolf shook his head, "You are a strange one but we will go along with you."

They led Star to the dais. I dismounted and approached the Emperor and Empress. I saw the joy on the face of the Empress and the thin-lipped smile on the Emperor. He was not happy and I wondered how much he had had to do with the attempt on my life. I had no doubt that he had used the Count to try to hurt me. As we waited for them to descend I glanced over and saw the Count and his men leaving the arena. I would have to watch out for him.

I knelt as the Emperor approached, "You have done exceptionally well, Englishman. That is the first time I have seen the Count unhorsed. He is never beaten. You are someone to keep an eye on." I was looking up into his eyes and I saw hatred. There was something else I saw, pain. The Emperor was not a well man. Perhaps this explained his dyspeptic nature. He held out the chest. "Here is your reward, rise." I rose and took the chest. "I am told you leave today."

"Yes, sire. We have to get back to Caen. The King may need us."

"Then I hope you have a safer and less eventful journey home than you had coming."

I wondered if that was a threat, but I smiled and replied, "As do I sire."

Matilda said, suddenly, "I have decided to reward the six of you for your services to me. I know that the Emperor has rewarded you but we would like to give you all something to remember me by." I could see that the Emperor knew nothing of this from the expression he bore but the silent arena and crowd meant that they had heard Matilda's words which had been spoken loudly enough for all to hear. She waved a delicate hand and two servants came across, each bearing a cushion.

"I have created an order of knights. They will be the Knights of the Empress Matilda. You six will be the first recipients. Kneel." We all fell to our knees and looked up at her. She began with the Swabians who were kneeling to my left and she placed what looked like a large coin or medallion around each of their necks. She spoke quietly to each of them as she did so. Then she went to Sir Guy at the other end of the line and placed one around his neck. After Edward, she came to me and put the medallion around my neck. "By this token you are sworn to protect me and to come to me should I need you."

As I looked up I saw that her eyes sparkled and there was more behind the words than within them. "I swear, as I did to your father, to protect you with my life; always."

Spontaneously the others all intoned, "We swear to protect you with our lives."

There was a momentary pause then the crowd all cheered and the moment was gone. The Emperor whisked Matilda away before she could say another word and we were left alone in the arena. I looked at the medallion. It had been cast in bronze and had the Empress' image on one side and Saint George slaying the dragon on the other. It seemed appropriate. As we compared them Rolf suddenly laughed, "It seems we are not all equal."

Sir Guy asked, "What do you mean?"

He held up his. "Do you see how each of us has a different colour stone in our medal? The baron has a blue one but if you notice it is placed in the heart of the Empress. Ours are in her hand. It seems the baron must be her favourite."

I shook my head. "I think you are wrong. They look to be in the same place to me. The man who made them must have made a mistake."

Gottfried said, "No mistake but it does not matter. We six are sworn to protect her. Let us take the blood oath."

Sir Guy looked confused, "Blood oath?"

In answer, Rolf took out his dagger and made a cut across the palm of his hand. The Swabians, Edward and myself all did the same. I knew the custom from my father. Sir Guy nodded and did the same. We then all clasped hands so that our blood intermingled. Rolf nodded, "Now we are blood brothers and oathsworn. He walked over to a brazier burning in the corner and, taking his knife, plunged it into the flame. After a few moments, he took it out and placed it on the wound. He repeated it with us all. "Now we are oathsworn in blood and fire. When the Empress is in danger then we must go to her side; no matter what."

After we had tended to Star's injury we returned to our quarters. Guy and Edward took off my surcoat. "Look at that sir. There is a dent in the armour."

I could see that there was a small dent in the armour. It was where the lance had struck me. It had not penetrated but the scale would need replacing. Just then Carl came in holding something in his hand. Gottfried and Rolf were with him

"I returned to the arena and found the lance the Count used. I found this in the broken end." He opened his palm and there was a narrow arrowhead. It would have been invisible at the end of the lance. Edward took it and placed it next to the dent in the armour. It was a perfect match.

Edward rolled the narrow arrowhead in his hand. "They didn't know you wore lamellar armour, Baron. If you had worn mail then this would have gone right through." He placed it next to his mail and I saw that it would have gone through. "The Count was trying to kill you."

"Keep that safe Edward. I shall return it to the Count one day." Turning to the Swabians I said, "And you three watch yourselves. Being associated with me may be dangerous."

"Do not worry, my English friend, we have learned about treachery the hard way and our comrade paid with his life. We will watch."

We parted from the Swabians and, after picking up the surcoats and supplies for the journey we left. It was in direct contrast to our arrival.

The streets were empty leading to the gates for people were enjoying the holiday atmosphere in the taverns of the town. We were able to slip out unobserved. The men were satisfied for they had enjoyed their stay in the town for they had had none of the politics to contend with. They had drunk and wenched. Some had spent all of their coins and were now eager for action and the prospect of more treasure. The three of us, who rode at the front, had much to think on. Harold and Alan had been on the periphery of the intrigue but Edward and Guy knew as well as I did that there were plots and intrigues going on here.

"Guy, you live in the Empire; how does it view France and Normandy?"

He shrugged, "We are in the provinces and it is hard to judge. As far as we can tell the Empire supports your King Henry. After all, his daughter is the Empress of the Empire but events in the last few days have made me question that."

Edward had an annoyed expression on his face. Since he had discovered the arrow head he had been silently fuming, "My question, Baron Alfraed, is how did those knights get so far into the Empire unless someone was giving them support. We were almost within sight of Worms when they attacked. And those two Teutons, Lothar and Konrad, who got them close to the Empress? This is a big conspiracy. No sir. I am glad to be rid of that place. Not the Empress mind, she is worth fighting for, but she has found herself in a nest of vipers there."

We rode in silence for a while. I did not want to think about Empress Matilda trapped there so far away from home and so vulnerable. I turned to Edward's squire. "How is the arm, Alan?"

"It aches a little but the physician we saw in Worms said that Wulfric had set it well. I am just pleased it was only my shield arm."

"Good. I would like to ride hard, Sir Guy, and get to your uncle's castle as soon as possible. I wish to question Lothar and Konrad. We now have names to put to them."

That night we camped on a small hill where we could defend ourselves. I divided the money we had won between Sir Guy and Edward. I knew they would use some to pay their own men. I would do the same. Sir Guy had used his reward from the Emperor to hire four more men at arms. There had been many in Worms and Rolf had chosen them for him. We were a formidable-looking force as we sped along the roads to Bar. I hoped that, without the Empress and with so many men, we would deter any attacker. I was proved correct for we reached Bar quickly and without incident. However, as we approached the gates of the town I saw, on top of the castles walls, the heads of Lothar and Konrad. We would question no one.

Chapter 6

"But the message came from the Emperor with the news of your good fortune, Guy. We were told to execute them as traitors. The rider arrived two days ago." The Count du Bar looked upset. He had given his word and the Emperor had forced his hand.

"That explains the games and the delay in holding them. They wanted us there. I wonder what they could have told us."

"Just before they died, Lothar shouted, 'Curse the Count! He has betrayed us. I guessed he meant the Count of Flanders."

Sir Guy shook his head, "We met two more candidates in Worms, uncle; the Counts of Aachen and Stuttgart. I am glad to be home."

His uncle smiled, "And now we can help you build your castle. Baron, will you stay awhile?"

"No, thank you for your kind offer but we must get back to Caen and I fear we have the more dangerous part to come."

"We will escort you as far as La Cheppe."

"You do not need to."

"It will not be any trouble and I am loath to lose your company."

Sir Guy laughed, "I think my uncle will be glad to have me off his hands! He just has one demesne to find for Raymond."

Raymond nodded, "Oh you need not worry about me. I am going to seek my fortune in the Holy Land. You have found fame and fortune when you left Bar, perhaps I will have the same good fortune."

"Besides, we need to help him rebuild the castle and this time we will do it in stone. It does not burn so easily. We can make a better castle than poor Guiscard did."

"I only made a few gold coins, uncle."

"We still have the gold from Lothar and Konrad. I feel I can use that to build a stronger defence. After all you will be protecting my western approaches."

We camped that night, at the desolate graveyard that was La Cheppe. I did not envy them their task. They would have to clear the site of the dead before they could begin their work. We now had to move through the land of France, skirt Flanders and find a way to avoid Count Fulk's men in Anjou. We left the encampment at La Cheppe at dawn. The farewells showed the bond that we had made. Three of us were Knights of the Empress. I was not certain how we would serve her but I knew that the three of us would never forget our oaths.

We did, at least, look like a real conroi. The blues of our gambesons and surcoats were almost the same colour and the two stars looked good. The men, even the archers, had liked them. We now had only five archers. This had been an expensive foray for archers were almost impossible to replace. I split them into three uneven groups. Being lightly armed their horses could ride further without tiring and I had three, under Dick, ranging far ahead while the other pair rode to our left and right protecting our flanks. We were also down to five men at arms. Our adventure had cost us good men. We shunned towns wherever possible. The Count had provided us with supplies of dried meat and we had water skins. It would be the rivers which would determine our course west. We had to cross the major ones and use the minor ones for drinking. That was how they eventually trapped us. We had not been forgotten. We had merely delayed their pursuit. We had headed to the north of Paris this time but we had to turn west otherwise we risked crossing into the land of the Count of Flanders and that was when they found us.

Dick came galloping back towards sunset. We were close to the tiny hamlet of Saint Nicholas d'Azy. Ahead was the River Nonette. There was a ford but once across we were clear to Caen and we would be home in three days. Dick's sudden arrival put paid to that.

He reined in, breathing hard. "There are men waiting on the other side of the ford, Baron. They are waiting for us, I think."

"How do you know?"

"I saw the knight with the red shield again. I recognised his horse." He shrugged, "Unless there are two such knights."

"No, you are probably right. How many are there?"

"Six knights. I counted ten men at arms and I think they have six crossbowmen. I could not be sure of the crossbowmen. I did not wish to get too close in case I was seen."

"You did well. Where are our other two archers?"

"They watch from the trees. I found John and Mark, the other scouts and they watch too."

I turned to the others. "Council of war." My men at arms, squires and Edward, gathered around me. "We have five archers and nine who can wield a sword." I looked at Alan. "I will not risk you. You can watch the spare horses. Someone needs to do it." He nodded.

Edward asked, "Dick, could we charge them?"

"You would be slain by the crossbows before you were half way across the river. It is narrow but the crossbowmen are well hidden in the trees."

"And the others are hidden?"

"They are all hidden."

"Then I have a plan." I gathered them around and explained my idea to them. It was risky but it was the only one I had. We had to get around Paris and the alternative was a hundred-mile detour south. Who knew what dangers we might meet in France?

As I led Harold and Wulfric towards the ford I was relying on the fact that our ambushers had not spotted my scouts. I had tried to envisage what they would see. They would see the three of us, the advance party, heading for the river. We would talk of setting up camp and letting our horses water. I doubted that they would attack until they had us all. Because we now wore surcoats they would just see a knight, a squire and a man at arms. I guessed they would be expecting more men. That was the plan but if I suddenly found a crossbow bolt in my chest then I would know that I was wrong.

We rode leisurely towards the water. I found it hard not to stare across the river and look for our enemies. I had stressed to Harold and Wulfric that we had to appear casual. I had also told them what to say. We dismounted and feigned checking our girths. In reality Harold was stringing his bow.

"I wish Edward would get a move on. Damn his lame horse."

"He is doing his best, my lord. Don't forget poor Alan's wound will delay them too."

I snorted, noticing that Harold had an arrow nocked already.

"Well, this looks like a good place to camp. When they come we will cross and set up camp. You two wait here and I will see if I can hurry them up." I mounted. I watched as Wulfric, hidden behind his horse slipped his shield over his shoulder. I pulled Scout's head around as though heading west and as the first arrows sped across the river strapped my shield close to my body, drew my sword and galloped across the river. I heard the hooves of Edward's horse as he galloped up to join Wulfric and me. I braced myself for the crossbow bolt which never came. My archers had hit them all and were now felling the men at arms who, seeing the trap sprung, were streaming down to the water to get at us.

This time we would approach them in single file. I was still not confident about Harold in combat, especially when facing so many knights. They came at me in a wedge led by a knight with a yellow quartered shield and a light green and yellow surcoat. He had a lance. He would need more than a little luck to hit me while riding down a rough slope. I heard a roar from the two flanks as my archers and men at arms fell upon the ambushers. I knew the crossbowmen were dead which made our numbers almost even and I hoped that the sudden attack would give us the edge. First, however, I had to fight my way through the four knights who were charging towards me. By lowering my head slightly, I avoided the lance which stabbed at the empty air above my helmet. I punched with my shield and the already unbalanced knight tumbled into the water.

A second knight came at me and I stood in my stirrups to rise up and bring my sword down hard on his helmet. Although he brought his shield up quickly it was not quickly enough and he fell backwards off his. He had not had time to make a strike with his sword. As he splashed into the edge of the river I heard a shout of pain as Edward finished off the knight with the quartered shield.

My archers were raining death with great accuracy on our enemies and the men at arms were fleeing. I saw the knight with the red shield. He turned and began to gallop up the slope. I spurred Scout on. He was one of the keys to these attacks. He had been at the last two and I would have words with him this time. I passed the bodies of some of the dead ambushers. Up ahead I saw Wulfric and his men as they laid into the remaining warriors with their swords. The trees, which lined the river, began to thin and I started to gain upon the knight in red. I hoped that Harold was still with me but I could not look around. I had to concentrate on the red knight.

Suddenly another knight came charging from the trees to my right. I do not know if he had waited there for me or was just lucky. His lance struck my shoulder and I felt myself falling from Scout. I kicked my feet from my stirrups. I did not want to drag my horse down with me. As I fell I saw a large tree to my left. I instinctively put my head behind my shield and when we struck the tree the shield took the worst of the damage. I rolled to my right just as the lance jabbed into the tree against which I had fallen. It proved to be the knight's undoing. He failed to release the lance and he fell forward as the lance embedded its head against the tree.

He fell in a heap some ten paces from me. I ran to him with my damaged shield and my sword. I was putting my sword to his throat and yelling, "Yield!" when he swept his foot and took my legs from me.

As I crashed to the ground I resolved to stab first next time; if there was to be a next time. He was on his feet in an instant and he drew his sword and brought it overhand to strike at me. It hit my shield and a huge rent appeared in it. I could see my life being ended here in this inconsequential valley in the middle of Frankia. That could not be. I had too much to live for. I brought my sword horizontally across his body. He countered with his shield but his feet were on the slope and the blow caused him to slip and stagger. While he was concentrating on balancing I swung vertically and when he brought his shield up my powerful blow made him lose the little balance he had. He tumbled backwards down the steep slope towards the river. I went after him, watching my footing for I did not wish to lose my balance too. I saw him crash, finally, to earth and he gave a sigh. A tendril of blood appeared at the corner of his mouth. I saw that he had speared himself on the broken stump of a tree. It grew from his middle like a red flower. He was dying.

"What is your name?"

"Roger of Conisborough."

He was from England. "Who sent you here?"

He tried to laugh but it was too much, "De Brus has a long arm and a longer memory he…"

His head fell off to the side and he was dead. De Brus haunted me still. Harold ran towards me. "Are you all right, Baron? I am sorry I did not stay close enough."

I laughed, "It was a plan riddled with risks. Find how many men fell." When he left, I searched the body. His sword was a good one and I took it. He had a jewelled dagger too. However, when I found his purse I discovered five gold coins and each one was from Charles of Flanders. He might have said De Brus, but Charles, Count of Flanders, had his sticky fingers all over the ambush.

I found Scout and the dead knight's horse was close by. I led them both back to the river. There I saw what we had gained and what we had lost. There were four good horses and a pile of arms. The bodies of Roger and Geoffrey told me that we had paid a price. Edward held out his hand; on it, there were eight golden coins. Each one bore the face of Charles Count of Flanders. "It seems he wants you dead, Baron!"

"But the knight I questioned spoke of De Brus. This is a complicated web. Let us bury our brothers and then make camp. This has been an expensive journey we have taken."

Wulfric nodded, "And yet, my lord, we are all the richer. I served with these two for many years. They would have taken the gamble any day. It is a risk we all take. Though there are but three of us left but when our time comes, Baron, remember us but do not mourn us. We do what we do because we can!"

The men had collected all of the weapons. I watched in amusement as the archers and men at arms smashed the crossbows into tiny pieces. "Why do you hate them so, Dick?"

"Crossbows are the work of the devil, my lord. They enable a pathetically weak man to release a bolt. God did not intend that. God wants archers who have spent years training and preparing to pull back the bow and release the arrow. He does not want a devilish infernal machine that can be used by a weakling!" In a final gesture of destruction, the pieces were used to feed our fire so that even the metal parts were rendered useless. Archers hated the crossbow.

It was a pathetically small conroi which rode into Caen. We had horses and we had gold but we had but two knights, two squires, three men at arms and five archers. I hoped that the King did not need us soon for we were in no condition to serve him as we should.

Robert of Gloucester commanded. "How is my sister?"

"We got her highness there but it was not easy." I told him of the plots, assassination attempts and the treachery. Finally, I gave him my losses.

"You have suffered and for that I am sorry. I know how valuable your men are to you. And I have no good news for you. The King cannot release you for we go to war against Charles of Flanders."

"And there you are wrong. That is good news for that man has paid for all the attempts on our lives." I held out a handful of the coins we had collected from his assassins. He nodded sympathetically. "Where is your father?

"He is in Blois gathering men for the campaign."

"It is late in the season to campaign."

"And that is why we shall go for Charles will not be expecting it. We have a truce with Count Fulk and this is our best chance to hurt him."

"Beware the Emperor, I think he plays a dangerous game, my lord. Your sister is not happy."

"I know, she spoke with me at length when she visited."

"Are there any men at arms for hire here?"

He shook his head, "No, my father is struggling to raise enough warriors. The Empire and the frontier are restless." He shrugged. "He will be glad that you have returned safely. It confirms his trust in you and gives him a commander he can rely upon."

"Me? I know nothing!"

"And yet you survive and you profit. I have heard of this Count of Stuttgart. If you defeated him then you are remarkable. Do not disparage yourself." He patted my arm, "On a personal note I am pleased that you saved my sister. I am more than fond of her. She served my father and has been ill served by her husband."

"What do you mean?"

"He sends the Empress with an escort so small that bandits could take them? I think he used her as bait to tempt out his enemies."

I had not thought of that but it made perfect sense. And I had done no better. I had left her with him. My only consolation was that my three brothers, the Knights of the Empress, were there and they would die before allowing harm to befall her.

The King was away for four more days which allowed me to have my armour repaired and a new shield made. I had the stable master check out Star's wound and he passed him fit. We would go to war with sound armour and horses. We had three spare warhorses now and four palfreys. I could, if they were available, hire more men at arms. What I needed was another knight. Harold was coming on but far too slowly.

It was relatively pleasant to be in the castle and enjoy the company of Robert of Gloucester. He might have been an illegitimate son of the King but he was the best general I ever served with and that included Henry. The fact that we both held Matilda in such high esteem also helped. The earl spent two nights asking me about the Empire and our travails crossing it.

"I knew about the Count of Flanders but these other enemies were a mystery to me."

"I hate to say this, my lord, but I am not certain that the Emperor holds your sister in high regard, for if we had not discovered the plot then the two Teutons would have killed her. She deserves a better man."

He smiled at me. "You are smitten, Alfraed, but you can do nothing about this. She is an Empress. Put her from your mind."

63

I nodded but my thoughts told me something different. How could I forget her? Our destinies were irrevocably bound together. My father and his oathsworn had spoken of wyrd, fate. This was wyrd!

When King Henry returned he looked weary. I later learned that he had had to bully and threaten many of his subjects to fight for him. In the past, I had been naïve enough to believe that the wives and children of his knights who stayed in his castle were guests. They were hostages. This time there were no hostages. He had brought ten knights and forty men at arms. I waited to be summoned.

"Harold, you had better prepare the men. If the King has returned then we will be campaigning soon." He nodded. "How is Alan's arm?" I worried about his ability to defend Edward.

"It is almost healed, Baron. He will be able to hold a shield. I had suggested putting padding there to cushion the shock of the blows. His right hand is stronger than it was."

That was no surprise he had been forced to use his right arm for all things. The wound had not been all bad. When his left arm healed he would be a stronger warrior.

"Baron Norton, the King will see you now."

The King was slumped in his chair and Robert of Gloucester stood behind him. He smiled when he saw me, "Come, and sit, the two of you." After we had seated ourselves he pushed across the pichet of wine. "You bring a little hope into my life, Alfraed of Norton. From what my son says you and your men were assailed all the way to Worms and back; yet you succeeded."

"Yes, your majesty. There are strange alliances being formed out there."

"I know. The Count Flanders I knew about. And I had heard that Louis was putting forward my nephew, William Clito, as a candidate for this land but I knew not about the Emperor." He shook his head, "I have sacrificed my daughter and I cannot trust the man she married."

"He appeared to me to be a complicated man, your majesty but I do not think he has control over his Empire."

I saw the interest in the King's eyes. "You think not?"

"He has some knights such as the Count du Bar who protect his lands but many others regard themselves as their own rulers. I can see the attraction of the alliances. He protects his borders. He is at peace with you, the French and now, it seems, the men of Flanders. I think he is like the duck which sails upon the pond. Upon the surface, it is serene but

64

beneath it is paddling like fury. He plots and he plans. He is a man to be watched."

"You use your eyes and your head. That is good. My son tells me that you have been made a Knight of the Empress?" I nodded, "My daughter has created her own order of knights. She is thinking then. I wish that she had been born a man and then I would have an heir after I die."

Robert said, "She still could be."

"What and leave my land to the Emperor? When I married her to him I did not think that my only son and heir would drown on the White Ship. I still have time for a son if God lets me live that long." He shook his head as though to clear the thoughts from within. "We leave tomorrow for Ghent. I will teach this Charles of Flanders that he threatens me at his peril. Had we more men then I could conquer his lands but the Welsh and the Scots are being troublesome."

My ears pricked up. Was my home safe?

"When this is over we will return to England to deal with these irritations."

To me, a threat to my home and my people was not an irritation. It was a cause for concern. The sooner I returned the better.

Chapter 7

This time we were able to leave some of our booty and our spare horses at Caen as we headed north to the land of the Flemings. It was not a large Battle which the King led. He had ten household knights and twenty others. Of men at arms we had a hundred but of archers we had barely fifty. They were a valuable commodity and I prayed that Wulfstan was training more at Norton and Stockton. I could hire men at arms, there were many of them, but an archer could only be raised on our island home. It was one reason why Henry was so successful. Our archers gave us an edge over the enemy but this campaign that would be an exceedingly thin edge.

The land through which we travelled was flat and well cultivated. It had been cleared of trees in the time of the Romans. It made it valuable land for farming. As we rode towards Calais I spoke with Robert of Gloucester about the small numbers his father led. This was more of a warband than an army.

"The problem, Alfraed, is that many knights from Normandy have joined the Hautevilles. They are carving out a kingdom in southern Italy much as grandfather did in England. There they can win great estates." He smiled sympathetically at me, "My father has only poor estates such as Norton with which to reward his knights. Hauteville slaughters the Italians and gives their rich land to his followers. Others have gone to the Holy Land. One reason that we can leave Normandy at this time is that Count Fulk is believed to be heading back to the Holy Land. So, you see this Battle is as large as it will ever be."

One of Henry's household knights came to me. "Baron Alfraed, the King asks you to take your conroi and discover what defences they have at Calais. The rear guard will watch your war gear and horses."

"Edward, let us ride." As I led my tiny conroi north I knew why Henry was making this deviation in the direction of Calais. Bruges, Brussels and Ghent were all fortified and this was the heartland of Flanders. If things went awry then Calais would provide an escape route back to England.

"Dick, take the archers and ensure that we are not surprised."

As they rode away Edward said, "They should not be expecting us."

"True Edward but my father always told me to expect trouble everywhere. I think that was why he survived so long."

"Aye, and it is sad that he died in his own manor."

"I believe that he was happy to do so. He was, for the first time in his life, actually defending his own home. He spent his youth fighting for Harold Godwinson and his adulthood fighting for the Emperor. At the end, he died defending something far more valuable; a tiny wooden manor at the very edge of the world. It is all in the perspective and how you view your world. The Empress is not happy and yet she jointly rules the second largest Empire in the world. Perspective."

Edward laughed, "You are becoming a philosopher Baron."

Dick halted us at the rise which overlooked the port of Calais. We could see the castle there. Although there were flags flying none of them were the yellow flag with the rampant black lion which would indicate the Count was present. "Aelric, ride back to the King and tell him that the castle is occupied but not by the Count of Flanders."

While we waited we examined the defences of the castle. The gates were open and there were just a couple of men at arms lounging by the bridge over the moat. "You know, Edward, I think that we can take this castle ourselves."

"That would be a bold move, my lord. How would we manage that?"

"Have the men sling their shields around their backs. Dick, keep the archers here. They would identify us immediately. Alan, put your left arm in the sling again and have the men take off their helmets. We are a party of Flemings returning from a raid on Normandy. Edgar, ride by me and use your German if they ask us aught."

I sensed the excitement as my men did as I had asked. We descended down the road towards the castle of Calais. We rode casually as though we had every right to be there. The town gates were open too and there were just two men standing guard. They looked suspiciously at us. "I am Guy de Brus sent with a message from Count Fulk for the castellan" The lie came out with such confidence that they waved us through. Our passage through the town of Calais also afforded us an easy approach to the castle. I made sure that we were on the bridge over the moat before we stopped. This time the guards crossed their poleaxes to prevent entry.

Edgar played his part well; he could have been a mummer! "This is Count Raymond from Stuttgart we have a message for the castellan."

As two of them turned to go into the castle I said, "Now!" The two remaining guards were quickly overpowered by my men and we rode into the castle. "Edward, take some men and hold the gate and signal Dick to bring the others!"

We galloped into the bailey. The door to the keep was open. "Harold and Wulfric, keep the door to the keep open." As we dismounted I almost laughed. Edward had most of our men at the gate and I was about to capture a keep with a man at arms and a squire. I put on my helmet and raced through the open keep door. This was the last refuge in the castle. I ran up the stairs expecting to meet someone coming down. When I reached the first floor I breathed a sigh of relief. The Great Hall was empty. Was the castle deserted? I found no-one close by and I headed up the stairs to the quarters of the castellan. I was beginning to work out that the lord of Calais must be with the rest of the Count's army at Ghent.

Suddenly I heard giggling. I walked towards the noise. It was coming from a room at the front. I stood next to the door and listened. From the voices, there were at least three people within. I hefted my shield around and pushed open the unlocked door. I leapt in expecting to find danger instead I found a small middle-aged man romping around the bed with two young girls.

He pulled the sheet up and said, with as much dignity as he could manage, "What is the meaning of this intrusion?"

I managed to hold back the laughter. The two girls were dressing, seemingly oblivious to the castellan and his predicament. "If you are the castellan then I have to tell you that your castle has fallen. I am Baron Alfraed of Norton and I have taken Calais Castle for my liege lord Henry of England, and Duke of Normandy!"

The castellan sank back into the bed. Whatever happened now he would lose his comfortable post. The Count of Flanders would not take kindly to his castle being taken without a blow being struck in its defence.

The girls gave a curtsy as they scurried down the stair. "I should get dressed if I were you. The King will be here shortly. It would not do to create a bad impression, would it?"

The castellan wrapped a robe around his body as he prepared to dress. I descended to the bailey. "You two can go up to the hall if you like. The castellan is dressing."

Wulfric grinned, "I have been a man at arms for ten years my lord and I have never seen a castle taken so easily!"

I shrugged, "I think it was just luck."

"No sir, you saw the opportunity and you went for it. You make your own luck!"

Dick and the archers galloped through the gates. They were laughing as they did so. "You should have seen the old men at the gate, sir, when we galloped through. They dived for cover!"

"Well done, lads. Now get those flags and banners down. The King will want his own up as soon as he arrives."

Aelric must have ridden like the wind for we soon heard the commotion as the King arrived with the rest of the army. I stood, with Edward on either side of the bridge. "You have Calais, your majesty."

He leaned down, "Perhaps I should send you scouting more often Baron Alfraed. Did you lose any men?"

"Nary a one. We tied up the guards and the castellan waits within."

"Then we will stay here this night. It means we have a base now. "Robert, go with Baron Norton here and stop any ships from sailing. We can use one to send a message to Dover. I would have this castle garrisoned."

We took my archers and men at arms with us. As we rode through the streets to the harbour Robert said, "A remarkable feat and it helps us immeasurably. We now have something with which to bargain. We may not even need to fight the Flemings."

I was not so sure but I held my tongue. They had tried so hard to stop us returning the Empress to her home; I could not see them allowing us to take Calais and then bargain a peace treaty. They would want their swords bloodied.

In the harbour, there were just fishing boats and one small trader. My archers swarmed aboard the trader as the captain tried to set sail. "Have your men prepare to sail to Dover with a message. I will write it now."

"Wulfric, how many men would you need to control this crew?"

"Me and Edgar could do it on our own, my lord."

"I think you had better take all the men at arms and three of the archers too. I would hate to lose you. Just leave me Dick and Aelric. We may need scouts."

"Right sir; come on lads, let's introduce ourselves to the crew eh?"

Robert returned a short while later. He boarded the small ship, "Deliver this to the Constable in Dover castle. He will send back some men with you. I doubt that you will be back before tomorrow." He handed Wulfric some copper coins. "This is for your trouble."

Wulfric knuckled his head, "Thank you, my lord."

I knew my men by now. Wulfric would pocket the money and take whatever the crew had stored below. This would be the spoils of war.

One of the unexpected finds was a map of the area. We had our own but this was a detailed one and showed the location of the forts and castles. We added Utrecht to our list of enemy strongholds. It proved to be invaluable intelligence. I was now considered almost as close to the King as his household knights and I was summoned later that afternoon.

"Alfraed, you have done enough by capturing this castle so easily and I will send Sir John de Warenne with his conroi to spy out the enemy dispositions but what I need from you is an assessment of the Flemish forces. You have come up against them a few times."

I nodded, "They like ambush. They use crossbows and not archers. They are a little reckless. I think that our knights have more control. When we fought them, they did not keep knee to knee and they use the line. When we used the wedge, they could not stand against us. They do not appear to have any flexibility. I also noticed that they have the older type of shield. They do not cover as much of their bodies as our shields do."

"Good. That tallies with what I had seen. Then when they are found I have my plan ready." He slapped his hand on the table. "An unexpected pleasure thanks to Baron Norton! We sleep in soft beds tonight."

Two days later four ships arrived back in the harbour. One had Wulfric and my men on board and the others brought over some of the garrison of Dover. We now had archers and men at arms. We could leave Calais in safely in our hands while we went to face the Count of Flanders. Sir John de Warenne had discovered them moving west to meet us. I felt guilty for not preventing anyone from leaving Calais when we had taken it. I had been so concerned with capturing the stronghold that I had neglected to hold the town gates. Someone had taken the news to the Count.

Robert of Gloucester put my mind at rest. "This is better. The Flemish army comes to us and they will be tired. We still have our castle in to which we can retreat and with the extra archers we have the edge once more."

We were also honoured for Dick was made captain of the archers. He led the one hundred men and would command them during the battle. We found the Flemish squarely positioned on a very low ridge. It was so low as to be almost indiscernible. The King saw that they had their crossbowmen arrayed before them. Their men at arms guarded their flanks and their knights sat atop the hill. Numbers did not matter. This battle would be determined by a right of arms. Robert of Gloucester took the King's standard and I escorted him as we rode to meet with the Count's men. Two knights rode forward. One carried the black lion rampant on a yellow field while the other had a red shield with a black fess. Had it just been a plain red then I would have been convinced that it was the mysterious knight who had plagued me for the past months.

As we rode across I looked at the knights and I saw the shield and banner of De Brus. I did not see his face for he had a full-face helmet. Next to him I saw the knight with the red shield. He had an open helmet and I saw his face for the first time. Although he was in the distance I could see that he was older than I was. I marked his features and his position. In the coming battle I would seek him out. Honour demanded it.

The Flemish knight spoke first. "Charles the Count of Flanders demands to know why you have invaded his lands and imposed your will upon our city, Calais."

Robert of Gloucester spoke calmly, "We are here for the many insults your master has heaped upon King Henry; not least of which was the attempt to abduct and harm his daughter the Empress Matilda."

For the first time, there was a reaction from the knight, "That is a lie! We did no such thing."

Robert of Gloucester looked at me and inclined his head. I spoke, "Do not call me a liar, sir, or we will settle the matter here and now. I fought with your knights and made them flee and yonder knight," I pointed to the knight with the red shield, "was present each time. Is he not one of your knights?"

The knight who had spoken had a choice; he could fight with me or accept my claim. He ignored my comments. "The Count of Flanders demands that you quit the field and abandon Calais. Go back to Normandy and he will allow you to live."

Robert of Gloucester laughed. He turned to me, "It seems Baron, that you may get the opportunity to show this knight that you are no liar." He turned back to the two Flemish knights. "This will be settled here and now on this piece of land."

We returned to King Henry. He was smiling, "I take it they are not willing to compromise?"

"No, my liege. They wish to fight."

"Send the archers in to harass their crossbowmen."

I felt my heart sink into my boots as the messenger rode to Dick. They would have to advance close to the crossbowmen and would be at great risk. Their advantage was that they could release up to eight arrows in the time to send a bolt upon its way.

I watched them as they moved forward. The crossbowmen knelt and levelled their weapons. Dick had been an archer in the woods of Sherwood. He had fought crossbows before. He had his archers release three arrows and then I watched as they all ran to the left and the right. There was a momentary hesitation from the crossbows as they picked out their targets. Another three arrows went on their way. Dick had them moving again. I saw five archers who had been struck but the crossbows had suffered, thirty dead. The advantage was with the archers and the next exchange left just one dead archer and another twenty dead crossbowmen. It was too much for them and they fled from the unequal contest. Dick was no fool and his archers raced back to the flanks before the men at arms could be launched.

King Henry nodded his approval, "Your archer is a fine leader, Baron. Robert, have the men at arms advance and your archers support them."

The archers were all mounted and they could move, dismount and then release their arrows. Their rate of fire would be lessened as they would require horse holders but they could loose over the men at arms. It was something the crossbows could not do.

King Henry shouted, "Knights of Normandy and England, let us end the threat from this upstart. Forward!"

The men at arms were moving at a canter and the Flemish army responded. They sent their own men at arms towards them. I saw that they had a small body, no more than fifty or so, of spearmen. King Henry had deigned to use infantry. He had wanted speed. The line of knights remained static on the ridge. I had Edward next to me and Sir Guy of Doncaster on the other side. I had never fought with Sir Guy but he rode tight to my leg and I felt confident about our charge. I saw the archers halt and dismount. The men at arms began to move faster and Dick's archers released arrow after arrow over the heads of the men at arms. They plunged into horses and men at arms. The whole line was thrown into confusion as horses fell and brought down others. The crossbows were felling but a handful of men at arms and soon they would be in danger of being overrun while our archers could maintain their rain of arrows.

72

"Trot!"

I levelled my lance across the cantle of my saddle. The tourney had given me an insight into my opponents. Each one had aimed for my head. I could use that to my advantage. The battle between the men at arms was one sided now and the English and Norman men at arms were driving the Flemish back into their knights. They were overrunning their crossbows.

"Charge!"

There was just a small gap between us and the enemy now. I spurred Star and he leapt forward. I had to fight to hold onto him. I saw a knight with a yellow shield and two red fess across it. I aimed for him. I was now accustomed to the speed of combat and I relaxed as I adjusted my lance across my cantle. I hoisted my new shield up and pulled back my arm. Success came with timing and I judged this one well. I punched forward and ducked my head. His lance skittered across the top of my helm but my lance plunged into his middle and threw him from the saddle. I released the now useless lance and drew my sword. Harold was just behind me with his spear and I took comfort from that.

Our line was no longer tight for we had broken their static defence. I saw the knight with the red shield to my right and I yanked my reins around to head for him. I could no longer see De Brus. The knight with the lion rampant suddenly darted towards me. I had not seen him but Harold had. He punched his lance at the shield and the knight had to veer in front of me. I stood in my saddle and brought my sword down. It hit his shield and his helmet. He fell to the side and pulled his horse with him. I yelled, "Up!" and pulled on my reins. Star was magnificent and climbed above the dying knight. As we were landing I saw a knight preparing to bring his sword down on Robert of Gloucester. I had less than a moment but I swung my sword horizontally and brought it across his unprotected back. He arched as his spine was severed and fell to the ground. I looked for the red knight but, once again, he had evaded me.

As I looked around for another opponent I saw my false knight, Richard. He had just unhorsed a man at arms and was preparing to bring his sword down. "Richard, you traitor! Today is your last on earth!"

He charged his horse at me. I had practised against him many times and we knew each other well. I had never fought him from the back of a horse before. That day Star came into his own. Perhaps the wound he had received in the tourney had changed him, I know not but, as I jerked his reins around he reared slightly and that made Richard flinch as Star's head came around. I did not strike at his shield but brought my blade across the top of his horse's head. He tried to bring his sword up to counter my blow but he merely slowed down the strike and my sword bit into his arm. As Star's head came down he bit into the neck of Richard's horse which pulled around to the left. I now had Richard broadside on to me and, standing in my stirrups smashed my sword across his helmet. I knew it was a good helmet, Alf had made it but my blow had the anger of betrayal behind it and Richard my first knight and my false knight fell dead at my feet. He would betray no one else.

The Flemish army was disintegrating. Our archers had weakened them and our charge had shattered them. All around knights were raising their arms in surrender. I raised my sword to decapitate a knight with a yellow shield and a red star. He dropped his sword and demanded mercy. I lowered my sword. He took off his helmet and shook his head, "I cannot fight a madman like you. It is true what they say, Alfraed of Norton is the devil incarnate."

"You know me?"

"We have all heard of the knight in blue with the two stars and the black horse which is spawned by the devil."

I turned and saw a grinning Harold, "Take this knight to our camp."

"Aye my lord, and he is right. It is like following the devil when you and Star ride. I would not like to stand against you."

In those days, before the civil war, it was a civilised kind of war and knights were more inclined to take prisoners. Count Charles was taken and I was there when King Henry addressed him. "You will pay me one thousand gold talents. You will do this each year for three years. At the end of that time I will return Calais back to you. If you forfeit once then I will keep Calais. What say you?"

Had the Count not tried to kill or capture the Empress then I might have felt sympathy but as it was I felt merely scorn. He acceded. He had little choice else. We all returned to Calais richer men.

The knight I had captured, Richard of Bruges, came from a rich family and I received twenty golden talents as ransom. My men also did well as they pillaged the battlefield. Dick was rewarded by the King with ten gold pieces. And the best news of all was that we had lost no men. God had favoured us.

Ten days later, as the first of the Autumn storms whipped the waves outside Calais and the last of the ransoms were paid, I was summoned to King Henry and Robert of Gloucester.

"You have done well for me, Alfraed Baron of Norton. As a reward, I free you from the Palatinate of Durham. You answer only to me in all matters military and financial." He handed me a document with his seal attached, "You are now a household knight and one of my closest fellows." He came to me and kissed me on both cheeks. He held out his hand and Robert handed him a seal on a bronze chain. "You are now my Marcher lord for the Valley of the Tees. I charge you with the protection of the river and my peoples." I flicked my eyes to Robert who shrugged. "You have fulfilled your duty. Take a ship and return to Norton."

I was dismissed. I sought Robert of Gloucester. "This does not sound good."

"It is not. The Scots have raided Carlisle and stolen cattle. Already they may have attacked the Tees. God speed my friend. You go from the pan to the fire! My father and I must remain here and consolidate our gains. We will return at Christmas. Until then it is up to you and lords like you to protect our land." He handed me a document with an official seal. "This is for you. You may demand service from any knights along the Tees and you have the authority to raise the fyrd. I pray you can hold on until we reach you."

"And the Empress, my lord, what of her? Is she safe now?"

"She is as safe as she can be. From what you say your Swabian friends will watch over her. She is Empress and you have a job to do in England."

We managed to find a ship which was going to London and could accommodate us and our horses. As we sailed down the Thames I reflected that we had needed two ships to take us to war but only one to bring us back. Edward mentioned our lack of numbers as we passed the castle which dominated the city. It had been William the Bastard's mark on the land. It showed the country that he ruled.

"We should get more men here in London. There will be more of them and they will be cheaper to hire than further north."

"But will they be men we can rely upon?"

"Wulfric and I were swords for hire for many years. Allow us to choose them. You could have Dick ride to his old forest and see if any others wish to become archers."

"I am anxious to reach home."

"I know my lord. Like you, I am worried about what we might find but that makes it all the more important that we have enough men when we reach there."

I nodded. I knew that he was right. And it made sense to do so in London. There were taverns and inns where we could stay. It was the only part of the country where we could guarantee a bed. As a household knight, I could have requested accommodation in the Tower but I would be viewed with suspicion. The Tower was the King's prison. His brother resided there; heavily guarded. The guards and the constable did not know me as a household knight. I did not wish to be viewed with suspicion. I would make my own arrangements.

I sent Dick and the archers north to find more of their fellows. "We will follow in three days. Do not worry about horses we have more than enough for the men you will find." We now had a string of rounceys and palfreys as well as five destriers. I had recovered Richard's. My father had paid for the animal in the first place. It sounded petty but he had betrayed both me and my father.

My father and his men had always believed that things happen for a purpose. We did, indeed, manage to recruit ten men at arms. That was down to Wulfric and Edward. Their names were well known. I also knew that the name of Alfraed of Norton attracted the right kind of warrior too. I managed to have short surcoats made for them. But it was when I needed mail for them that we struck really lucky. There was an armourer who had a forge hard by the river and the Tower. One of my new men, Arkwright, told me of him. He had some mail for my men but, after speaking with him, I discovered that he could make mail gloves rather than the mittens I wore. The mittens protected the back of the hands well but the palms were exposed. Even better were the mail leggings he showed us. My greaves protected the front of the legs but not the back. He made leggings for Edward and me. There were flexible metal knee pieces which divided the weight. The whole contraption was much lighter than I had expected. Even better was the fact that we did not need boots and the mail leggings made riding easier. We cheerfully parted with some of the ransom we had collected. Money was no object for good armour. We rode north better protected than we had ever been.

We were close to Doncaster when Dick emerged from the forest with our four new archers. It was not as many as I would have wished but I knew that if they came from the forest then they would be good men. It was a powerful conroi which headed north up the Great North Road. We made good time despite the increasingly wet weather. Our surcoats protected the armour from the worst of the rain although the rust we accrued would still need to be removed. As we approached the Tees I began to think, for the first time, of my home on the river. I had left as an impoverished knight. Now I had gold and, more importantly, I had power. With that power came responsibilities. I would need to administer justice and I knew that could be time-consuming but I resolved to be a fair arbiter of the law. My father had taught me that. As we waited for Ethelred and the ferry I wondered when I had changed from the headstrong and wild youth who had not wanted to leave Constantinople into the knight who had been given this valley to rule.

Part 2 The Border War

Chapter 8

Stockton 1123

Our homecoming had been joyous and that first Christmas in my castle at Stockton had been both festive and enlightening. Wulfstan had protected my land well in my absence. There had been threats from the north but the vigilance from the men I had left behind meant that we suffered no harm. I was relieved.

Despite my misgivings on the way back from Caen my home still stood. Faren was with child again and she had blossomed. Adela had been overjoyed to see me when I had stepped from Ethelred's ferry. I could see that she had wanted to throw her arms around me but she did not. I suspect that was due to my reserve. I merely smiled at her. I had changed in more ways than one. I had met the Empress and all others would now be compared to her. Norton, too, had prospered. Osric and Athelstan had both done well in spite of their self-doubt when I had appointed them. They had transferred their loyalty to my father to Norton. They would serve the manor equally well. An unexpected and welcome surprise was that Aiden had managed to train a hawk for me. I could now be a real lord of the manor and go hawking.

As the days began to lengthen, imperceptibly at first, I sat with Edward and Wulfstan in the west tower looking towards the hills that rose in the distance, watching the sun set on a snow-covered land. We had brought wine back with us and, as long as it lasted, we would enjoy it. "So, Alfraed, you are to rule the Tees. You have done well. That is a mighty leap from lord of the manor."

"I think rule is too strong a word, Wulfstan. I was charged with protecting the Tees from the Scottish raids."

"It is rule in all but name." I inclined my head in agreement. "There are lords at Normanby, Yarm, Gainford and Piercebridge. They are all the men you can command. Hartness has people but no lord and Guisborough is still in the hands of the De Brus. How will you deal with them?" I knew that Wulfstan was doing what he always did; he was testing me and my mettle. How would I deal with problems which might be just around the corner?

As with many things I had yet to think things through. I would not have much of an army without the De Brus knights. "I will have to visit with the De Brus clan but I would rather see the other four lords first. I hope they have knights."

Edward stood to pour some more wine while Wulfstan placed another log on the fire. "We only have three my lord. I know that our men at arms and archers are the best for we have seen them fight but if a large force comes south to raid we cannot sit behind our walls. We must go and meet them. King Henry wants the valley protecting from the ravages of raiders; not just Stockton and Norton. "

"I know." Neither was telling me anything I did not know. Doubts assailed me from each direction. My chain of office felt like a leaden weight. We drank in silence for a while listening to the logs crackling on the fire. I changed the subject. "Your son has grown, Wulfstan."

My old mentor smiled, "Aye, Edward, he is a proper little boy. Perhaps God will grant us a daughter next."

I was surprised. I had thought that he would have wished for another son. "A daughter Wulfstan? I would have thought you would have wished for another son to follow you."

He shook his head. "I have changed, Alfraed, as you have. You still have a journey to take but you are getting there. While you were away I saw Adela grow from a frightened young girl into the lovely creature you have ignored since you came back. I would have a daughter so that she could become like Adela."

"Ignored?"

"When you went away you looked at her with soft eyes and she with you. She gave you a token to protect you while you campaigned and you have come back indifferent to her. She is hurt you know. Faren has told me she has heard her crying in the night."

"But I gave her no promises."

"Not with your words but you did with your eyes." I knew he was right and I could not meet his gaze. I stared at the fire. Wulfstan was as close to me as my father had been and I did not like to be criticised by him. What made it worse was that he was right. I had neglected her and there had been an expectation. He was right; I had changed.

Edward's quiet voice broke the uncomfortable silence which filled the room. "It is the Empress is it not?"

I looked up and stared at Edward. Did he know of my feelings? Wulfstan asked, "The Empress?"

"Aye, I think our young lord became infatuated by her when we journeyed to Worms."

Wulfstan shook his head, "She is an Empress. Put those thoughts from your mind. I saw men broken on the wheel in Miklagård for even looking askance at the Empress of Byzantium."

"Aye and the Emperor was none too pleased either. He took against the baron."

"It was nothing and we are here now far from any entanglements."

Wulfstan leaned over and tapped my chest. "You still have them there. Rid your body and your mind of them. No good can come of them."

"I will do so but that will not make my feelings towards Adela, return."

"Alfraed, your father charged me with making you a warrior, a knight, someone he could be proud of. There is more to being a knight than just fighting and riding a horse. It is in the way you behave and the way you treat people. Generally, I think you have become such a knight save in one regard; women. There you fail to meet the standards. Your father would not be happy with your treatment of a vulnerable young girl. Think on that!"

I found it hard to look at Adela over the next few days for I knew, in my heart, that Wulfstan was right. During a break in the weather I took the opportunity to visit Norton. I took Edward and our squires. I was also feeling guilty about neglecting what had been my father's home. I visited his grave in the church before I did anything else and I silently said a prayer for his soul.

Father Peter found me kneeling still. "We say prayers for him and the others who died defending us each day. Your father was loved, Sir Alfraed."

"I know and he had his wish. He died here in England. He is at peace now and this grave in his church is somewhere I feel I can be close to him. And how are you, Father Peter?"

"The church in Durham is still unhappy that they did not appoint me. The Dean himself came to chastise me." He shrugged, "I have been ordained and I know that I do a good job here. What care I for the politics of the church?"

"So long as I approve then do not fear. The King has appointed me defender of the valley. I will visit the Dean and speak with him. How are the people? Do they prosper?"

"They do. Osric and Athelstan are good men and they care for the people here." He hesitated. "You should speak with them, lord, for they have received disturbing news of late."

I hurried to the hall where I found my father's oathsworn laughing with Edward. They rose and each gave a slight bow. "Edward here was telling us how you captured a castle without losing a man. Would that I had seen that. It was the sort of thing your father would have loved."

"It was luck."

Edward shook his head, "I keep telling him that we make our own luck."

"As the new defender of the valley I will be visiting all of the manors along the river. I need an accurate number of men who might be available. How many are there in Norton?"

"We have ten spears and four bows."

"Good. Are any of the bows young men who might join my conroi?"

"Young Alan, son of Garth, is someone who might suit. He needs work for he is still growing but he should be ready for war by summer."

"Good."

"Father Peter said that you had heard disturbing news of late."

"Aye, Alfraed; there is no lord at Hartness yet but it prospers and armed men have passed along the road north to Hartness. If we had had the men and the authority then we would have visited."

"Thank you. I will take my men and pay them a visit in my new position as defender of the valley. Hartness guards the estuary."

My final visit was to see Aiden and my hawks. They were both beautiful birds. Aiden told me how their mother had deserted them when they were chicks and he had hand-reared them. "When will they be ready to hunt?"

"By the summer my lord."

"Good." I looked at the young man who had been bought as a slave but whom I had freed. He was growing quickly. The outdoor life had made him both strong and athletic. "Tell me, Aiden, how would you feel about coming to war with me the next time I go? You would be a great asset as a scout."

"I would be honoured, my lord, but I could not leave my animals without care."

I nodded, "I can understand that. Then find someone you can train up." We had slaves in both Norton and Stockton. When buying slaves, I had tried to buy families for I hated the thought of splitting up a mother from her children. There would be many boys who were similar to Aiden. He would be the best one to judge who they were.

"If I might suggest two, my lord."

I smiled, "You have two in mind already eh?"

"Yes, my lord. At the moment Osric has them as swineherds. It is a waste for they both know animals and understand them. Swine are clever. They care for themselves."

"I will see Osric."

We came back through Wulfestun and the Hart Burn. I was particularly keen to see how my fletchers Tom and Old Tom were getting on. I was impressed with the small hall they had built. There were many large trees along the becks which crisscrossed that part of my land. They had chosen stout timbers for the roof and walls from the many trees there. They had built it so that the door was reached by some steps. It made it more difficult to attack. I knew, without looking, that the bottom level of the house would be the place they kept their animals in winter. I also saw that Young Tom had a wife who was with child. "An impressive home, Old Tom. I see you are beginning to fill it already."

"Yes, Baron. I hope to raise fine archers. I know you lost some in Normandy."

"We did and we missed your strong backs and arms there too. We have taken on four new ones and we shall be needing arrows for the spring."

"We have a good stock of wood laid in and the geese have been busy too."

I laughed. The goose feathers were essential for good arrows. "This is a good place here. You are happy?"

"Yes, my lord but we are vigilant. If the Scots come again we will be ready."

"And I will be vigilant too. As soon as the snow goes I shall take my men and inform the other lords of their duties then we shall hunt for the raiders and not wait for them to come to us."

William, my mason, had still to finish my castle. Yet as we approached, from the west, I thought how solid it looked. Having been in Caen and Worms, I knew it was not the largest of keeps but it would be hard to take and would deter raiders. I wondered what other work I could put his way for I was loath to lose such a good workman. As we rode home I asked Edward and the others for their views. Harold came up with an answer. "The church in Norton, my lord, it was barely finished when he began work on the castle."

"Besides, baron, the castle still has work which needs completion. The curtain wall and the gatehouse could be much improved. It is your coin."

"You are both right. While the weather is inclement I will send him back to Norton and then we will use the gold to make an impressive gatehouse and a sturdy wall."

William was happy when I told him, "I have to confess, Baron, that I was feeling guilty being inactive. But my family are happy here. This has been the longest time they have spent in one place and they are settled and happy."

"I would keep you here as long as you wish, William. I want a castle which stands as a rock against whoever tries to take it from us."

Despite my visits and the progress being made all over my manor I could not shake the feeling of guilt. Edward and Athelstan were both correct; Matilda was unobtainable and yet I did not love Adela. At least not in the way I loved the Empress. I knew then that I should have spoken with my father at his grave. After he had died his voice had come into my head. Perhaps it could come again. I decided to make the effort and be as I had been. I no longer avoided Adela and I began to speak to her each day. At first it was uncomfortable but, gradually, it became easier.

My days were filled with practise. My new men at arms needed to be welded into one and Dick needed to show the new archers how to fight with men at arms. They were coming on well.

"We need helms my lord."

"For the men at arms, Edward?"

"Aye and the archers too."

I went to visit with Alf. I took the new gloves we had purchased in London. He bowed as I entered his forge. I noticed that it was busier than it had been when first we had arrived and he had four men working within it. "It is good to have you back my lord. Was it a good campaign?"

I laughed, "You mean did we make enough gold to help you pay for your new workers."

He had the good grace to nod, "I would be lying my lord if I didn't say that your patronage is appreciated."

"Well, you are right. I have coins. We need helmets for my archers and my men at arms."

"Helmets for archers, my lord?"

"They are as valuable as my destrier in war. I want one without a nasal for that would impair their archery."

He nodded, "That makes them easier to manufacture and cheaper too. But you wish nasals for the men at arms?"

"Yes, and a protection for the back to the neck."

"That can be arranged."

I handed him the gloves. "I bought these in London. How easy would it be to make them?"

"Not easy at all. This is fine work." He nodded to a young boy who was working the bellows for one of the smiths. "I could train Ralph to make them. Will you need mail for the men at arms?"

"No, Alf; they have their own but it would not hurt to prepare a shirt or two in case we have damage."

"That will incur a cost for me, my lord."

"And I will pay." I smiled wolfishly at him, "And I hope you keep good accounts for the tax man when he comes. I will certainly be keeping a record of my costs."

His face fell, "Yes my lord. When will you require these?"

"You have a month. I shall send the men over so that you may get an idea of sizes."

That evening Wulfstan and Edward joined me to watch a particularly fine sunset. Its red rays spilt over the Tees making it look as though it was bathed in blood. "I hope this is not an omen."

Edward shrugged, "If it is my lord then it is the same omen for everyone."

"Tomorrow we will begin our journey around the key manors. We will begin in the east at Normanby. Wulfstan, what do you know of Sir Mark?"

"Nothing. I have never met him or heard of him. However, there appears to be little danger to him being south of the river. It may be he thinks he is safe."

"Then my orders from the King will come as a shock to him. We will visit Yarm and then return here."

"You can do them both in one day?"

"It is but ten or twelve miles to each and we can travel swiftly."

"Whom will you take?"

I smiled at Wulfstan's question. Faren was coming close to her time and he was fretful. "You may stay here my old friend. I will take Edward, Wulfric and eight men at arms. We do not go to war."

As I was leaving Adela came to me, "May good fortune attend you today, my lord and may God watch over you."

"Thank you for your concern, Adela. It does you great credit."

She hesitated, "Do you still have the lucky charm I gave to you? The jet deer?"

My hand went involuntarily to my neck. "I do. Do you wish it returned?"

She shook her head vehemently, "No, my lord. I was just making sure you had not discarded it."

Perhaps I was being overly sensitive but her words sounded to me as though it was she who had been discarded. I knew I would need to find some answers to my questions soon or go insane.

We crossed on the ferry. Ethelred was even more prosperous than when we had left. It was reflected by the fact that he no longer charged me. He realised that it was due to me that he had a business and he could not afford to lose my patronage.

The road east was more of a track which followed a low ridge which wound around the marshy swamps which lay to the south of the river. We made good time. I saw the farms which dotted the fertile soil but the people who lived within remained hidden. I had never travelled in these parts and, I suspect, I was an unknown quantity. News rarely reached this remote border.

I saw the motte and bailey castle which was on a knoll in the foothills of the moors. It was a good site and overlooked the Tees. I frowned. On a clear day I expected that you would be able to see all the way to Hartness in the north.

The gates were shut as we approached. I was not surprised. I had never visited with Sir Mark of Normanby. As far as he was concerned then I could be a raider although our shields were on our backs and we carried our helmets on our cantles. A number of faces appeared at the gate tower. Crossbows were pointed at us.

"I come at the orders of King Henry. Who commands here?"

The knight who was in the middle of the crossbowmen took off his helmet. There was something familiar about him. "I am Sir Mark De Brus, Baron of Normanby."

That explained much. I now knew why he looked familiar. This was the cousin of the traitor. "I am Baron Alfraed of Norton and I am charged with the protection of the Tees valley." I took the parchment from Harold. "This is my authority from the King. May we enter or are we to shout at each other?"

His scowling face told me that he would prefer to stand and shout but he also wanted to check my credentials. He shouted down and the gate was opened. Edward said, "This is a good start, my lord. I thought we would have to fight our way in."

"Who knows Edward, we may have to fight our way out. Keep your eyes and ears open."

There were no longer crossbows pointed at us but they had been replaced by surly looks. I dismounted and strode up the steps to the hall. Sir Mark awaited me. I turned to my men, "You may stay here, Sir Edward."

Once inside I unrolled the parchment and allowed Sir Mark to read it. Not every knight could read but I saw that he was actually reading. When he had read it, he rolled it up and handed it back to me. "I do not think that this applies to me. The river is to the north of this castle."

"You can see the river and you live in the Tees Valley. The King wants it protecting from Scottish raiders. That applies to you too."

"They never bother us here. Nor my cousin in Guisborough."

"And what of your cousin who is named traitor by the King?"

He flashed me an angry look, "He is no traitor!"

"And I say differently. I will happily put this to a trial by combat if you wish for I am already tired of you and your whining."

I could see, in that instant, that he was a coward and liked to intimidate people. He backed down immediately. He said, flatly, "What do you require of me?"

"How many knights do you command?"

"None. There is just me."

"Crossbows?"

"Ten."

"Men at arms?"

"Six."

"And the local fyrd?"

"We can muster twenty yeomen."

"You have no archers?"

"They are hard to train."

"Then train some! When I send my instruction to you then you will muster your men at Stockton, by the ferry. I will expect you to set off as soon as the instruction is sent."

I took a candle and dripped it on to the table. I pushed my signet ring into it. "This is my mark! Heed it well. I am not a patient man."

As we headed west I shook my head, "The De Brus family seems fated to haunt me!"

"They will be of no use to us, my lord. Wulfric tried to speak with them. They never practise and none has mail. Their helms are made of leather! We would not be able to rely on them."

"You may be right and we have yet to see the others. If this is typical of the men we are to use then it does not bode well for me. I may well have merely my own men to command."

"That is not necessarily a bad thing."

"I know Edward but why should my men die to protect others who cannot be bothered?"

The castle at Yarm was a tiny wooden affair. It stood on a hill overlooking a bend in the Tees. This time, however, the gate was open. As we approached a knight, in livery, and some men at arms, wearing just tunics and carrying staffs emerged. It was obvious that they had not seen us for they halted and looked at this column of men who approached them.

I dismounted and held out my hand. I determined that each of the knights would be given the chance to shake the hand of friendship. "I am Baron Alfraed of Norton and I am here on the King's business."

"And I am Sir Richard of Kirklevington. I have heard of you." He waved a hand down his soiled tunic. "I am sorry for my appearance. We have been practising with staves and were on our way to the river to bathe."

"Then do not let us stop you. We will come with you and talk as we walk."

I explained what the King intended. Sir Richard seemed more than happy. He did not ask to see my authority but nodded eagerly when I explained that he would be summoned to the ferry at Stockton. "Good. The Scots have taken my people before now. My garrison is too small to beard them but they have yet to breach my walls."

"And how many men do you have?"

"Not as many as I would wish for. I have a squire." He smiled self consciously, "It is my son but he is a good lad. I have these four men at arms and eight archers. It is not much of a conroi I am afraid. This manor is poor."

"If they are of good heart then their numbers matter not and perhaps we can make money from these Scots who come to take from us." I took him to one side and spoke quietly. "I do not intend to sit and wait for them to attack. If I hear they are heading our way then I will take the war to them. I would fight on land to the north of our home."

"As would I but what of my family if I leave?"

"I have a stone castle at Stockton. They could stay there. I intend to leave my home with a garrison."

He grinned, "I like you, Baron Alfraed, and I will be ready for the call."

"How many men in the fyrd?"

"We have ten who have pole weapons, two old soldiers with swords and four who can use bows."

We left in a better frame of mind. We forded the river and headed back the five miles to our own castle. We rode along the bank of the river and, as ever, I was amazed at the game and the fish with which the valley teemed. This was a land worth defending. When we ate that night, I told Wulfstan what had happened. Adela looked up in horror when I mentioned Sir Mark. "I remember him. He was a horrible man."

A cold chill spread down my body, "Did he..."

She shook her head, "No but enjoyed belittling me and he was... well he made my flesh creep. He was very close to the lord of the manor of Hartness."

"Thank you, Adela, that gives me more information than I had before and insight into my new knight. He will not be invited here now."

"Sir Richard is a different matter, we liked him didn't we Baron?"

"We did. It is a shame he has not more men. I offered his wife and family the protection of this castle. It is close enough to us so that they could be here swiftly."

"You have not said what you intend, Alfraed."

"I intend to take the raids to the Scots. The Bishop of Durham appears content to have his see protected but not the road south. The castles which defend the border are along the coast and the Scots can skirt them. This valley is ripe for the picking. We have good crops and fine animals. We are sheltered and that is why the raiders come."

Adela said, quietly, "And the raiders are not always Scottish, my lord." We all looked at her. She continued. "Some knights and their men came from the north to stay at Hartness. They raided cattle and brought them back to Hartness before returning north."

"If they went north then they were Scottish."

"No, Sir Wulfstan, they were Norman and came from the land between the Tyne and the Wear. I recognised some for they had visited my father in more peaceful times."

"Now it begins to make sense. We assumed because they came from the north then they were from Scotland but de Mamers should have been a clue. They are bandits, pure and simple."

"I urge caution, Alfraed. You are now a knight with much to lose. If you make war on your countrymen it will mean more than a loss of revenue. You could pay with your life."

"I know and I am not foolish enough to think I could just attack my countrymen. However, as keeper of the peace for the valley I would be within my rights to question any strange knights who crossed my land, would I not?"

"Just think before you act, my headstrong young friend and do not let your hatred of De Brus blind you."

"I can see clearly, Wulfstan."

Sir Guy of Gainford and Sir Geoffrey of Piercebridge proved to be as keen as I was to rid the valley of the raiders. Both had suffered losses although, like Sir Richard, their castles had yet to be breached. That was the problem; the people could shelter within but not the animals. The raiders, whether Scots or renegades, happily left the defenders behind their walls, just as long as they could take their animals. The isolated farmers and their families were taken as slaves. We could not stop it before now. I had to make the difference. It rested upon my shoulders.

I sat with my two knights and tallied our forces. If we called up the whole of the fyrd then we could muster a hundred and thirty-two men but half of those would be farmers fighting with pole weapons. I had sixty men at the most that I could use. When we had the tally, I leaned back. The only ones who can reach us quickly will be Sir Richard and Sir Geoffrey. I think that Sir Mark will dally and Sir Guy has a longer journey."

I strode to the fire and poked the wood to make it burn a little better. "I will take a journey north tomorrow and visit with the Dean at Durham. I should inform him of my new position. Then I shall travel east to Hartness and let them know that, until the King appoints a new lord of the manor then I will be responsible for the administration of justice. It will also give me the opportunity to assess the Manor. Osric and Athelstan had fears for it. Wulfstan, we will have quarterly sessions. The first will be at Easter. We will hold them here in my hall."

Chapter 9

I left half of my men and my archers at the castle. I took Edward and the other half with me. I did not wish the Dean to think that I was trying to intimidate him. The town and castle were prosperous. The gate at the bridge had now been finished and would give an attacker their first problem. The winding road which led to the main gate was also protected by a wall and any raiders would have to run the gauntlet of arrows. Once the main gate was taken then the garrison could hold out in the keep but I doubted that would happen for the Cathedral lay on the other side of the Green. St. Cuthbert and his bones needed protection too. After I had delivered him my news I left. It had been an acrimonious meeting. Edward laughed as we descended to the Wear. "I do not know what upset him the most, the fact that you were now in charge of the Tees or the fact that he had lost a valuable income."

"I do not think we have heard the last of this. I think the priest will be sending a message to the Bishop. We may yet have to deal with the Bishop of Durham. Like his Dean, he will not be happy that he is no longer the only dispenser of justice and all that entails." We both knew that there was profit to be made from the law by unscrupulous people. I knew that Bishop Flambard had manors and lands in the south and, at the moment, he was busy with them but one day he would return. I had yet to meet the man.

The gates of Hartness were opened as soon as my gonfanon was seen. I had left them in no doubt, on my last visit, that I would not brook any delay in gaining entry. I saw the masts and spars of four or five small ships bobbing in the anchorage. Trade had returned. The port and the town looked more prosperous.

A new headman came scurrying to greet us. He was a younger man than the last one. "My lord, this is an unexpected honour."

"What is your name?"

"Harold of Elwick, my lord."

"Well, Harold of Elwick, King Henry has appointed me the guardian of this area. I am ordered to protect the valley and that includes Hartness. Until a new lord of the manor is appointed then I will administer the law.

There will be a session at Easter. Any cases you wish me to hear must be brought to my castle at Stockton. Is that clear?"

"Aye my lord. That is a good thing. We need law."

"As the King needs taxes. The tax collector will be escorted by my men when he comes." This Harold of Elwick seemed quite obliging. Perhaps there was a change in the air. This time, there were nods and bows as we left. The people, indeed, appeared more prosperous than they had been under the rule of the De Brus, yet I felt a sense of disquiet as we headed south. Osric and Athelstan were no fools. They had said armed men had travelled to Hartness and yet I had seen no sign of them. Where had they gone?

It was getting dark as we approached Norton. "Edward, take the men home. Harold and I will follow shortly. I wish to visit the church."

"We can wait, my lord."

"If I cannot travel the few miles from Norton to Stockton safely then there needs to be another lord of the manor. I will be safe."

I spoke to Athelstan and Osric before I entered the church. "I visited Hartness and saw no sign of the men you saw. That does not mean they were not there. They may have been in hiding. Remain vigilant and ask those who farm closest to Hartness to keep their eyes and ears open.

Osric nodded, "I will take some men hunting in the marshes. The seals make good eating in winter and I can speak with the fishermen who use the salt marshes."

"Harold, watch the horses." I took off my helmet and handed it to him and then entered the church. My father's tomb was quite close to the door. I closed the door behind me and knelt down. His tomb lay beneath the carved stone in the floor.

"Father, I have need of your advice. I fear that I have misled a young maiden and I do not know what to do about it. You must see all in heaven can you advise me what I ought to do?"

The silence seemed to weigh upon my shoulders in the dim church lit only by a solitary pair of candles at the altar. I had paid Father Peter to keep them burning there for my dead father. There was no reply from my father just the flickering of the candles. I was about to leave when Father Peter appeared from one of the recesses. "Perhaps I can help, Baron Alfraed. I am a priest. Would you like to confess?"

I looked around fearfully. What had the priest heard? I was about to rise when the young priest's hand touched my shoulder.

"You were asking your father for help. Perhaps he will answer through me."

"You are kind, Father Peter, but I need advice from someone who is a man of the world."

"And not a young barefoot priest who rarely leaves Norton?" He walked around the grave towards the altar.

"I meant no offence."

"I understand your reluctance, Baron, but if the lord of the manor cannot trust his priest then I might as well leave. I thought I had the trust of all but it appears I am wrong."

"No Father Peter…" It may have been a trick of the candlelight or the shadows cast by the priest but the stone effigy of my father on the stone seemed more at peace. The priest was right. I had to trust him. My father had when he gave him the church and his body to protect. "When I rescued the Lady Adela there was a joy in both of our lives. Then I went to Normandy and since I returned I have brought her only pain."

"And you would have her joyful once more?"

"I would."

"What made you change, my lord?"

I remained silent. I would not betray the Empress. I bowed my head and closed my eyes. *'Father, give me an answer to my question. The priest is kind but he does not understand.'*

"I am guessing that war did not change you. Lady Adela is more than fond of you. I am a priest bound by the confessional and I can say no more. I am guessing that you have met someone in Normandy and, for whatever reason, she is unattainable." Father Peter was shrewd.

I opened my eyes and stared at the priest, framed in the candlelight and watching me. He knew. But how?

"Your face is honest my lord and I can now read the story in your face. What you have done is not a sin. In fact, it shows that you are an honourable man. Let me give you some advice. You may take it or leave it. I am a young priest and you are right I know little of this world. However, I know the Lady Adela and from your deeds and words I know you. Make the Lady Adela your wife. It will make her happy and I believe it will not make you unhappy. The alternative for the young woman is not attractive. She would stay a ward in your castle, watching you each day and knowing she could never be with you? That is not kind. Send her to a nunnery? That would remove your problem but she would not be happy either. Ask yourself this. Would it make you unhappy if she were your wife? Would it make you unhappy if she bore you children? You cannot attain what you left in Normandy. Would you resign yourself, as I have had to do, to a childless life?"

That was when the voice came into my head, *'He is right, my son, heed his advice.'*

I stood and walked past the grave to the priest at the altar. I clasped his hand, "Thank you for your advice, Father Peter. I will think on your words but you have comforted me marvellous much."

Harold and I rode back through the night to the sanctuary that was Stockton. I had not yet made up my mind but I slept well that night. And that was the first time in a long time.

At breakfast, I told Wulfstan, Edward and Adela of my two visits. Adela frowned. "Harold of Elwick was a friend of the de Brus, my lord. They went hunting in the woods to the north of Hartness. He bought many of the slaves which were taken by those like de Mamers. Were there ships in the port?"

"There were. Why do you ask?"

"Harold of Elwick owned ships. He has a fine house at Elwick. I never visited but I know that De Brus stayed there and he liked his comfort."

"I see a plot here my lord. We have removed one of the heads of the hydra but another has grown and from what you say this one is equally devious."

I hated inactivity and I hated waiting for things to happen. "Edward, we will ride today and take all of our men. Wulfstan, would you ride with us."

I saw the worried look on his face. Faren patted his hand. "Go my husband. Your child will not enter the world this day. You have been cooped up here all winter. Go."

It was good to have my old mentor with me. He was still the finest warrior I knew. I had learned much but he had forgotten more than I had learned. His advice and his wisdom would aid me.

We rode north on the track which led to Hartness. Where it forked we took the northern fork to head towards the Wear. That route would take us past Elwick and the tiny village of Hart. I did not know what we were looking for but it was good to be out with my conroi. "Dick, take one of the new men and scout Elwick. Carry on to Hart and then rejoin us."

The land rose steadily as we headed north. Where the trees allowed we had a fine view of the sea. We even saw the masts of the ships in the port. We halted where the land flattened out and afforded us a good view of the track leading north. The Romans had not built a road here and the track we trod could be impassable in winter. If this were my manor I would have had a road built which could be used in winter. Hart was a huddle of huts on a slight rise. It had a fine view of the sea and yet was sheltered.

Dick and Wilson joined us. "What did you see?"

"Both are prosperous my lord. They have cattle and swine. The hall at Elwick is a fine one and there is a ditch around it."

"Did you see any armed men?"

"No, my lord but…"

"Go on Dick."

"Well, my lord the track which led north was well-trodden." He pointed over his shoulder. "The last part had had few hooves upon it but a mile or two to the east there are signs that both horses and men have been making use of that way. We saw cattle by the houses."

"You have done well." I saw my old mentor looking north and rubbing his beard. They were sure signs that he was thinking. "Wulfstan?"

"A puzzle indeed."

"If there are cattle there then the Scots have not been raiding them. Have they been raiding the Scots?"

Edward shook his head, "If that is true then there is naught for us to do. King Henry charged us with stopping the Scots raiding our lands."

"But there have been raids. Sir Richard. Sir Guy and Sir Geoffrey all told us that their isolated farms had been raided. Suppose those animals had been taken first to Elwick and then distributed north?"

"We would have noticed."

"No, we would not. The Bishop of Durham does not keep the northern road patrolled except for five miles around his domain. If they passed to the north of Wulfestun they could cross the track near the fork and head to Hartness. We will ride east and follow this track."

I sent out four archers as scouts.

Sometimes we know not why we make decisions and they turn out well. Sometimes they do not. It was just after the weak early spring sun had passed its zenith that Aelric rode in. "My lord there is a band of warriors heading south. They have their war gear on."

"What banners did they carry?"

"None, my lord."

"Were they Scots?"

He shrugged, "They could have been but there were at least four knights with them and they held shields such as you."

"How many in total?"

I was fortunate in that Aelric could count well. Many of my men could count but not using numbers. "I would guess at thirty or more. They were travelling loosely."

"Horses?"

"Half of them were mounted, the rest were afoot."

Loosely suggested a warband of raiders out for what they could take. I looked to Wulfstan for guidance. He shrugged, "They could be friendly knights."

"Then why travel this track which just goes to Hartness? This is a path you tread if you wish to remain hidden but we will be cautious." I spied a clearing and a dip ahead. I led the conroi forward. At some time there had been a couple of huts there but all that remained was a jumble of daub and wood.

"Wulfric take half of the men and hide in the woods to the east. Await my command. Aelric take the archers and hide in the woods to the west." I turned to the other six men at arms. "You six form a second rank behind me. If we charge then you follow up." As they did so Wulfstan and Edward flanked me and Harold and Alan took post at each end of the line. As we waited I lifted my helmet to the back of my head so that I could be seen. It also enabled me to see clearer too. I knew that Dick and my other scouts would be trailing them. If fighting began then they would come in from the rear and give the warband a nasty surprise. My men could be right and these could have peaceful intent. My mind told me otherwise. I formed our line up at the edge of the clearing so that there were a hundred paces for us to use.

Alan asked Edward, "Why is it significant that they do not have banners?"

He pointed to my gonfanon. "This marks Baron Alfraed a banneret knight and tells others who he is. It identifies him. These warriors are coming hidden; in disguise. They may be peaceful but it is unlikely." Alan looked at my blue banner with the two stars, seemingly for the first time. I smiled. He was learning what it meant to be a knight. Harold, who held the gonfanon, seemed to sit a little straighter at those words.

We could now hear them as they approached. The clearing was on a slight rise. Whoever had lived here had chosen well. I later discovered that there was a stream just ahead. I heard the splashing as the hooves of their horses crossed it. When the knights' heads appeared, I wondered if we were the only conroi to send out scouts. Had they had scouts they would have seen us earlier. As it was I saw the looks exchanged between the knights which showed that they had not expected us. Their leader made a rapid decision. He yelled something and they charged at us. It was a mistake but it took away the decision I had worried about making. I lowered my helmet and my lance. I saw that the four knights also had lances but they were not riding knee to knee. Behind them were a motley mixture of men at arms and light horsemen. There were twenty, at least. As I prepared to launch our counterattack I saw the foot soldiers spreading out. I could ignore them.

I waited until the knights were halfway across the clearing and approaching the uneven ground where the huts had stood. "Charge!"

It was the first time in a long time since I had charged next to Wulfstan and I took comfort from his presence. Although not a natural horseman he was a born warrior. I pulled back my lance as Scout thundered ahead of the others. We had not brought our destrier and Scout was the best of the horses we had. It meant I was the one who struck first blood. I aimed for the middle of the knight with the red shield and yellow star. His lance was well-aimed but it came for my head. I trusted my left arm and my shield. They took the blow although my left shoulder rocked around. My lance struck him a moment after his and the movement of my body brought the lance head around so that it struck the knight's left side. He was already slightly unbalanced and he tumbled from his horse.

I pulled my arm back as I steadied Scout and I punched forward at the warrior who came at me with a long spear. He did not pull it back before his struck and the weak blow merely clattered off my shield whilst my lance tore into his middle and came out of his back. I released the now useless weapon and drew my sword. I was in the heart of the horsemen and I knew that I had a wedge of warriors behind. My men were well trained and we were fighting a rabble. Discipline would overcome numbers.

I spurred Scout and he leapt towards the next man at arms. Instead of stabbing, I swept my sword around my head. The man was concentrating on stabbing me. The tip of his blade touched my surcoat and the lamellar armour beneath as my blade took his head. And then I was through the horsemen. I saw two spearmen lying with arrows in their backs as I swung my sword into the face of the surprised swordsman. I reined Scout in and turned. Behind me I could see the effect of our charge and our ambush. There were just four men who had surrendered. The rest were fled or dead.

Wulfstan reined in next to me. I saw that he had suffered a wound to his leg. "Wulfric, we need your needle."

"It is nothing Alfraed. I had suffered worse sharpening my sword."

"Nonetheless it will be tended to. I would not risk the wrath of Faren."

I saw that the others who had been in the front rank were unharmed although two of the men at arms who had followed me were injured. I took off my helmet and rode back to where Edgar and my men at arms waited with the prisoners. There were just four of them. I glanced at them as I rode past them to the knights. Three were dead already. Brian had his sword at the last one who was not long for this world. He had a black shield.

I waved Brian's sword away. This knight would hurt no one. "What is your name?"

He tried to hold up his shield. He could not manage it. "I am the black knight and you must be Alfraed of Norton. We were warned to avoid you."

He spoke in Norman. "Then you were not the leader."

"No, Lord William thought we could avoid you if we came this way. He…" Those were his last words and he died.

"Well, we know one name at least."

"Aye Edward, perhaps we can get more from the prisoners."

The four of them were poorly prepared for war. They each had a shield and an axe. Two of them had metal helmets but the other two had leather caps. All had a wound of some description.

"Where did you come from?"

The four of them stared insolently at me. I tried them in Saxon and had the same response. "Anyone speak Scottish here?"

One of my new men at arms stepped forward, "I am Thomas of Ulverston, my lord. I understand a couple of words."

"Good man. Try them."

He spoke to them and this time there was a brief flicker of reaction and then they retained their stone faces. "Sorry my lord."

"Oh, they understand all right. Tell them that if they do not speak I will have them executed." He nodded. "Say it slowly so that there is no mistake."

He did so, enunciating each word. This time one of them spat at my feet. Wulfric went to hit him but I restrained him. "No Wulfric. These are brave men, misguided but brave. Bind them and bring them with us. Strip the bodies of anything useful and pile them in the middle of the clearing. Fetch brush and we will burn them. We have no time to bury them and I would not have the animals dig up their bones."

There were just eight dead. The rest had fled. I knew that more were wounded and I guessed that some would die on their way north. We could do nothing for them.

As we headed south, Wulfstan, who had a heavily wrapped leg said, "You have grown Alfraed. Your father would be proud. Where is the arrogant young knight who thought he knew it all?" He laughed. "I watched your men. They followed you as we followed your father. They may be paid warriors but they are your oathsworn in all but name."

"Thank you, Wulfstan. Those words mean more to me than you can know. What concerns me now is the origin of these raiders. The knights were not Scottish but the men were. What were they after? Is there still a connection with Hartness? I fear this will be a long summer. It is barely spring and already they are raiding. Whoever this William is he must be close to the Scottish border."

"We are victims of our own success. The Welsh cattle you brought from King Henry's Welsh wars will prove to be a lure for every ragtag warband who thinks we are an easy mark. If you want some advice, I would speak with Osric and Athelstan and warn them of the dangers. They will be the first to suffer an incursion."

I nodded and rode in silence. We passed the track leading to Hartness. I had not managed to see what was in the harbour of Hartness. I would leave that for another day but the proximity of the manor without a lord was worrying. I was safe behind Stockton's stone walls but Norton had wooden walls only. Edward must have been reading my mind. "My lord, you are sending William to work on the church, why not have him build a tower next to the church. It could be a refuge. With a beacon on the top, they could signal Stockton and we can be there swiftly. It need not be a large tower."

"That is a good idea. We need not his skills to finish the curtain wall."

Wulfric was behind me and he murmured, "Aye, my lord but we need a gaol. If we are to have sessions we need somewhere to put those who are convicted."

"You are right Wulfric. We will give thought to that when we reach our home."

As we rode through the gates I knew what we would do with these prisoners. "Wulfric get four ropes and string these up from the gates. Their bodies can act as a warning to all who would steal from us."

As soon as the four ropes were thrown over the gate leading to the town the men began to struggle. They knew what was coming. They shouted at me. I wondered if they were telling me what I needed to know. "Thomas, what are they saying?"

He looked down, "My lord, they are cursing you." My men crossed themselves.

The eight men at arms holding the ropes all pulled at once and the four Scots' wriggling, writhing bodies were jerked up into the air above the gate. Their necks did not break but they were slowly strangled until the last leg stopped twitching and my men tied off the ropes.

Wulfric shook his head, "Next time, my lord, we cut out their tongues first!"

The next morning, I had to pass beneath their bodies. I noticed the smell. They had fouled themselves as they had died. I would have to have the bodies cut down. It would not do to upset Faren and Adela. I went to Alf and negotiated two sets of mail in return for the armour and weapons we had collected. It suited Alf for he would pay no taxes and yet he would profit.

We began work the next day on the gaol. We had enough space in the bailey. We attached it to the keep on the village side. It would afford more protection from an attack. We made the entrance on the top so that it could not be used by an attacker. It was six paces square. We would be able to accommodate ten men at a time. We deduced that it would be unlikely that we would need room for more. William went each day to Norton to begin work on a tower which could be attached to the church. Privately I thought that it would make a good bell tower. I would ask Alf if he could cast one in bronze for us. It would not need to be large but it could be used to summon us if danger threatened. Norton was where my father rested and it needed protection.

As spring made the river come alive and Olaf and the other ships began to ply the river more I saw that trade was increasing and I detected signs of prosperity. More houses were being built and William and his sons began to be asked to make some of the houses in stone; at least the lower levels. I felt quite proud of the progress we had made. It meant that people felt safer. The moneyer, Leofric was now producing not only copper coins but also silver ones. They each bore the face of King Henry. I had used the treasure we had collected from the dead raiders and I was able to pay my men a little extra. They had shown their loyalty and this was the best way to reward them and encourage them at the same time.

When the gaol and the curtain wall were finished, I held a feast. We were close enough to Easter and I was keen to reward all. I sent my archers out to hunt in the woods around the Hart Burn and along the river. I had crude tables constructed and we laid them outside my walls in the middle of the settlement which was burgeoning. Faren had just given birth to Wulfstan's daughter, Judith, and so Adela had to take on much of the organisation. She did a fine job and the feast went off without a hitch. I walked down the river with Wulfstan and Edward. We had all had plenty to drink.

"Adela did a good job there, my lord. It went off without a hitch. Your people are fed and replete. This has been good for Stockton."

"Perhaps I should have done something for Norton too."

Wulfstan laughed, "Poor Adela had enough to do organising one such feast. Wait until the Midsummer Festival and Faren will be able to help."

"Unless she is with child again!"

Wulfstan laughed, "And she may well be! It has taken me many years to sire a family. Do not blame me if I take advantage of a fecund wife."

I laughed too. My two household knights were easy company.

Wulfstan stopped at the bend in the river. On the other bank, we saw a pair of herons. They were engaging in the mating ritual. Wulfstan belched. "Better out than in! And what of you and Adela?" I flashed him a look of irritation. Edward was there. He laughed, "Edward knows of the situation, all of your men do. What have you decided? Will you be fair to the girl or no?"

My shoulders slumped in resignation. "I spoke with Father Peter and I know what I ought to do. The problem is broaching it."

My two friends looked at each other and Wulfstan shook his head. "Do it the way you did the other day against those raiders. Tackle it head on. Just tell her what is in your heart. You will not be disappointed."

The two birds disappeared into the bushes which lined the river. "Should I do it now?"

"No, my young friend. You have had a drink and your words might be misconstrued. Choose a quiet time and make sure you are alone."

That night, as I lay in bed I knew it would have to be the next day. I had the first of my Easter sessions coming up and I would need a mind cleared of clutter by then. The next morning, I approached her. "Adela would you care to go riding today? It is clement weather and you have not ridden this year. I would talk with you and thank you for your efforts yesterday."

Her enthusiasm almost knocked me over. I had one of the gentler palfreys saddled and I rode Scout. I rode towards the Hart Burn. There were wild parts near there where I knew we would not bump into anyone. I wanted just to be alone with Adela. If I had to say something then I wanted no one there to mock me or see my foolish efforts. It was almost as though she knew what I was going to say for she listened intently to what I said about my land and showed a remarkable insight into the manor. I almost forgot what I was going to say. We found ourselves at the shallow valley a half a mile from Old Tom's house. We dismounted and let the horses graze. We watched a kestrel as it hovered before plunging down on a water vole.

"This is a good place, my lord."

"The whole manor is and I know that you are a large part of that Adela. I wanted you to know that." She said nothing but looked intently at me. She was not making it easy and there was a silence which had to be filled. "Before I went away to Normandy I felt that there was something stirring between us."

"For my part, there still is my lord. Have I displeased you?"

"No! Of course not. Events happened in Normandy which, well let us just say they complicated matters."

"Not for me. You have my heart and I shall give it to no one else."

I was out of my depth. "What would you have?"

"You."

"Even though I cannot promise that you will have my heart?"

"You will have mine and that is good enough for me. When we have children then I will have their hearts and they are part of you. I will be content but one day I will have your heart. I know that."

I shook my head. "You are a remarkable girl. Think on this until this time next year. If you feel the same way then we shall be wed. Does that please you?"

Her answer was to throw her arms around me and to kiss me. "Aye my lord. Today you have made me a happy woman."

I was surprised by the warmth with which the news was greeted by all in my castle. It seemed I was the only one who had not seen what was before my eyes. It certainly made my life easier for I could now concentrate on being Lord of the Manor. I held my first sessions at Easter and I became the knight my father had wanted me to be. Life was good.

Chapter 10

War came before we could reap the benefits of Spring. The men of the north, Gospatric's men, came a month after Easter. This was not a handful of hopeful raiders. This was a large warband who came to ravage the land in King Henry's absence. Gospatric had lands which straddled both England and Scotland. King David and King Henry had both given him lands and manors to make him loyal. The winter barley had been a poor crop and the harsh winter, further north, had killed many animals. Gospatric took himself off for a pilgrimage to Rome. His lieutenants came raiding. I knew, for Wulfstan told me, that the absence of Gospatric was deliberate. He could avoid any blame. He could punish his men if things went awry but if they were successful then he would have more lands and more animals. He would be richer. Of course, we only discovered this much later. What we did know was that refugees fled from the north, first to Norton and thence to Stockton. They spoke of fierce warriors who slaughtered men, took the women and enslaved families. They gathered the animals and drove them north. It was not one army but like the fingers of two hands it was columns of warriors heading south and avoiding such places as Durham, Bamburgh, Alnwick and Raby. Too many knights were serving in Normandy or had taken the cross. There were not enough men to oppose them.

I sent riders to Sir Richard and Sir Mark asking for their men. I warned Sir Guy and Sir Geoffrey of the dangers and told them to get their people within their walls. With seven or eight columns heading south I could not afford to have those two river crossings abandoned. We would have to face whatever came our way with less than a hundred men. We had no idea how many were coming. We just knew that the columns of warriors were sweeping all before them.

While I awaited the arrival of my two knights I rode with Edward to Norton. Osric and Athelstan had begun their preparations. The closest farmers had been prepared while those who were isolated had been urged to enter the walls for protection. Some chose to take their chances. I knew that we had to have as many within the walls to provide warriors on the walls.

"We are prepared, Baron. Tom the Fletcher has provided many arrows. The ditch is deeper and William's gate, while not finished is stronger than the wooden one." He pointed to the half-finished tower. It stood the height of a man. "And we have that refuge too. Father Peter will shelter the women and children in the church. Your father will protect them there."

"That is good Athelstan."

"And what will you do, Baron? Are you going to let them waste their strength on your walls?"

"No Osric. I have enough horses to mount our men and meet them far from the Tees. I want none of my people hurt by these savages. I was charged with protecting the Tees. I will do so." I hesitated, "There is room enough behind Stockton's walls."

Osric laughed, "While your father's body lies in the church we are still his oathsworn and we die to protect it. Fear not. We will hold."

I did not tell them that I feared for them. They were as dear to me as my father had been and I wanted them to end their lives peacefully in their beds and not fighting Scottish raiders.

I returned to Stockton. I would leave Wulfstan to command. My fyrd would watch the walls. I had enough horses to mount all of Sir Mark and Sir Richard's men. Mobility would be our strength. Sir Richard arrived on the same day that I sent my summons. He brought, as I had told him he could, his family. His son, of course, would be with him as his squire.

It was the first time he had visited my castle and I saw the envy in his eyes. "This is fine stone. You must have a rich manor."

Wulfstan had laughed, "He has a fine sword and sound men. Sir Alfraed here makes more from his warring than his ploughing." When Sir Richard realised that I was leaving a knight to protect his family he was relieved.

"But where is Sir Mark?"

"He has not arrived yet. If he has not arrived by the morrow then we will leave without him. However, he will do that at his peril for I will raze his castle to the ground if he fails to heed my order."

"Have you the power to do so?"

I shrugged, "No one has told me I may not. If I am punished then so be it but I rule as I see fit."

In the end, Sir Mark did arrive but it was with a pathetically small force. He brought only three men at arms and five crossbows. I brought him before the other knights and squires in my hall. "Sir Mark, did you misunderstand my message?"

"No, Sir Alfraed but I had to leave some men to protect my lands."

"Why? The raiders can only get to your lands across my ferry. The nearest ford is at Gainford and that is protected by Sir Guy. Your lands would be safe. I fine you one silver piece per day for each warrior you failed to bring and one penny a day for each of the fyrd."

"That is outrageous. You have no authority."

I held up the parchment. "I have the King's authority but if you wish to ask a jury of your peers there are three of them here. Ask them if they think I am being unjust."

He retreated a little. "They are your men," he said sulkily.

I smiled, "And I thought you were my man or did I misread the instructions from the King?"

"I am your man."

It was as close to obeisance as I would get. I dismissed his behaviour from my mind. I had to focus on the task in hand. "We are a small conroi but I intend to strike at these raiders whenever we can. We strike and withdraw. I want them to go elsewhere and raid. We need them to fear this valley and our knights."

"With five knights?" scoffed Sir Mark.

"No with four knights for I intend to leave Sir Wulfstan to lead the fyrd in case we fail."

"Then it matters not that I left my fyrd at home, Sir Alfraed."

"It does because it means that Sir Wulfstan has twenty fewer warriors."

Wulfstan snorted, "If they are all as spineless as this popinjay then it as well they are not here."

Sir Mark coloured, "Are you questioning my honour?"

"Of course I am. You insubordinate apology for a warrior and when this is over if you wish satisfaction then seek me out I will not be hiding!"

Sir Mark fell back.

I held up my hands. I was a leader and had to begin to act like one and not become annoyed because I did not like Sir Mark. "Peace. We do not fight amongst ourselves. I will tell the men later but you all need to know my tactics and plans. We have only four knights but we have three squires. They are dressed as we are and may be mistaken for knights. We charge in a tight line. I shall have Sir Edward and Sir Mark next to me.

My squire, Harold, shall flank Sir Mark. Sir Richard will be on Edward's left with his son and then Alan. It is a great responsibility on Alan and Harold but I know they are up to it. Wulfric is my sergeant at arms and he will command the men at arms. Dick is my captain of archers and he will command the archers and the crossbows of Sir Mark. We ride mounted. I do not believe that the enemy will be a mounted force. We will speak with the men and then we ride before dawn's early light."

When all had retired I sought out Wulfstan. "I would have you leave Sir Richard's fyrd here and take mine to Norton. The walls of this castle will come as a surprise to any raider but Norton is still vulnerable. We have enough horses to get you back here should danger strike."

"You are right Alfraed although I like not leaving my family."

"Alf and Ethelred are not fyrd and they will be in Stockton. They are both sound men. They will hold Stockton with the other burghers. They have a vested interest in its survival."

We reached Norton while it was still dark. Dawn would break in an hour or so. We did not enter but I summoned Aiden. "Come Aiden and bring your dogs. You will be our eyes and ears. Go to the north and find the enemy."

Dick knew the worth of Aiden and he, like me was happy to have the youth and his dogs ranging far ahead. Dick, as captain, had to delegate the scouting duties to others and Aelric led the four archers who were behind Aiden, watching for our foes. I had spoken with Dick before we had left the castle to warn him to treat the crossbows with respect. Our numbers were too few to disregard these weapons and the men who used them.

By the time the sun was warming the earth Aiden was back. He pointed to the west. "My lord they reached the fork in the road from Hartness and they headed west."

I had been outwitted. My arrogance had led me to believe that an enemy would raid me first. Of course, I was wrong. By sweeping west these raiders had the soft underbelly of the valley to ravage. They had avoided Durham and could raid the fertile lands as far as the stone castle at Barnard. The land was well tilled and teemed with animals now that spring was finally here.

"How many?"

"It was hard to tell but they have a mixture of horses and foot. I would estimate a large warband."

"Take my archers, find them and follow!"

We spurred our horses west. We spied the still burning houses of Seggesfield. It was a small community. I suspected the raiders would be disappointed. They made pots there and other objects from clay. The few animals they had would not be what they sought. That was confirmed when Atheling returned.

"They have killed the men, eaten the animals and taken the families as slaves my lord." He shook his head, "They smashed their pots!"

I had been right. That was not what they came for. That was mindless destruction borne out of the frustration of not finding what they sought. "Which way have they gone?"

"They are heading south west, towards the river. Aiden and the others are closing with them."

I sent him to rejoin the other scouts. Spurring my mount on I began to berate myself. They could be heading for my castle which was held by a handful of men from Yarm. In stripping it of Wulfstan and my fyrd I had laid it open to attack. Sir Mark seemed to read my thoughts. "If we head back to Stockton, Sir Alfraed, then we could be there before the enemy."

"True Sir Mark, but they could just as easily head towards the bridge over the Tees at Piercebridge. Until we know where they are going we have to follow but we can, at least, follow quickly."

We rode hard to catch up with them. Each step to the south west took them further away from Stockton but I was surprised at their speed. They were travelling at least as fast as us. It was past noon when Atheling returned. "We have found them, my lord. They are heading for Piercebridge. Aiden and Aelric are watching them. They have started to raid the farms."

For the first time that morning, I allowed myself a smile. Sir Geoffrey would have collected in all of his farmers and animals. By raiding Seggesfield first they had allowed Sir Geoffrey to save his people. They would come away with little to show for their raid.

We saw the smoke from the farms some two miles from the river. That both saddened and angered me. They were just destroying for the sake of it. There was nothing to be gained save alerting Sir Geoffrey. Perhaps that was their intent, to draw Sir Geoffrey on to their blades. Even Sir Mark hurried to follow me as I led my men towards the sound of the screams. Not all of the farmers and their families had heeded Sir Geoffrey's warning. Aelric and his archers awaited me.

"My lord the force has split into two. One half raided the farm just over there the other half headed towards the river. Aiden has followed them."

"How many are there?"

"There are forty or more here. They have but two knights and most of them look like the wild men of the north. They fight with long swords and axes."

"They shun shields then?"

He grinned, "Aye my lord."

"Dick, take the archers and go with Aelric to the north. When you are in position then rain death upon these wild men. We will wait. I will ambush them when they flee towards the river and the rest of the warband."

I kicked Scout on and we rode just four hundred paces to the south. There were many open fields surrounded by ditches. This land had been farmed since the times of the Romans and was fertile. We crossed the ditch and waited in one long line. I could see the farm on the other side of the small copse of trees. I saw the arrows as they soared in the air. Men who do not wear armour and have no shields are vulnerable to arrows and the hidden archers caused mayhem. The raiders burst from the trees. They were led by three mounted knights and eight men at arms. I guessed that the rest would be on foot. We charged obliquely across the field.

I urged Scout on for I wanted a wedge formation. We outnumbered their horsemen and I wanted them despatched before the wild men with the axes came. Because of our oblique attack we struck them like a hammer on their shield side. They had no lances to counter our attack and two knights were hurled to the ground. The third was far enough away to avoid our lances and he took off west like a startled deer. The other riders had suffered equally. I caught sight of Richard's son, Tristan, as he struck his first enemy in battle. His lance was held high and it speared the Scot in the throat, throwing the lifeless body to the ground and breaking the lance.

"Draw your sword boy!" I heard the father's voice, filled with pride as he looked to his son.

The wild men with the axes, hammers and long swords were finally free from the bites of the arrows and they fell upon my men and horses like demons. One of Sir Mark's men had his leg severed and his horse gutted like a fish by a Scot wielding a two handed Danish axe. Edgar ended his life by spearing him with his lance.

"Do not let them get too close! Use your lances and wait for the archers!"

I had too few men to risk losing them to wild men from the north. The main warband was still ahead of us. It was only my men at arms who had brought lances and spears. When the arrows and bolts fell amongst the survivors, they fled to the south. I waved the men at arms on. "Pursue them!"

This time Sir Mark and Sir Richard's men could engage the wild men for they had their backs to them. Our horses had carried greater weight and we needed to rest them.

"Dick, take the archers and crossbows. Find the main band!"

We had not escaped unscathed. I saw that at least one of my archers and a crossbowman had fallen. I knew that others would have wounds too. The two Scottish knights lay where they had fallen. Their horses had remained by the bodies. These were not destrier but palfreys. They would come in handy. Three Scottish men at arms lay dead and eight of the half-naked wild men. I dismounted to examine the bodies. They were heavily tattooed and their hair was limed so that it formed a hard cap. It did not replace armour but it made them look fearsome.

I saw the three squires talking. "You squires did well. Especially you, Tristan. Next time, aim for the body. It is a bigger target and punch as you strike."

Sir Mark seemed more confident now that he had emerged unscathed. "They were easy enough to defeat."

I shook my head, "We surprised them and it was not the main band. Wait until they are all despatched before you begin crowing. Come we had better see to the people of the farmstead if any remain alive."

We found three women and six children who emerged from the woods. Their men lay dead. I dismounted and went to the elder of the women. "I am sorry that we came too late mother."

I think my Saxon surprised her. She fell to her knees, "Thank you for coming my lord. Sir Geoffrey offered us sanctuary but my husband was a stubborn man. He has paid the price with his life."

"Will you stay?"

She adopted a defiant pose. "A few barbarians will not stop us. Thanks to you they did not have time to steal our animals. We can begin again."

I nodded. These were my father's people and they had iron for bones; especially the women. "My castle is at Stockton. If you need aught then go there and ask for help. King Henry has charged me with defending this valley and I take that seriously."

"I thought that the King cared little for us."

"He has many enemies but he cares. Trust me."

My men at arms returned. I saw that we had four of our men who were wounded. "The wounded men stay here and help these people. Collect the Scottish weapons and wait for us."

Conan the Irishman and William of Deal were among the wounded. "What will you do my lord?"

"We will follow them and finish them off. Take command William until I return and help them to repair their defences."

Although our numbers were depleted by leaving such good men there I knew it was a risk to have them fighting in a weakened condition.

It was late afternoon when Dick found us again. "Aiden followed them and found them at Sir Geoffrey's castle. The Scots have learned that they cannot attack such a well defended castle. They have moved west towards Gainford."

"Then we have a chance."

We hurried to the castle where Sir Geoffrey greeted us with a grin. "We showed those Scottish bastards that we have a backbone. My men did well."

I pointed north. "You lost two farms. We managed to save the women and children at the closer of the two but not the other."

He shook his head, "Richard of Headlam was like his father. He was headstrong and believed he and his family could see off raiders."

"I left men with them. The raiders have headed to Sir Guy's castle."

"That is not good for it is not as strong as mine. It is further from the river." He patted his gate. "We have stone which the Romans left."

"Then we will rest now and leave well before dawn. Leave your fyrd to watch your castle. We know where they are and we can surprise them at camp."

He nodded. "I am sorry that my hall cannot accommodate all of your men at arms."

I laughed, "We are warriors. We will cope."

Sir Mark huddled with his own warriors. He was still unhappy about having to serve with us. The lack of any coins amongst the dead Scots had done nothing to make him any happier. Edward and I lay with our backs to the wall of the hall and talked with Sir Richard.

"It was good to see my son blooded today but I was fearful for him. Those warriors were savage fighters. They went for the horses!"

"My father was one of Harold Godwinson's housecarls and he told me that they did the same thing. The Danish axe is a fearsome weapon and can take the head from a horse. It renders the rider vulnerable."

Sir Richard nodded, "And that is why you stood off from them."

Edward nodded in my direction, "You will learn, Sir Richard, that our leader is a careful warrior. We are never reckless but we survive and that is important. There are too few of us to waste lives."

"But we have taken little in the way of horses and treasure."

"That will come. We have some horses. They are not the best but we have learned that a mounted conroi has more chance of success than one which is afoot."

"And tomorrow? What will that bring?"

"I know not who commands this band of raiders but I would assume that they did not leave their best warriors to take that little farm. Whoever we meet tomorrow will be stronger than they were but we are no longer alone. We have Sir Geoffrey's men and I hope that Sir Guy will have others to help us."

Suddenly Aiden and his dogs materialised from nowhere. Sir Richard actually jumped, "Is your scout a ghost that he can appear from nowhere?"

"He is good. What have you found?"

"The Scots have camped at a farm a mile or so from the castle. It was empty. They have a band of twenty watching to see that no one comes to the aid of the castle or leaves."

"You think they are waiting for the morning?"

He nodded, "They have cut down a mighty oak and are hardening the end in a fire. They will attempt to breach the walls at first light."

"How many are there?"

He shrugged, "I counted fires only for it was dark but there must be a hundred or more men. They have eaten well this night. They slaughtered one of the cattle they had collected and there were screams from the women."

He said no more but it became clear that we had to get there as early as we could. I did not expect that we could surprise these. The ones who had escaped would have warned them of our presence. This time they would be ready.

Chapter 11

It was pitch black when we left. The difference with our previous long march was this was less than a few miles and we had a better force. We had nine more archers and seven more men at arms. Sir Geoffrey brought his squire and, like, Sir Richard it was his son. With five knights and four squires we were more of a force to be reckoned with. Before we left I gave them my instructions. "This time we use four lines. The first line will be the knights. The squires, the second. The men at arms the third and the archers will be the reserve. They can release their arrows over the heads of the knights."

Sir Mark pouted, "My crossbows cannot."

"And that is why we have archers. Your crossbowmen can guard the archers' horses." Sir Mark was getting a lesson in warfare. He should have known the limitations of crossbows. They were best suited to defending walls and not being used on a battlefield.

The land was a patchwork of fields surrounded by ditches. Here and there were woods which had yet to be felled. The motte and bailey castle was a hundred paces from the river on a small rise in the land. Around it I could see the burnt-out houses of the small settlement which had surrounded it. The wooden walls of the castle were scorched and blackened where the Scots had attempted to fire it. However, the banner of Sir Guy still flew about the gatehouse. I did not know any of my knights well enough yet to know how they would react in a given situation. I hoped that he would sally forth, come to our aid and attack the host which now faced us in the flank. This was not the best position for us. For their leader had chosen a piece of land which rose gently and was free from trees on either flank. The only places of concealment were the few folds and hollows. I would not be able to hide my archers. I had to use the little that the land had to offer us. We drew up just above the road which led north. There were two drainage ditches running alongside. They would be an obstacle to the unwary.

Their leader had drawn his men up with his men at arms on one side and his knights on the other. The men at arms were closer to the castle. In the middle were a mass of the wild men as Edward had called them. There were ten knights and twenty men at arms. The bulk of his men

114

were the eighty Scots wielding a variety of weapons. I suddenly remembered my father's men talking about Hastings and how the Norman army had pretended to retreat making the fyrd charge after them. That would have to be our ploy.

I turned. "Dick, Wulfric, I am going to entice the wild men on to you. Dismount the men at arms and present a wall of spears. Dick, have your archers behind the men at arms. We will charge and then retreat as though we are fearful. Squires you will charge the left of the line; closest to the castle. You will come back around the archers and form an echeloned line behind them. Knights you follow me. We charge and when we use our lances we stop and I will yell, *'fall back we are beaten!'*" I smiled, "I will not mean it." I had our spare lances and spears jammed into the ground on either side of the men at arms.

I formed the squires and knights into a solid line so that the men at arms could dismount unseen and have their horses led behind them. I heard the Scots banging their shields and shouting to us. I guessed that they were insulting us in some way, shape or form. As we lined up I said, "Keep your formation and when you retreat, gallop as though the devil himself was after you."

I spurred Scout and we began to move forward. We held our lances aloft. It was easier that way. "Trot!" As we moved towards them I saw the knights ahead in conference. They were wondering what we were doing. Were we going to be so foolish as to attack a large warband with just a handful of knights? The mass of men before us were now banging their shields even harder and chanting something. I could not make out their words. "Canter!" We were now a hundred paces from them and I lowered my lance as I yelled, "Charge!"

I could see that they were laughing at us. There were nine of us charging at eighty warriors. I pulled back my arm and I saw my target. He was a huge half-naked warrior with a war hammer. He was already whirling it over his head. I would have to time this right or Scout would be struck. I pulled back my arm and, standing in my stirrups, leaned forward as I punched my lance into the middle of the warrior. I twisted as I pulled it out and shouted, "Fall back. We are beaten!"

The weight of our horses and the hole we had made with our nine lances allowed us to turn in two different directions. The knights might have seen what we were doing but the wild men just saw us running. We had killed or wounded a tenth of their men and I suppose those we had struck had been the leaders. They yelled something and ran after us. It was why I had told my men to gallop hard. We were in danger of being caught. The wild men saw knights running from them. They had the blood lust coursing through their veins and they lost control. They charged after us screaming their war cries.

I glanced over my shoulder and saw that the knights had yet to move. That was a mistake on the part of the knights. Some of the less disciplined men at arms had followed their fellows. The enemy leader had had his force of horsemen split. The ones who charged came, not in a line, but in a disorganised mob. We turned and formed two lines on the flanks of our dismounted men at arms. Dick and his archers loosed flight after flight over the heads of the men at arms and their hedge of spears. Half of them had found a target. Having run the gauntlet of goose feathered death they ran into the twenty lances and spears of my dismounted men at arms. Dick and the archers were able to release their arrows at point blank range. They were so close that I saw one arrow enter a Scot's head and come out at the back.

Finally, the knights and the men at arms who had remained behind charged. I worried about the squires but I had to concentrate on the line of knights charging us. We had all replaced our lances but our mounts were not as fresh as the Scots. We moved forward. I saw arrows being loosed over us as some of Dick's archers made life difficult for the knights. As I lowered my lance and aimed for the knight with the green and yellow shield I heard a cheer from my left. I had no idea what it meant. I kept my eyes on the knight. I saw his lance wavering. It told me that he was not using his own cantle for support and that he had not done this too often. It gave me confidence. When we were twenty paces apart I stood up and then squatted down as I punched forward. His lance went into the fresh air above my head. Mine ripped and tore into his stomach. The lance was broken as he fell from his mount. As I drew my sword I risked a glance to the left. Sir Guy was leading his men at arms to aid the squires.

I turned back and it was just in time for a sword came down towards me. I barely parried the blow. The edge struck my hand. If it were not for the mail gloves then I would have lost my hand and with it, my life. This was a powerful knight. I took him by surprise when I wheeled Scout around, presenting him my back. He had already started his turn and I saw that we were shield to shield. I punched with my shield as I brought my sword overhand. He reeled. As I readied myself for a second blow he jerked his horse around. His surviving knights and his men at arms were fleeing north. They had baulked at the wall of spears and the rain of arrows. He spurred his horse and he joined them. We had the field.

My own men at arms were dismounted and there was no way that our weary horses could follow. I had to content myself with holding the ground before Sir Guy's castle. Some of the men with axes and hammers had almost gone berserk. We surrounded them with a wall of spears and my archers filled their bodies with arrows. When the last body stopped twitching my men gave a huge cheer. Against the odds, we had won.

I took off my helmet and surveyed the field. We had not escaped unscathed. I saw that, although Sir Guy's intervention had been timely, Alan lay dead, transfixed by a spear. Tristan was nursing a wound and I saw blood pouring from Harold's head. As I looked around I saw Sir Mark's horse dragging his dead body around the field, his foot still in the stirrup. There were four dead men at arms but the cost had been lower than we might have hoped. Four of the knights who had tried to ravage my land lay dead, ten of their men at arms and fifty of their wild men would not return north.

"Dick, take the archers and follow them until they are beyond our land. Return to Sir Geoffrey's manor."

"Aye, my lord." He paused. "This was a great victory. Men will talk of this for many a year."

I pointed to Alan's body, "But not all." He nodded sadly. "Wulfric, see to the wounded."

Sir Guy came over to me and clasped my arm, "I wondered what you intended when you fled. That was masterly."

I shrugged, "Duke William did the same at Hastings. We were lucky. Had the enemy been more disciplined we would have lost. Thank you for your intervention."

"Your squires fought bravely. I am sorry for your loss."

"Alan died a warrior." I nodded towards the enemy dead. "Have your men strip the bodies of valuables and then burn them. If we leave them then it will attract carrion." He nodded and strode off, "Edward, lay out our dead and we shall bury them with honour."

I summoned Ralph, one of the two remaining men at arms from Normanby. "Your lord is dead; would you take him home to bury or will you bury him here with the other dead?"

Ralph was as surly as his master had been. "We will take him home."

I nodded. I could understand that. "Has he children?"

He shook his head, "He was unmarried."

"Then I will write to the King and the Bishop and inform them of the loss of the lord of the manor of Normanby."

"His cousin is lord of Guisborough."

"He does not gain the manor by right. That is for the King to decide and not his cousin. I leave you to command his men until a new lord is appointed." The remaining men of Normanby trudged home with their dead. They shared not in the spoils of war.

Sir Guy insisted that the knights and squires use his hall. He was the eldest of us and I could not refuse. In my heart, I wished to share the open fields with my men but we had been saved by his prompt action. We divided the spoils of war although they all deferred to me expecting, no doubt, that I would have kept the lion's share. We each gained a horse from the fray. One of the swords was given to Tristan for his bravery and a second to Harold. His head wound had not been as serious as it had looked although Wulfric's stitches would leave a wicked-looking scar down one cheek.

"I hope that this has dampened the enthusiasm of the Scots for their raids but it may not. We need to be vigilant. We cannot rely on Normanby any longer. Until the King appoints new lords to Hartness and Normanby we will have to rely on our own resources for the defence of the valley."

Sir Guy looked at Sir Geoffrey, "I believe I will try to hire more men at arms. But your son fought well. He could be a knight as could Tristan here."

Sir Richard said, "I would have my son become more experienced before he is knighted. Edward's squire, Alan, was a brave warrior and he fell. It will not harm my son to become more skilled."

"And I feel the same. My son has time to improve. It is a pity so many young knights took the cross. I would rather have a knight who brings his own men at arms. My people are becoming more prosperous. With more taxes, we can employ more warriors; if they are there to be hired." He was right. A good knight was more valuable than a pile of gold.

We left the next day. Each day we kept the fyrd armed was a day less for them to work in their fields. News came to us, later on, that other parts of the border, including the castle at Barnard, had suffered privations at the hands of Gospatric's men. We had suffered less than the others but it was still too much. Sir Richard and his men stayed an extra

day at Stockton. He wished to speak with Wulfstan about the best way to train his son. "Your mason, William, would he work for me?"

I laughed, "He works for coin but aye he would work for you. He is keen to work in the valley. He likes it here and his family is settled in the town."

"It has grown much. I was last here five years ago and it was barely a hamlet."

"Do not be a stranger. We are close neighbours. Your wife seems to have got on well with Faren and Adela in our absence."

"She is high born and she misses speaking with ladies of quality."

I glanced at Wulfstan's impassive face. He was proud that Faren, who we had bought as a slave, had become a lady of quality. After they had gone I noticed that the castle seemed a little emptier. With men and horses to heal and armour to repair I was kept busy for the next few days. It was Wulfstan who took me to one side. "I think you need to speak with Edward. He is brooding over Alan's death. He thinks he did not train the youth well enough."

"That is nonsense. I was to blame for putting him in such danger."

"No Alfraed, that is how a man becomes a warrior. Speak with him."

Wulfstan was right. Edward was one of my knights and I owed it to him to watch over him just as he protected me. I went to the town to visit with Alf. My mail glove, which had saved my hand needed repair. He turned it over in his hand. "I can have this ready in three days my lord."

"That quickly?"

He nodded, "Would that we could repair men as quickly eh, my lord?"

He was correct and I decided to do something about Edward. Aiden had now come to live at my new castle. He had his two boys whom he was training to look after the hawks and his other animals. John son of Godwin and Leofric son of Tan were fine boys and they proved to be almost as skilled with animals as Aiden. I decided to use the new hawks as an excuse to go with Edward and talk with him. Harold was still recovering from his wound and it would seem natural.

John was the bigger of the boys and he had the honour of carrying the cadge. As he had never done this before we just went down the river a mile or two to the woods close to the Hart Burn. It was a new experience for the boys. I decided to hunt a little before I brought up Alan's death. The two hawks were fine birds. "Aiden, have you named them yet?"

"No, my lord, they are your birds. I just trained them. Besides, I think it is better if they name themselves. That way they will answer quicker."

"Name themselves?"

"Aye my lord, the way Scout did. He has sharp ears and eyes and is a good scout. Let us see what they do when they hunt." We left the horses tied to a tree at the top of the steep bank. I took the first hawk from the cadge. He had sharp eyes and he stared at me. I had known, in Byzantium, some nobles who would have got rid of such a bird. I liked its insolence; it was showing that it too was a warrior. Its beak gave it the look of a Roman Emperor. I searched for prey and saw a dove which suddenly darted from the trees across the river. I lifted my arm and the hawk followed the fast-moving bird. It rose, almost lazily, and then swooped imperiously down to snatch the dove in its talons. Aiden whistled to fetch it back. I was impressed with the way it dropped the dead bird at his feet and allowed him to place it back on the cadge. He gave it a morsel as a reward.

"Caesar. He is Caesar!"

Aiden had never heard of Caesar but when I told him that he was a Roman Emperor who conquered Britain he was impressed. "It is a good name." He handed me the second bird. "Now this one is different to Caesar. She is slightly smaller, my lord, but do not let her size fool you. She is a good hunter."

We made our way to the river. This hawk kept watching all around her. She was curious. A duck suddenly took fright and flew along the river, keeping very low. I let the hawk go. This would be a harder kill for the duck kept moving from side to side and was very low over the water. The bird flew under trees so that the hawk could not get above it. The hawk seemed to lose interest and rose high above the river. They were almost lost from view. I wondered at Aiden's words. This bird did not seem as good as Caesar. The duck flew in a straighter line and the hawk dived, almost vertically. The shock was so great that it broke the duck's neck in an instant. She brought the dead bird back to Aiden.

Even Aiden was impressed. I watched as she tore into the titbit Aiden had just given her and I nodded my approval, "She is a killer! But she is regal. I shall call her Sheba!"

Edward had begun to smile as he had watched the hawk working her prey. As we moved up the slope, going slowly for the cadge was not easy to manoeuvre, I brought up Alan. "You still grieve for your squire?"

His face fell, "I am sorry, my lord, I did not know it showed."

"Edward, you are one of the most honest men I know. You cannot disguise your hurt nor should you. But you must temper that with the knowledge that we are all warriors and none of us is invincible." I held up my right hand. "I came within a sword thrust of losing my right hand and if that had happened then the Scot would have finished me. I was spared. Alan was not."

"Perhaps I did not train him well enough."

Perhaps. I think you did but you may be right. That means that you do a better job with your next squire."

"Next squire?"

"The Scots and other predators will not go away Edward and we need knights. So long as the Holy Land and its riches are a lure we will find it hard, in the poor north, to recruit knights. Perforce we must make our own."

We had reached our horses and we mounted. We rode along the ridge towards Stockton. The top of the tower could just be seen in the distance. "You are right my lord and, perhaps, I should take wife too. I am not getting any younger and I envy Wulfstan his son. He has a youth he can train from an early age to be a knight. Much as you were."

I said nothing but he was right and perhaps this was my father's way of telling me to marry Adela and begin my own family.

Deciding upon the need for a squire and finding one were two different matters but Edward was happier and he threw himself into the life of the manor. We had stopped one Scottish incursion but there would be another. The three of us took it in turns to take some men north each day and patrol the northern approaches and look for signs of newcomers. It honed the skills of all of our men and made them all better scouts. The days we did not ride north we trained. There were youths who were on the cusp of becoming archers and we had others, men at arms, who sought employment. Not all were suitable and Wulfric weeded out the ones he thought would be a liability. Men at arms were expensive and although the two manors were doing well there was a limit to the number we could hire.

I had had another expense too. With the sessions, the taxes and the correspondence I had to write I needed a clerk. I had little enough time to myself. Adela did it for a while and it drew us closer and softened the barriers I had erected between us. It was Osric who came up with the solution. Leofric the Moneyer had a son who could not only read but write quite well. He had thought to train as a priest but a dalliance with a maid, before I hired Leofric, put paid to that ambition. His carnal desires would get in the way of his religious duties. Osric brought him to Stockton when he heard I needed a clerk.

"My Lord Alfraed, this is John son of Leofric. He is an ambitious young man and would be your clerk if you would have him."

The young man looked presentable enough. He had soft hands. He obviously did not help his father overmuch and I wondered what he had been doing. "Tell me, John son of Leofric, how do you occupy your days?" He looked up at me in shock at the directness of my question. "If you work for me then you must know that I speak my mind and do not suffer fools gladly." I smiled at Osric, "I was brought up that way. If you do not like my bluntness then I suggest you go back to doing whatever you have been doing."

He nodded, "I help my father. I have nimble fingers and I help him make the dies for the coins. He needs a regular supply. When I do not do that then I sometimes teach some of the children who wish it, how to read."

"They are good answers and are testament to good character. Osric here says you are ambitious. What do you wish?"

"I have watched my father handling money every day and I would be rich."

"Then this is not the job for you for a clerk will never be rich."

"With respect, my lord, you will be paying me and I do not intend to waste that money. There are opportunities to use that money and to make it multiply. The story of the talents from the Bible tells us that. I will be patient and I will serve you well but I will also serve myself. A man may do that may he not?"

I laughed, "I like you, John. You answer directly and with honesty. You may use your coin for whatever you wish so long as you work hard for me. You will have much correspondence to write for I find writing tiresome. You will also need to organise the pay for the others who work for me and you will need to keep an account of the taxes and the money. There will be other tasks I set for you but we will discuss those as time goes on. What say you?"

"I will be happy to accept the post, my lord and I promise that I will serve you as well as any knight or man at arms."

I nodded and took his right arm. "Then you will now be my clerk. Welcome to Stockton Castle."

He proved as good as his word and I had more time to be with my men. I think the only one who was saddened by the appointment was Adela for we were together less often. I found that I missed our times together. It was just another sign of what I knew was inevitable. We would be wed but I had set myself a date and it was still more than half a year away. I regretted my words and, when my young couples married at the Midsummer feast I found myself looking at the lovely young woman and wishing that I had made the decision to wed.

Being in the far north we had little news and we heard nothing from London. Europe and the court of the Emperor might as well have been on the moon. Matilda was unobtainable and she was far away. I now realised that I had been a moonstruck youth and Wulfstan had been right. I needed distance to help me to see clearer. The courts of Europe were not for me. I was a marcher lord and I was happy to rule my two manors in the far north. There was less danger from a Scottish blade than in the politics of the court and I was happy to be away from such intrigue.

Chapter 12

It was late summer when Robert of Caen, Earl of Gloucester, arrived with a large conroi. He arrived at the ferry. Ethelred rubbed his hands when he saw the number of men. I shook my head, "This is the King's son, Ethelred. Make wise decisions."

He tapped his nose, "Thank you for your sage advice my lord. This may be the first of many!"

I shook my head. He was irascible. I sought Faren. "We will have guests tonight. The King's son comes. Have we food enough?"

She nodded, "Aiden and Dick were hunting yesterday. We have some deer. I will send to Ralph. He has some beans which might be ready."

"Thank you Faren." She was invaluable; my father had made a wise choice in buying her and Wulfstan an even wiser decision to marry her.

"I fear your cellar will be much depleted when they are gone. It is fortunate we made fresh ale yesterday but as these are Normans I am thinking that only the men at arms will drink something as base as beer!"

Adela rushed in. "Do we have company?"

"We do and you shall be much sought after by the bachelor knights."

She looked at me seriously, "There is only one knight for me and I only have half a year to wait for him."

I surprised myself by the good feeling I had after her words. I returned to my gate as Robert and his household knights landed. I knew all ten of them and had fought alongside them. They were good warriors one and all. I trusted them as I would trust my own knights. Robert clasped my arm. "I am sorry to spring this upon you, Alfraed, but my father sent me when he received the news about the incursions from the north."

"We did not suffer too badly here."

We strolled through my gate into my inner bailey. "But we did further west. Many farms were ravaged and manors destroyed. Had it not been for Carlisle Castle and Brougham Castle things would have gone ill for us."

"Do we know who caused the mayhem?"

"From some prisoners, we understand it was the men of Gospatric from Lothian and Northumberland."

"Does he not have lands in Northumberland?"

"Aye he does and his father was Earl of Northumberland until my grandfather took it from him and gave it to Siward." He leaned in, "We go north to his holdings in the borders and question him. If he is found to be guilty then I have the power to take his lands in England from him."

We had halted in the bailey so that he could talk quietly with me. "How many men do you take?"

"Not enough to cow him. I have my household knights and fifty men at arms." He paused, "We need your men. The ones who defeated the raiders."

I nodded. "I will send for them but the King needs to appoint a new lord of Normanby."

"There is one on his way from Normandy; Sir Guiscard d'Abbeville. He is a good knight and served the King well in the recent wars. We will leave when your knights arrive. I hope we will not inconvenience you."

"Do not worry, my lord. It is good to have some company. It will take Sir Guy and Sir Geoffrey a day or two to get here although Sir Richard can be here by the morrow. I will send riders now." I waved over Dick, "Send riders to Gainford, Piercebridge and Yarm. I have need of my knights and half of their men at arms and archers." After he had gone I explained, "All three are small manors and I would not leave them undefended. We still get Norse raiders in these parts."

"Those numbers should suffice." He looked up at my keep. "This is a fine castle and well built. Who designed it?"

"I had a mason and I just used ideas I had seen here and in the east. I know it is not large but we can extend." I pointed to the curtain wall. "I have left enough space to build towers on the town side and I can enlarge the barbican if I choose. Now come and meet my knights and my ladies."

As I expected Adela enchanted them all but I felt secretly pleased that she only had eyes for me. Faren proved to be a hostess to match any in Constantinople and the knights and Robert were pleased with the hospitality of my castle. John would tell me the cost.

Towards the end of the evening, the earl said, "I need to speak privately with you tomorrow without arousing suspicion amongst my knights and, I fear yours."

He had me intrigued, "We could go hawking. I have two hawks and a competition between them is something I have planned."

"Excellent and your falconer and codgers, you can trust them?"

"They do not speak Norman my lord. They are safe."

125

I told Aiden immediately and he kept the birds hungry. Faren insisted that the three of them be dressed in their best clothes as they were serving the son of the King. I shook my head. "But Faren we are hunting!"

"It matters not, my lord. We do not want these people to think we are savages!"

We rode while John carried the cadge and the hawks. Aiden scouted ahead to find us some birds to hunt. Robert turned to me as we left the castle. "This is a fine manor. I know it cannot support wheat but it has a good river and the woods seem to teem with game." He pointed to the tracks left by the deer heading down to the river.

"I am happy enough, my lord."

"You would not wish a grander one further south? The King favours you. If you asked for one I am sure he would grant your request. Here you are isolated."

"It is a kind offer but I will earn something larger. I am still taking small steps. I would not wear boots which were too large for me. What of Hartness? Has the King taken it from De Brus yet?"

"Politics, Alfraed, politics. The De Brus family is powerful and my father can use the threat of taking away the manor to gain support."

I shook my head. "Another reason why I am happy here."

He laughed, "I, for one, am glad. Now there are things you need to know. I have spoken with my half-sister and I know that you are both loyal and trustworthy." I flashed him a look. He held up his hand. "I speak plainly for the kingdom is in a parlous state. Since my half brother died in the White Ship there is no male heir. The King's new wife does not bear him children. I am testament to my father's fertility." He shrugged, "It must be God's will."

"Why cannot you be named heir? You would make a good king."

"That is kind of you to say but I am illegitimate and such a naming would result in a civil war. Until the King has an heir or names an heir then there will be discord and plotting. Already Louis is supporting the claims of William Clito and there are others who dispute his claim to Normandy. My uncle, the Curthose, still languishes in the Tower."

"Then what can we do?"

"That is why I have come to speak with you. You are a Knight of the Empress." I must have looked startled for he laughed, "I know that unlike the others that means something special to you. There is a bond there beyond words." He held up his hand. "I do not judge. The Empress may be in danger and it is likely that she might be named heir. It would either be her or Adele's son, Stephen of Blois. We need to be ready to go to the aid of my sister if events force our hand."

"How do you mean?"

"There was another attempt on the life of the King. You and your father saved his life once and this time it was his household knights but he is in danger. The visit to Gospatric is a ruse so that I may speak with you and so that we can wield a big stick and frighten those in the region who might seek to take advantage of the King's absence. King Henry wishes you to protect the Empress. He does not ask an oath for you have already sworn one."

We had reached Aiden.

Robert said, quietly, "Now you see why I mentioned a manor further south."

"Fear not, my lord. I can sail across the German sea and travel up the Rhine. It would be a speedier journey than one from London and less obvious. Is the threat to the King and the Empress, imminent?"

"Who knows? Part of my job is to keep my eyes and ears open and yours is to be ready. My father gave you authority. Do not be afraid to use it."

"The Bishop of Durham?"

"Forget Durham! He is too busy plotting to become Archbishop of Canterbury and my father has that dangling before him. He will not interfere in aught that you do. Besides I will visit with him and explain the necessity of your authority. He is no fool despite what others say." He smiled, "What say you?"

"I am the King's and the Empress' man. You can trust me."

"Good, and now let us see these hawks of yours."

By the time we had returned, after a successful hunt and a pleasant morning, Sir Richard and his son were there with four men at arms and four archers. I know that Richard felt badly about having so few men for he said, "I could have brought more."

I shook my head, "And leave your wife and home undefended? I think not. We go not to war but the Earl of Gloucester has need of knights. We go to impress the knights to the north."

He and his son now wore surcoats like my men and the men at arms all had the same coloured shield. It made for a fine display. I think he was overawed by the presence of Robert of Gloucester and he remained silent when we ate and just listened. As my father might have said, there was nothing wrong with that. A man who listened learned more than a man who never shut up.

We prepared to leave the next morning and Sir Guy and Sir Geoffrey arrived together. We had a fine array of knights who rode north. Every man at arms and archer was mounted. The Earl had been impressed by Aiden as a woodsman and concurred with my request to bring him. His keen senses were invaluable. We headed towards the New Castle on the Tyne, built by the King's brother, Robert, over forty years ago. Originally built of wood it now had a stone gate and it was where the Gospatric, the would-be Earl of Northumbria lived. The Roman Bridge which crossed the Tyne was protected by the castle.

We rode hard and reached the bridge by sunset. As we had been riding north Sir Richard had asked me if we thought we might have to fight. "I doubt it. The Earl is the son of the King. An attack on us would be tantamount to rebellion but I am not certain of the reception we shall receive."

"Do you think that the men we fought came from here?"

"The knights and men at arms did. They had weapons and armour such as ours. They spoke Norman did they not?" He nodded. "However, they did not fight under a banner and can deny everything. I think that the use of the Scots was deliberate to throw us off the scent. It will be an interesting meeting."

We were not delayed at the bridge and we clattered over the stone structure. The Royal Standard with the Norman lions assured our safety. We were in the second rank of knights. There were just six of us but I felt proud that three of us all wore the same livery. The gates were opened and a younger knight than I was expecting came to speak with the earl. After a few moments, the Earl dismounted.

When he turned to us his face was angry, "The castle is, apparently, too small to accommodate our horses. Tell the men at arms to camp over yonder on the high ground to the west of the castle. He will speak with us inside."

We sent the squires and the horses with Wulfric and Dick. I knew that our sergeant at arms would gain a good campsite and dry feet. We followed the household knights and Robert of Gloucester into the Great Hall. I saw that whoever we were meeting had his own knights prepared and there were fifteen knights in armour on the other side of the table. The atmosphere was tense. I wondered if they would be foolish enough to attempt bloodshed. Suddenly I recognised one of the knights who had fled from Gainford. I said, quietly to Edward, "Isn't that one of the knights we fought?"

He nodded, "Aye it is. Shall I tell the earl?"

"No, we shall wait for a judicious moment." I saw that we were recognised too. I wondered if swords would be drawn. I now knew that these men had raided the valley. It would not do to pre-empt the diplomatic discussions which were about to take place.

"So where is your father, William of Morpeth?" I remembered that the knight who had died had said, '*William*' before he died. Was this the same William?

The man who had greeted the Earl spread his hands and gave a smile such as a carpet seller from the bazaar in Constantinople might give, "He is on pilgrimage to the Holy Land. He has been gone these five months."

"And you command in his stead?"

"He has left his sons to run his lands."

The answer was evasive and, without even seeing his face, I knew that Robert of Gloucester was not happy. "Then whom do I ask about the men from this land who raided the border recently. The ones who killed the men, raped the women, took animals and enslaved women and children." He said it quietly but there were threatening murmurs from the knights who faced us. One or two laid their hands on their swords. The household knights of the earl close by began to draw theirs. The Earl's voice barked, "Keep your swords sheathed. The first man to draw one answers to me!" Weapons were returned to scabbards and the Earl continued, as quietly as before, "Who ordered the raids? Who is answerable?"

The smiling snake continued to smile, "I know nothing about raids."

The Earl was clever and he changed tack. "You were not raided here?"

William of Morpeth fell into the trap set by the Earl, "No, my lord. We have enjoyed a peaceful summer."

"Then explain how almost five hundred men could have travelled from north of here and raided as far as Carlisle in the west and Piercebridge in the east and every manor in between."

For the first time, the mask fell away and he looked discomfited. "I cannot explain but I can swear that none of my father's knights participated in the raid."

I moved towards the earl and said, quietly in his ear, "My lord we have recognised one of the knights we fought and who fled."

The earl kept his face impassive and continued to stare at William of Morpeth. He said equally quietly to me, "And he is here?"

"He is the knight standing behind William of Morpeth. The one trying to move away even now."

"You have done well." He smiled at the knights who faced him. "So, none of you raided the Tees or the Eden? None of you attacked the castle at Barnard?" They shook their heads, "Do you swear?" This time there were no nods. "I can fetch a Holy Book if your wish or we can do it the old Saxon way."

William stood up and began to bluster, "I give you my word. There is no need to impugn the honour of these men. You must be satisfied with our answers, my lord. We will not be made scapegoats because other lords cannot defend their lands."

Robert of Caen, Earl of Gloucester, now stood. You could see the royal blood of the Conqueror coursed through his veins. William of Morpeth had underestimated this warlord. "You speak of honour but there is at least one man behind you who I know has no honour." He jabbed his finger, like a sword. "You there! The knight trying to slink away like a dog in the night! Stand fast!"

The man had no choice and he stood glowering at me. "I did not raid." His voice was flat. "Who says that I was there?"

The Earl stood aside and I stepped forward. "I, Alfraed, Baron of Norton, say that you were there at Gainford."

He was about to say something when Edward stepped forwards, "And I Edward of Stockton saw you."

"He is your household knight. He lies as you do."

Before I could say anything Sir Richard, Sir Guy and Sir Geoffrey all said, "And I saw you."

I took off my mail glove and held it in my hand. "Take back your words or eat them!"

He leaned across the table, "You lie!"

I whipped the mail glove across his face. The metal links ripped open his cheek and blood was spilt. Before a battle could ensue, the Earl said, "There is but one way to settle this. Trial by combat!"

William of Morpeth had regained his smile, "I should warn you, my lord, that Odo of Hexham has never lost in single combat yet. Have your headstrong young knight apologise and we will forget this."

It was my turn to smile, "Fear not my lord, I have crossed swords with liars before and in my experience, a liar is normally a poor warrior. I expect Odo to live up to his name!"

The knight's face contorted into a snarl as he tried to get at me. William of Morpeth shook his head. "There is a piece of open ground close to where your men have camped. We meet there in an hour."

As we left the Earl said, quietly, "I know you have fought in a tourney but can you best him?"

Wulfstan snorted, "My lord he will beat him before that treacherous knight knows what has hit him. Alfraed is the fastest blade I have ever seen."

"I know but this is single combat."

Edward chuckled, "That was what the Count of Stuttgart thought and he ended up on his arse, my lord! If anyone is taking wagers, my money is on the Baron."

We had brought our war horses this time and Harold saddled Star for me. As I was waiting I watched as they prepared Odo's arms. He had a short battle axe hanging from his saddle. Edward saw it too. He asked the Earl, "My lord is he allowed a second weapon?"

"If he wishes. You can have one too, Alfraed."

I shook my head. "I will use the one with which I am familiar and besides I am not certain if an axe is an advantage on a horse." As the Earl left us to go to meet with William I said quietly to Edward, "Have our archers ready in case there is treachery." In answer Edward smiled and pointed behind me. I saw Dick and the others stringing their bows. It was not dark yet for it was still the time of the long days but the knights held torches along both sides. It gave the arena an eerie feel. This was not Worms and there was no dais. Nor was this for a pot of gold. This was a fight to the death. There would be no herald to tap me on my shoulder and tell me that the combat was over; there would just be the angel of death.

Star was keen to be in action again. Since our return from Normandy, he had grazed and been groomed. He was a warhorse and he wanted war. He stamped his foreleg and snorted. I checked that my sword slid in and out of its scabbard easily. Its edge was sharp enough to shave with. The lance was straight and true. Edward himself had chosen if from the supplies we had brought. It was now up to me.

William of Morpeth stood in the centre. There would be no preliminaries and no request to reconsider. Neither side could afford the loss of face. His hand dropped and I waited a heartbeat before spurring Star on. Odo did not wait. He was keen to close with me and knock me from my horse. I put my spurs to Star. He took off as though he was leaping a fence. I rested the lance across the cantle of my saddle and watched the approaching knight. This time we would not be able to return and get a new lance. When our lances broke then it would be hand weapons. I needed to ensure that he had no lance to use. Star had not yet built up to full speed but Odo had. I pulled back on my lance and stood slightly in my stirrups and leaned forward a little. It meant I could no longer use my spurs but Star was beyond needing them; he was going to war.

Odo was an experienced knight and I saw him adjust his lance and raise it slightly. He was going for a hit to my body. As we closed I squatted down as I punched with my weapon. His lance struck me first but my move had fooled him a little and his spear shattered against my shield. His blow was so powerful that it almost knocked me from my saddle. My lance slid along his side. I felt it grate against the links and then it was broken as his body came across it. I heard a grunt as the stump hit him in the stomach.

I was drawing my sword as I reined around Star. It was now down to our skills with hand weapons and horses. It was not one against one it was two against two. As I turned I looked to see which weapon he favoured. It was the axe. I hoped that was a mistake. I had only fought men on foot who wielded an axe. I did not know how this would aid him. I knew it was a heavy weapon and so, as we approached to meet shield to shield as was usual, I flicked Star's head to the left so that we met sword to axe. He had committed to a blow on the other side and his backhand parry was weak. I stabbed forward. There was a rent in his surcoat where my lance had struck and my blade went along the tear. I must have severed some links for this time I felt my sword slide along something soft; his gambeson.

I wheeled to my right as he struggled to turn his own horse. His axe was unbalancing him. My quick hands and magnificent horse allowed me to close with his back and I brought my sword sideways across his back. This time he did shout out. I had hurt him and he veered away from me to gain some composure. I, too, turned to face him. I had had three hits and only one in return. This time it would not be so easy. He approached me more slowly this time, ready to react to any tricks from me. I had no choice but to face him shield to shield. He brought his axe around with great force and it smashed against my shield as I struck him on his helm. His had been a powerful blow and my shield and arm both shivered with the shock. Our horses were also experienced and they pushed against each other. As he pulled his arm around for another blow to my shield I stood in my stirrups and brought my sword over my head to strike across his front. Wulfstan had praised my quick hands and my right hand certainly saved me. It bit into the haft of the axe as he tried to smash my shield again and it cracked. He was committed to the blow and the haft broke in two as the axe hit my shield. Pulling the thong from his wrist he threw it at me as he pulled his horse away to allow himself time to draw his sword.

My left arm was numb from his blows. I steadied Star. He had a sharp sword with which to come at me and an undamaged shield. My blows to his back and his side had not been mortal. I needed to finish this quickly. If he began to pound on my shield I would lose. This time I spurred Star on. I needed speed and I needed him to be a warhorse. As we approached I veered towards his shield side. He readied his sword. As we closed I pulled Star's head up to make him rear as I stood in the stirrups and brought down my sword. Star's mighty hooves made the knight flinch but he stabbed at me anyway as I descended towards him. He could not get his shield up in time and my sword smashed into his helmet. I felt his sword slice into my side. As his head fell back I saw his eyes roll into his head. His arms went out to the side and he fell from the back of his mount. There was a sickening crunch as he hit the ground. If he was not dead before he fell, he was when his body hit the ground. As the cheers on our side erupted I felt warm blood trickling down my side. I had been hit. I had to stay upright in the saddle until the verdict was returned.

The Earl came to me and held my right arm up, "God has favoured Baron Alfraed! He spoke true and this dead knight was a base liar." As more cheers resounded he added, quietly, "You did well there Alfraed I thought he had you."

"He did, my lord, I am wounded."

His face showed his concern and, as Edward and my men came towards me he said, to Wulfstan, "Your lord is injured, take him to a tent and see to his wounds and I will continue my discussion with William of Morpeth!"

Once behind the tents I was helped to the ground. Harold held up his hand and it was bloody. I gave a weak smile. "I hope we brought a spare surcoat! I fear this one is spoiled somewhat."

My knights and Harold took me into a tent while Wulfric took out his needle and catgut. I heard Sir Guy say, "I have some Eaux-de-vie I shall fetch it."

When the surcoat came off they could see the extent of the damage. Wulfstan tut-tutted me, "It was a clever strike from you, Alfraed, but your armour is designed to stop blows from above and not from below. His sword went between the lamellar plates. Had you not killed him then you would have become weaker. I think we will have Alf make you some new armour when we return to Stockton."

By the time Sir Guy returned they had my armour and gambeson off. My undergarment had soaked up much of the blood. I felt woozy. "This will hurt my lord." There was a flash of pain as the fiery liquor was poured over the wound. I was lying face down and waiting for the pain to subside. Wulfric sounded concerned. The wound is too deep to stitch. I cannot staunch the bleeding."

"Hold him." It was Wulfstan who took charge. Wulfstan who had protected me since I had been a child now took charge. I could not see what he was doing but I felt Wulfric wipe away the blood and dry the skin and then I felt heat. When I smelled burning I knew what he was going to do. He must have plunged a torch into my side to cauterize the wound. Mercifully I passed out and all went black.

Chapter 13

When I awoke it was light and Harold and Wulfstan's faces were above me. I tried to sit up and it hurt. "I would rest, my lord, or wait, at least until you have some food inside of you. You leaked a great deal of blood last night. I will fetch some food."

When he had gone Wulfstan said, "You were close to death last night. The priest hovered close by ready to give up the last rites. Our men prayed for you to live and I suspect that Gospatric's men prayed for you to die. God won in the end and you lived."

"And William of Morpeth? Did he confess?"

"No. He is a sneaky one. He blamed it all on Odo. His men fled last night and William said that was sure evidence that he and his father were innocent and it was Odo who had taken the law into their own hands. He said his family could not be held to blame." He laughed, "The Earl is a clever man. He should be named heir. He fined the Gospatric family five hundred head of cattle and a thousand gold pieces. He said it would teach them to manage their men better. We leave as soon as you are fit and able to ride north after his men."

"But it could not be just them. They did not have enough men."

"I know but it cannot be proven. The loss in cattle and gold will weaken them and teaches them a lesson. The Earl has perilously few men to do anything else. I think he has done the right thing and we are all richer because of it. The Earl said that if we did not find the slaves who were taken in the raids at Hexham then we would return and demand more answers."

"What happens now?"

"The Earl has sent your knights, men at arms and archers to follow Odo's men. He and his household knights are waiting here to collect the fine."

I struggled to rise. "Then let us join my men; I would not have them take risks whilst I lay abed."

Wulfstan pushed me back down. "I will decide that. Aiden will watch over you while Harold and I ensure that we share in the profits from this fine."

"How will it be shared?"

"The Earl appreciates what our men did and, more importantly, what you did. We get half of the cattle and half of the gold. Your knights are happy. They are suddenly richer."

I closed my eyes. Perhaps Wulfstan was right. I did need my rest. Wulfstan and Harold left. Aiden fetched me some beer and then asked, "Could I take Wolf and go hunting, my lord? I hate to be inactive."

"Aye, of course. I shall sleep now."

When I awoke it was almost dark. Aiden was seated next to my cot. Wolf slept at my feet. As I stirred he rose and smiled. "You have more colour, my lord. That is a good sign. I shall fetch you some food. Wulfstan will have me if I do not feed you."

"Are they away still?"

"Aye, my lord. There are just ten men at arms guarding the camp. The rest are within the castle. They have been counting coins all afternoon." I could hear the lowing of cattle. "And the animals are being brought here too. They should all be here by the morrow."

"Then you must ensure that I am ready to ride by the morrow for I will not lie idly by while others risk their lives for me. Tomorrow we ride to Hexham."

After he had left I managed to struggle to a seated position. Wolf heard my struggles and came over to lick my hand. He was a faithful hound. The food, which Aiden brought, was hot and nourishing. I was hungry and I ate two bowls of it and quaffed a jug of ale. I felt much more human after I had eaten.

"Help me up, Aiden, I need to make water." He looked dubious. "Would you that I soiled myself instead?"

He helped me to my feet and, leaning on him we left the tent and went to the stone wall which lined the field. After I had made water I felt a little weak. "Perhaps Wulfstan is right and I do need time to recover."

When we reached the tent, Aiden examined me. "I think Wulfstan healed you well. There is no sign of bleeding. Wulfric was worried that exertion might induce bleeding but the wound appears to be sound."

"Fetch me my armour."

"Why, my lord?"

"I am not going to wear it if that is what you mean."

He brought over the armour I had brought from Constantinople. I examined it and saw where the sword had struck up through the scales. I favoured a strike from above and it would happen again. Until that day it had served me well. It was lighter than mail and gave good protection. I knew that if I had had mail armour then the sword thrust would not have penetrated. Perhaps it was time for new armour. I would just have to learn to wear the heavier mail.

Wulfstan and Harold joined us later that evening. "We have done well from this, Alfraed. They are good cattle. They are smaller than ours but they look to be tougher. You have, as was promised, half."

I nodded, "And the same for the gold?"

"Aye for I have spoken with them and they are good lords. They will use the gold wisely and become stronger. That makes your strength more too."

"I just serve King Henry."

"And when we have a new monarch? What then?"

"I will serve him."

"Suppose that it is William Clito, the puppet of the French king?"

"He is landless. How can it be him?"

"Because he has a claim and if the King dies without a male heir then he will be considered. He will have support." I wondered who had been talking for the Earl's secret was safe with me. Wulfstan gave a sly smile. "There is much gossip amongst the men of the Earl. In London, it is the sole topic of conversation and already people are choosing sides."

"How can they choose sides? No one knows yet whom the King will decide upon."

"The King may decide but others can make decisions too. King Henry chose to be king and the man who should have been king now languishes in the tower." He rose. "You have much to think about while you rest. Our tent is the next one down. If you need aught then send Aiden for me."

The food had made me sleepy and I lay down. Aiden covered me with a fur. "Wolf will be at the bottom of the cot, my lord, and I will be here by your side. If you call out then I will wake."

I was soon asleep but my sleep was filled with dreams which seemed so real that I feared for my sanity. Suddenly I heard barking and I opened my eyes. In the half gloom of the tent, there were four armed men. I saw that Wolf had fastened his teeth around the arm of one while Aiden had his knife out and was struggling with another. I reached down and drew my sword from the side of the bed. I managed to hold it up and block the sword which arced towards me. I saw a second blade coming for me and I rolled off the cot. The sword smashed into it breaking it in two with the force of the blow.

The man whose sword I had parried ran around the end of the cot. I kicked out and took his legs from him. As he fell to the ground I rose to my knees and pushed the sword up into his rib cage. I kept pushing as he shouted. There was a yelp as Wolf was thrown to the ground and an axe came towards me. My sword was stuck inside the man and I could do nothing. Then a blade erupted from his middle as Wulfstan's sword ended his treacherous life. Harold swung his sword diagonally and hacked into the neck of the third of the murderers and then the two of them slew the man who was trying to kill Aiden.

Lights appeared from outside and Robert, Earl of Gloucester stood there. One of his knights held a lighted torch and viewed the bloody scene. "Are you safe, Alfraed?"

I nodded, "Aiden are you hurt? Wolf?"

Aiden shook his head. "I am unhurt thanks to Harold and Wulfstan but Wolf..." He ran over to his dog. He knelt over the animal and stroked it behind the ear. He smiled, "He was winded that is all. Good boy." He took a morsel from his pouch and fed the dog.

Wulfstan rolled them over. "Anyone recognise them?" No one did. He looked at me and then glared at the household knights. "Whether you are fit or not we ride tomorrow. You will be safer amongst your own men!"

One of the household knights of the Earl moved forward but Robert of Gloucester snapped, "He is right! How four assassins got through our sentries speaks either of incompetence or treachery! Perhaps my knights are only fit for herding cattle or collecting gold!" His men had the good grace to look shamefaced. "I am sorry, Baron, this should not have happened. You and your men will be safe now."

All five of us slept in Wulfstan's tent. I had no intention of sleeping in a bloodbath and I was not about to have my men clear away the bodies. We rose before dawn and Aiden and Harold helped me to dress and to arm. I rode Scout and we headed for Hexham. The Earl and eight of his household knights rode with us as well as half of his men at arms. The rest guarded the cattle and the gold until our return.

After an uncomfortable silence Robert said, "Why did they want you dead? It makes little sense to me."

"I think that I spoiled William of Morpeth's plans, my lord. I think there is a conspiracy here which reaches all the way to Hartness and beyond. The De Brus family also has lands in Scotland and England. They must think that I am a danger and should be eliminated. After all, they did kill the previous lord of the manor and we have been attacked on at least three occasions now. It is the only answer which makes sense."

"Perhaps I should have taken hostages."

Wulfstan shook his head. "That would have played into their hands, my lord, and made your father's position even more precarious. It would be seen to be vindictive. I, for one, would be happier if the King was in England."

"As would I. But he is not and we must make the best of the situation."

Hexham was half a day away and when we drew close we could see that my men had made a camp and surrounded the motte and bailey castle. It was under siege. Edward smiled when he saw me on my horse. "My lord, the last time I saw you I thought you had bled away completely. It is good to see you up and mounted."

I waved towards Robert of Gloucester. "Tell the Earl the situation."

"There are fifty or so men inside. The ditch is well made and we have not, as yet, tried to breach the walls. They are surrounded and there is but one gate. If they come out it needs must be this way."

"Good you have done well." The Earl studied the walls looking for a way in. There was a gate in the outer bailey and then another at the keep. It would mean two assaults. "Any suggestions?"

Wulfstan took off his helmet and rubbed his beard. "I can see no smoke which suggests that they are not heating oil or water. All of our men at arms and knights have mail and have good shields. With Dick and his archers to keep their heads down I think we can take the first gate. If we achieve that then they may be willing to surrender."

The Earl asked, "Surrender? Surely we kill them all."

"I would say yes, my lord, but they may have slaves they took from the valley. If they think they are going to die then they might kill them. Surrender may be a way out for them." Wulfstan shrugged, "But you command my lord."

Robert Earl of Gloucester was a pragmatic man and he saw the sense in the plan and the thinking behind it. "Very well," he turned to his lieutenant. "Have half of our knights and ten men at arms make a Roman tortoise. We will try to gain some honour this day."

I knew that I would be an observer that day but I determined to be as close to the action as I could and I went with Harold and Wulfstan to within a hundred and fifty paces of the walls. We had our shields but it seemed those within were not confident about their archery. Dick arrayed the archers in a line before us. The men behind the walls were using cover to avoid being struck by missiles. Dick was too canny a bowman to waste arrows. Until the knights and men at arms were attacked then they could wait.

The sixteen men began to move forward towards the ditch. Above them they held their shields and they also protected their sides. The ones in the middle all carried faggots to place in the ditch. When they were fifty paces from the ditch the defenders began loosing stones and arrows at them. They had little of either. As soon as their heads appeared Dick and his men began to release their arrows. It was an uneven contest and, after losing eight or nine men, the defenders had to hide. As soon as the knights reached the ditch they flung in their faggots and then stepped across. This was the most dangerous time for the cohesion of their shields was lost. As soon as a spearman stood to throw a spear he was struck by an archer. Once at the gate those men at arms with axes began to hack through the gates.

In a short space of time the axe men did their work and the gates were shattered. Edward led my knights and men at arms and they charged through the open gates. The defenders had already fled to the safety of the keep. This had a bigger gate and higher walls. The ditch was deeper but I knew that those inside would have seen the ease with which we had broken through and would already be worried. All that we had done was breach the outer wall and we just held the bailey. The keep would be harder to take.

We all moved closer. Two of the Earl's men at arms were down. They had been struck by spears through the gate as it was broken. The survivors formed up inside the bailey and waited for Edward and our men to form the second attack on the inner agate. This time we had many more faggots and while my men attacked the gate the rest of the Earl's men would cross the ditch and scale the walls. With our superiority in archers, I hoped that we would have few casualties.

Wulfstan and Harold dismounted to take their place amongst the other others who would attack once the gate was breached. Earl Robert led these men. I nudged Scout forward so that I could speak with Dick. "Keep our men safe, Dick. I would not lose any."

"And we will not, my lord. We heard of the attempt on your life. That was a cowardly thing to do. They will pay."

This time the defenders were more reckless and showed themselves more. The ones who had died in the attack on the first gate were joined by another eight as Edward and Sir Richard hacked at the second gate. My archers moved forward ready to pick off any who tried to halt the efforts of their comrades.

A number of things happened all at once. As the walls were scaled, the gate was thrown open and five riders galloped out. My knights were hurled to the ground but not before they had dragged one from his horse and butchered him. Wulfstan and the Earl ran with the assault party to intercept them. Two were halted and attacked but two came directly for the gate and all that stood in their way were Aiden and I. I drew my sword and galloped towards the two of them. Aiden would not die so long as I lived. I pulled back my sword and held it at chest height out from my body. My shield was gripped against my aching side. If I had the chance I would thrust into the chest of one of the men at least. The two knights must have thought that they had an easy victory but they reckoned without the skill of Aiden and my archers. One was thrown from his saddle as Aiden's arrow struck him in the chest and as I swung my sword in an arc the other knight was hit in the back by four arrows. He rode directly into my sword and his head was removed.

I reined in Scout before I fell from him. Aiden ran to me. "My lord, are you hurt?"

I was aching and I was not sure if I had opened up my wound but I was safe. Had my archers not reacted so quickly then I am not sure if I would have survived another combat. God must have been watching over me that day. "No, Aiden but I shall be pleased to get back to Stockton!"

The castle fell a few moments later. The last defenders fell back to the hall. They were offered surrender but they refused. They were overwhelmed and slaughtered. I waited for my knights to emerge. Sir Guy and Sir Geoffrey led twenty captives from the burning castle. They had found some of those who were taken. Every knight and man at arms who emerged brought out some treasure or weapon taken from within. The last two to come out were the Earl of Gloucester and Wulfstan. They both threw a burning brand into the keep and it flared up as a bonfire pyre for the treacherous knights who had fallen. As all had died we would never find out the true perfidy of the Gospatric family but it had served as a warning that they raided my valley at their peril. With cattle, captured horses and captives to slow us down we made our weary way south to the New Castle. We could go home.

Part 3 Wolf Winter

Chapter 14

We took six days to return to Stockton. Before we left the Earl spent a day closeted with William of Morpeth. He spoke in private but left him under no illusions about the future. Any further incursions from the north would be dealt with severely. The slaves we had recovered had not been able to identify their abductors but the Earl had told the son of Gospatric that he knew of his role.

By the time we reached the river I could stay in the saddle without too much pain. The Earl stayed but one night for they were going to sell their share of the cattle at Northallerton. I had to admit that I would not have wanted to drive them further south. Those who herded cattle for a living had my admiration. My three knights stayed a day longer. I suspect they wanted to show their appreciation for what we had achieved together. All of them had become rich men overnight. Each one would be able to pay for better armour, weapons and men but more importantly, they would have cattle with which to feed their people in the coming winter. In the event that proved to be the crucial result of our travail north.

We arranged that they would visit with us again at Christmas when they would bring their families. I was satisfied with the way events had turned out. These three fitted in well with Wulfstan and Edward. Together we felt like my father's oathsworn. When they left I felt slightly saddened and my castle was emptier.

Adela was more than concerned that I had been wounded. I glared at Wulfstan for I was certain he had told her of the seriousness of the wound. "You must take greater care, my lord. It is not just I who am dependent upon you. If you were not here then this town would shrivel and die. Like your father before you, you are the heartbeat of this town."

"I think you exaggerate Adela."

Faren backed her up. The two were close and more like sisters. "She is right, my lord. I have spoken with those like Alf and Ethelred who lived here before you arrived. They tell me that it was a handful of crude huts and they could barely make a living. Now new people arrive each day. Prosperity oozes all along the river. Why last year Ethelred has hired a tanner for the cattle you captured from the Welsh. Now we have provided fine hides and we can profit from them."

"They are right Alfraed, you are a natural lord of the manor, as was your father. I know not if you know what you do but sharing out the majority of the cattle amongst your people endears you to them." Adela gently touched my arm as she spoke.

John, son of Leofric, was sitting at the table scribing the numbers of animals we had taken. "It is also good business, my lord, for it makes more taxes. By doling out the cattle then the people become liable for more taxes and everyone benefits. You please the people and you make money. It is inspired business."

I shook my head, "It is just the right thing to do."

Wulfstan laughed, "And as I have said before that, in itself, is a mystery, for you were never taught those skills."

"You are wrong Wulfstan for I watched my father. I just do what he would have done."

I took a turn around the town the next day, with Adela and John son of Leofric. I was interested to see these incomers. Everyone seemed delighted to see both myself and Adela. Many of the women giggled as we passed them. I found it disconcerting. They also asked after my health. Word had spread of my wound. I found the new tannery. It was to the east of the town and I could see why. The smell was acrid for they used urine to tan the hides. The prevailing winds took the smell over the river or towards Hartness. Ralph the tanner seemed a happy fellow. "I hear, my lord, that you have brought more cattle. We'll soon make hides out of them. This is a good place to live now. Not as crowded as York."

"You came from there?"

"Yes, my lord. We heard that Stockton was a growing town. York is shrinking. Many knights have either gone to Normandy or to the Holy Land."

As we made our way back towards the smith's I saw that the town was indeed burgeoning. The land was flat until the shallow valley between us and the Hart Burn. People had room to build and yet were close enough to the castle for protection. Norton, in contrast, was a little more cramped. The swamps, which offered protection on three sides, restricted the land which could be used for homes. Here it was the opposite.

143

John had a wax tablet and he made marks upon it as we toured. "What are you doing, John?"

"I keep a record of who lives where and when I return to the castle I transcribe them into my ledger. I do it once a week and it is an accurate record of who lives in the manor. When they leave, or die, then I scratch out their name."

Adela asked, "What of those who live just beyond the town. Like Tom and his son at the Hart Burn?"

John was an assured young man but Adela, who was as bright as they come, had spotted a flaw in his plan. He frowned. "I had not thought of that."

"Ask Aiden to take you to visit them. Once you have done it once then you will know your way around."

"There is, however, one thing missing, my lord."

"And what is that, my lady?"

"There is no church."

"We have Father Peter in Norton. Why need we a church?"

"When the weather is clement such as now then we do not need another one but when winter comes then those few miles can seem interminable. We need one."

"I will give thought to that." We had reached Alf's. "John, escort Lady Adela to the castle. I think I must have words with Alf."

He nodded and Adela said, "Thank you for this morning, my lord. It is the most pleasant morning I have spent in a long time."

She looked at me with her deep blue eyes so intensely that John looked away in embarrassment. "And I too, my lady. We shall make this a weekly event. What say you to that?"

She curtsied, "I thank you, my lord."

When I entered Alf stopped work. "Sir Edward told me that you were wounded, my lord."

"I was Alf. My fine armour let me down. I would have you make me a suit of mail. I want it as strong as my lamellar armour but can you make it as light?"

"No, my lord. I can make it lighter and stronger than most mail. But it will be expensive. I would make it from rings which were tempered longer and I would rivet them so that they would be hard to shear."

I nodded. I had resigned myself to making my body stronger over the winter to carry the extra weight. "And I would have the coif an integral part of the mail, not separate as it is now."

"I can do that my lord and I could strengthen the front by fitting a band of metal which would support your helmet. It would mean you would not need a full-face helmet. I will make a new helmet too." I had seen, in Normandy knights whose coif fitted closely around the head with strengthened bands around the forehead. It would provide more protection for me.

"And the leggings."

"Of course. If you let me measure you now, my lord I can begin work." He hesitated, "I can start as soon as…"

I laughed and took out a bag of coins. "Here is a deposit to enable you to start. If I like this then I may have a set made for my squire, Harold."

He rubbed his hands together, "If we go on like this, Baron, then Stockton shall soon be larger than York!"

I was kept busy for the rest of the day by John, my clerk, who had many decisions for me to make. "And I must see Leofric, your father. The gold we received from William of Morpeth can be made into our own coins and I will use some of it to buy copper and silver. Those coins will be more useful."

By the time evening came, I was exhausted. Wulfstan came to see me. "I have good news, my lord. Faren is with child. I am to be a father again."

I clapped him on the back. "Then I am happy for you." I noticed his serious face, "And yet you look not happy."

"Alfraed, when your father asked me to watch over you he said I should do this until you were a man who could stand on his own two feet. I believe I have done that. You are ready to stand alone."

I was crestfallen. "You would leave my service?"

He laughed, "No, Alfraed, never. It is just that I wish my own hall. I am wealthy now, thanks, in no small part to you. I can have my own retainers and servants. I wish to be with my family." He waved his arm around the castle. "Here I am dependent upon you. It is your coin which buys my food and we are, well we are crowded here. Faren and I wish to have quiet times sometimes. I want to enjoy my children."

I breathed a sigh of relief. He was not deserting me. "Then choose your plot of land."

"I have done, my lord. I have spoken with Young and Old Tom. I would live close to the Hart Burn. It is a sweet valley and yet close to the castle. I would like my hall to be there."

"Then go with my blessing and be my Lord of Hartburn."

Those months, after we returned from the north, were peaceful and settled. We were able to make the manor more comfortable. William the Mason was much in demand from my fellow knights. My warriors toiled building Wulfstan a house which was both stout and comfortable. We were helped by the weather which proved to be perfect for the harvesting of crops and animals. Father Peter, at the celebration of harvest, was able to speak of a bounty given by God for the good works we had all done. That was a rarity, had we had any poor in the manor then we would have been able to provide food for them for the winter. In that, we were lucky. Widows did not stay widows for long. There were many landless men who sought land and work. We were blessed.

When my men were not building Wulfstan's home I had them finishing the walls before winter. William, the mason's son, was able to help us with the gatehouse and it was in stonework where we had the most frenetic activity. As soon as the frosts came then all building in stone ceased. That time could come any day. William and his son would have to spend all of their time indoors carving intricate pieces for the spring. Such was our cycle of life.

I made sure that both Norton and Stockton each had a large building, within the walls, to store our surplus food. The one enemy we found it hard to fight was the rat army which seemed to grow no matter how many dogs were used to catch them. This was where we brought our knowledge of the east and we built buildings which were easier to protect from rats. They had a gap between the floor of the store and the ground. The small terriers Aiden used to hunt rats were able to scour any vermin from beneath our granaries. We still lost a little but not as much as we had. What we had gathered I intended to keep!

The time of the bone fire was always a difficult one for me. In Byzantium, we had not had to cull our animals. Winters did not cover the grazing in a white sheet of snow and ice. I rode with Aidan around our lands and visited our farmers ten days before All Hallows Eve. He had an eye for the land which I did not possess. He was, in many ways, a throwback to the time before we had become so civilised. He understood Nature. We rode a circuit which took us towards the Hart Burn so that I could see the progress being made by Wulfstan and then we would swing around to see the many tiny farms tilled by the villeins. As we crossed the beck which marked one edge of the land watched over by Wulfstan we saw many women and children harvesting the last of the blackberries, damsons, sloes and other wild fruits. It was a bounty which would not last long. We stopped and spoke with them. It was the best way to gauge the mood of the people.

As we left Aiden pointed to the banks which ran down to the beck. "The rabbits your people introduced when the Conqueror came now run riot over yonder land, sir. They should be hunted. At the moment they just breed. We need their numbers to be thinned."

"Good. The meat will augment what we have and the fur can be made into cloaks and mittens for the winter."

"I will set traps. It is easier than wasting an arrow and the beasts are not intelligent!"

Wulfstan's Hall now had a roof and walls. He would be cosy within. I spoke to him of the rabbits. I was gratified by an approving nod. "We brought many cattle back. Is there no alternative to slaughtering them?"

Wulfstan stroked his beard. He pointed to his hall. "I am keeping my cellar for animals but I can only keep a few there."

Aiden was walking through the long grass which still surrounded the hall. Eventually, the ground would be cleared and made into a plot for vegetables. He ran his hands through it. "We could cut this grass down, my lord. It would dry and provide feed during the winter."

"A good idea Aiden but we would run out eventually."

"Yes, Baron Alfraed, but it would keep the animals alive longer and when we had to kill them then the meat would be fresher. It would save us salting." He was right for sometimes salted meat spoiled and was good for nothing save burning.

Faren had come out with a jug of ale and heard the last part. After she had poured us a beaker each she pointed to the barn where Wulfstan's workers were separating the grain from the husks on the barley, rye and oats. "All that we do with the husks is throw them away. If we store them and then mix them with water and the dried grass they might feed the cattle over winter. They would not deteriorate. It would save waste too."

Faren had more common sense than anyone I knew. Wulfstan nodded. "It means we must build a stockade to keep the animals close. When I have used my scythes to clear the grass I will build a wooden wall and bring my cattle and sheep here. I must gather them from the fields anyway to cull them."

As we passed the tiny farms which dotted the land to the west of my manor we told all the villeins the same. Most barely existed. They hand ploughed a few strips of land and kept a handful of animals for their milk and their eggs. Many of their animals would not survive the winter. The huts they lived in were little changed from the ones the people had used before the Romans came. Even though they all had so little they were incredibly grateful for the few gifts I had sent their way. I told them of the rabbits and Aiden's advice. They looked surprised. Alan of the High Waite said, "But, my lord, the hunting of deer and rabbits is forbidden to all but the lord of the manor."

I turned to Aiden who nodded, "It is my lord. Only the king and the lords he favours can hunt deer and it is accepted that only the lord may hunt rabbits. Why villeins cannot even have a dovecot."

These laws and rules seemed pointless to me however I dared not break the law of the land. That did not mean that I could not bend it a little. "I see. Now suppose Aiden here, my man and," I smiled as I conceived of a title for him, "my gamekeeper, were to organise a hunt of rabbits and each of my farmers joined him. It would then be up to Aiden how many animals and their skins he brought back to my manor would it not?"

Alan of the High Waite and Aiden grinned, "Yes my lord."

"Then we will designate the next Saturday as the day that Aiden and his workers will harvest the rabbit harvest! We shall make it a weekly event until the weather deteriorates and the animals sleep for the winter."

Such a small gesture had an immeasurable effect on the poorer farmers. To them, the meat of the rabbit was a luxury. It would provide a richer diet before the ravages of winter made them suffer.

When I returned to Stockton I had John organise the clearing of grass and its drying and the creation of enclosures for animals. Athelstan and Osric did the same in Norton. One short ride had had a dramatic effect on my manor. It proved to be crucial as the year drew to a close.

The time around All Hallows Eve was a busy one. Despite keeping more animals than normal, we still had to slaughter the weaker and older animals. Nothing was wasted. The skins were dried. The hides were sent to be tanned. The offal was eaten quickly or cooked and mixed with fat to make pastes and pates which would last longer. The fat we rendered was kept to seal the jars of meat we preserved and make it less prone to spoilage. The intestines and guts were kept to make sausages. Even the hooves of the dead beasts were rendered down to make glue. Finally, the bones were gathered and, after the goodness had been extracted from them in soups and broths, were added to the piles of leaves which had fallen from the trees. The Bone Fires we burned on All Hallows Day were a sign that winter was coming. The ash was distributed and spread over the fields. Fertility would return to the ground for the following year. It was the cycle of life.

When my father had arrived, he had begun a tradition on All Hallows Day of distributing some of the precious spices we had brought from Constantinople. I used Olaf to bring more from our contacts in our old home. I knew how to pay less than most merchants. We were better stocked with the precious spices than many and the women used them with homemade elder wine and bramble wine to soak into spoiled fruit and dubious meat to make into a pie which could be eaten over the Christmas period. As we had travelled the manor the sweet aromatic smell had pervaded every hut. It was a sign that the seasons were changing. The nights were drawing in, the leaves were falling and winter was approaching.

It was shortly before Advent that things changed. It was Captain Olaf who acted as the harbinger of doom. He was in port collecting some tanned hides and sheepskins to take to London to sell. We had a particularly cold night and there was a sheen on the river. It happened to be the day that Adela and I used to walk the town. He waved us over. "My lord, I shall leave on the noontide today."

"Why the rush?" I pointed to the blue skies.

"That is the reason. The river had a sheen of thin ice upon it last night and the weather is coming from the north. I come from Norway and we learn to notice such things. That weather means that ice is coming. This will be a harsh winter. I do not want to be trapped here."

I laughed. "You think the river can freeze over?"

"I know that the river can freeze over." He shook my hand. "I will return in the spring, my lord and I beg you to take care. This winter will be hard."

"An icy sheen on the river and a blue sky tell you that?"

"No, my lord, they do." He gestured towards the birds. They too were flying south in large numbers. He showed genuine concern, "My lord prepare for a hard winter. This is not Byzantium. Last year was bad but this one will be worse."

"Thank you for the warning."

I sought John and Edward. "Olaf tells me that it may be a hard winter." They looked at me in surprise. I nodded, "I know the skies are blue but Olaf has rarely let us down. Send riders to warn Norton and Hartburn of the prediction. Send out woodcutters while we may. The exercise will be good for my men. We need to lay in a store of wood. Cut down as much as we can. It will not hurt to dry it out before we use it. John, check that we have enough fresh food in for at least a week. Adela will need help now that Faren has gone. Find any grass which has yet to be cut and have the terriers hunt the rats. What we have we keep."

While they went to do as I had instructed them I found Alf and told him of Olaf's news. He took it seriously straight away. "I will tell the rest of the burghers. We need to prepare. With the short days coming we have to be ready. Thank you for the warning, my lord."

I looked at him in surprise. "Why should I not warn you?"

He laughed, "Many lords would ensure that they were prepared and not care about the people without their walls."

"But you are my people."

"And that is why you are so respected. You are not as other lords. Many of those who lived in Hartness came to live here after you rescued the Lady Adela. They told us a different story of cruelty and neglect. The Lord De Brus cared not if his people starved so long as he ate well. We will not take our good fortune for granted."

Olaf's predictions came true but not for three days. I had begun to think I had wasted the efforts of my men and my townsfolk. We woke, with just two weeks to go until Christmas, with a blizzard which blew all day. The snow piled high against the gates. I had the men clear it but stopped them after two hours when I saw little reward for their efforts. The storm raged all night and all the next day. William the Mason barely struggled, with his men, into the town having taken all day to travel from Yarm. I did not speak with him but I saw them struggle against the white wall of ice as they entered the town.

Three days into the blizzard I woke and found that I could not see where my ditches were but the snow had temporarily ceased. I had every able-bodied man, John and me included, clearing the snow from the gates and, where possible the roads in the town. I did not want the people trapped within. It was as we were clearing the track near to the tanners that Aiden observed something.

"Have you noticed, my lord, that the ground is not churning up? The air is filled with cold. We have not been aware of the cold for we are working but it is still cold and the snow has stopped. It is too cold to snow."

That sounded ominous. I had never seen snow until I had sailed from Constantinople. It was an unknown phenomenon. Each time it snowed I learned something new. I wished that I had paid more attention to my studies when I had been younger. I am sure that those who taught me would have mentioned something about snow and ice.

I woke in the middle of the night and I was shivering with the cold. The fire had died. I wrapped a fur around my shoulders and went to build it up again. I could have summoned a slave but I was awake anyway. I saw, as I took the firewood over to the fireplace, that there was ice on the inside walls. This was truly cold. I placed some wood on the embers of the fire, which seemed barely glowing, and I blew on the embers until a few weak yellow flames licked the wood. It took some time to get the fire going. By that time sleep was beyond me and I dressed. The fur I had used for initial warmth I kept about my shoulders as I left my room. I also donned a cloak. The rest of the castle was so cold that my breath appeared before me. I pulled the fur over my head and I headed for the battlements.

When I opened the door to the tower I was hit by an icy wall. It actually hurt my face. I regretted not having a full beard like my archers. I saw the glow of the brazier in the corner and headed for Roger of Lincoln who was on guard duty. He was so close to the brazier that I thought he might actually burn. He looked at me in surprise. "My lord, is something awry?"

"No Roger I just awoke with the cold."

He pulled a blue hand from beneath his cloak and pointed to the river. "It is so cold, my lord, that the river has frozen."

I looked and saw that the river was like a black and silver road shivering in the moonlight. I saw that he was so cold that he was actually shaking. "Come Roger. We will go and get you warm. If any enemies are abroad this night then they are not human for only the animals who hunt will venture out this night."

He obeyed, gratefully, my orders. As soon as we went back into the castle I noticed the rise in temperature. We hurried down to the kitchens. The slaves were all asleep, huddled together and the fire there was just a glow. The two of us began to feed the fire. Seara awoke and looked startled at the two shadowy figures in her kitchen.

"My lord, what is amiss?"

"It is cold outside, Seara. I am just getting Roger something warm to bring him back to life."

Roger had managed to get a roaring fire going quickly. Here the wood was not frozen and he began to thaw out. Seara went to wake the other slaves and servants. "No Seara let them sleep. You go back to bed too."

"No, my lord. It is not right that you work while I rest."

She swung the black pot over the flames and, taking a ladle, she began to stir it. Then she took a long iron poker and placed it in the fire. Pointing to the table she said to Roger, "Sit there and I will fetch you some hot broth."

It was rare that I came down to the Stygian depths of the kitchen. Adela visited frequently but I was always too occupied with other matters. I realised that there were some advantages to working here. It was marginally warmer than the rest of the castle and the huddle of bodies sleeping under their blankets emanated warmth. Seara ladled some of the broth in a bowl and placed it on the table. Roger was about to use the bone spoon to eat it when she put her hand across it. "It is not hot enough yet." She went to the fire and, taking out the poker from the fire, plunged it into the broth. It hissed as it went in and when she withdrew it, it steamed. "Would you like some, my lord?"

The smell was too appetising. "Aye Seara."

The broth was not the soup we had in the main hall. This was the everyday fare of the slaves. It was water and whatever had been left over from our plates. That night it tasted like ambrosia. I felt more human after eating it. When Roger finished he said, "I will get back to the walls my lord. Wulfric will have my..." he grinned, "he will not be happy if I have deserted my post."

"I will join you and watch what passes for sunrise this day. Thank you, Seara and that was fine soup."

It was just as cold as we stepped out on the castle walls but the soup within kept us warmer. It was still some hours from dawn and we had not even reached the shortest day. That would come just before Christmas. It would be a long time until spring.

Roger put more wood in the brazier; we would need more timber cutting soon. He rubbed his hands in the warmth of the flames. "You are right, my lord, no men will be out this night. It is only the animals clad in fur who will be abroad."

"It is a small comfort, Roger, but I fear this will be the conditions we have to endure for some time."

"We can learn to live with this my lord. If no enemies travel then we will have a peaceful winter; cold but peaceful."

It was then we heard the wolf pack howl. It was south of the river in the hills above Normanby but we both heard it. Its chilling sound carried over the icy river. It was a pack and they were hungry. That was the start of the wolf winter.

Chapter 15

The sudden cold and the sound of the wolves shocked and surprised all. We were trapped now by a sea of white. I went to the hall my men used. "You are all soldiers and you fight for me against my enemies. The enemy now is winter and the cold. When the snow abates I want the bailey clearing and then we will help the townspeople to clear their houses. Wulfric and Dick, I want four archers and four men at arms to accompany me. I must visit Wulfstan and Norton." I paused, "Aiden has hunted many rabbits. I want each of you to take the skin of a rabbit and make yourself a pair of mittens. Roger of Lincoln almost lost his fingers last night with the cold." It kept them busy.

I sought my clerk. "We must husband our food and I think there will come a time when we have to bring the farmers in here. I will keep the bailey clear for just such a purpose. Have we willow and hazel within the castle?"

"Aye my lord. We gathered it before the Bone Fire to encourage new growth next year. I was going to keep it for firewood when we ran low."

"No, John. If there are any breaks in the weather then we send woodcutters out. The days are so short now that we use every moment of daylight that God sends." Use the willow and hazel to make hurdles and pens within the bailey. We can use them to make shelters if the people need them."

The break in the snow was brief. The grey scudding clouds promised more and so I led my eight men, along with Harold, towards the now frozen Hart Burn less than a couple of miles away. Our horses struggled through the snow. We were only a short distance from Wulfstan but it took an hour to reach there. In places there were drifts up to our girths. As we passed each farm I told those within that if the weather became too bad then they could shelter within our walls. The first ones lived within sight of the reassuring stone walls of Stockton but I knew that those who lived further north would struggle to reach us.

Wulfstan had also cleared his land of snow. He only had two men at arms to help him but Old and Young Tom lived so close that they were part of his retinue. "I fear this winter will be a harsh one, Wulfstan. I know that we are well prepared but some of our people are not. I have told them to come within my walls when things become too bad. And I heard wolves howling across the river."

Wulfstan looked up sharply, "I thought that was a dream or a nightmare."

"They were south of the river but the river has begun to freeze. It will not support weight yet but if the cold continues then we may have more trouble than we can handle. If they cross the river…"

"We will be ready for them." He took me to one side. "I fear for Norton, Alfraed. We have friends like Richard and Guy to protect the south and the west but if this winter is harsh then human wolves will descend. Others will not have prepared as well as we and they will come to take what we have."

"I know. I go there next."

We make plans and then God, or in this case Nature, interferes. By the time I had visited every farm and hamlet it was almost dark and we barely made Norton before the snow came again. The last mile to Norton we endured cold so biting that my men were looking for the animal which was sinking its teeth into their faces. We would have to spend the night in Norton.

Athelstan insisted that we stay, "Alfraed, you are blue and Harold here looks like a corpse already. Come into the hall and warm yourselves."

I was pleased to see that my father's old comrades had planned well and the manor looked to have prepared as well as it could. As we warmed ourselves by the fire in the Great Hall I voiced my fears and those of Wulfstan. Osric nodded, "I too heard the wolves but they were to the west and the river and swamps have frozen here. Any enemy need not fear them now."

"I hope that our enemies will be kept away by the cold."

"That will only be so long as they have food enough but other lords do not care about their own people and if men become hungry they will take from anyone. We need vigilance."

"How many men do you have to defend Norton?"

"There are six men at arms and we have twelve men who can fight."

"That is not enough. I have invited those farmers who live far from help to seek sanctuary with us. Better that we feed them and then use them to protect what we have. You know that they will not leave their homes until things are desperate. If you have more men within your walls then you all have a better chance of survival."

"Aye," Osric chuckled, "When we left Miklagård to come home we forgot what the winters were like."

"Would you be back there?"

"No, but I would have better winters."

Father Peter had joined us, "This is just God testing us."

Athelstan shook his head, "The land tests us enough without his help."

The snow fell all night. It was a blizzard. The night watch told us that it stopped before dawn and then the sky cleared and was filled with stars. The snow which greeted us in the morning was not the soft freshly fallen blanket we expected, it was a hard crust of frozen ice. We left as soon as we could and it took us all morning to reach the walls of Stockton. The horses' hooves gained no purchase on the slippery surface. We had to dismount and lead them on the steeper slopes. It was treacherous underfoot. So long as the cold remained no one was moving on our land.

As we approached our land from the north I heard the sound of axes. We came through the woods to the east of the manor. They were thin and spindly and the ground was too poor for farming. Alf and the men of Stockton were hewing the thin trees which had grown there in recent years. He paused as we approached. "I know it is cold, my lord but I fear it will get colder before it thaws. These trees are thin and easy to cut. We have burned much already. I would not have us run out."

Harold had lived in the forests of Sherwood and he said, "In the forest we dried out animal dung and burned that. It burns for longer than wood. If you mix the two then we will be warmer for longer."

"Thank you. We were wondering what to do with the animal waste. They are warm to be close to and the milk is nourishing but we wondered what to do with the dung."

It was another example of how my people's skills married together. As a community, we were all greater than had we been isolated individuals. I think that was what helped us to survive the winter.

The days were cold and the nights colder still. The river became frozen so hard that a warrior in armour could walk across to the other bank. That was the first warning sign. The river had been our defence. If there was no river to halt an attacker, animal or human, then we would have to increase our vigilance. With three times more night than day we had to have three sets of sentries to keep watch. We all dreaded those times when we have to leave the relative warmth of the draughty castle to endure the biting cold outside. All of us now wore the rabbit mittens. I never ventured out without my fur cloak which I wore over my head. If a man was outside for any longer than an hour then his beard would be rimed with the white frost making him look like an old man.

The wisdom of keeping the animals within our walls was soon obvious. Although not as healthy as grass-fed cattle and sheep, they survived better than we could have hoped. Their diet was not the best but then neither was ours and they lived. Their waste was dried and provided fuel. The milk was the lifeblood of the manor. We continued to make cheese. However, inevitably, some animals succumbed to the poor diet and we had to slaughter our first cow a week before Christmas. It fed us all for that week leading to Christmas Eve. It was a blessing. The bones were not burned but placed in a huge cauldron and simmered to extract every morsel of goodness. Every shrivelled vegetable we could find was used to add to the flavour of what we termed Christmas broth. Our Christmas feast would be this strange soup. As we hunkered down on Christmas Eve the rich smell of the bubbling broth permeated the castle and drifted across the still air to the town. We all felt warmer.

And then the wolves came.

They came silently across the river. Wolves do not know what day it is. Were it not for our priests then we would not. They came on the night when all were comfortable and looking forward to our feast of Christmas when the spiced treats we had saved would be brought out to savour on the feast of the birth of Christ. They came when the nights were so long that we seemed not to have any daylight. They came when we hoped for joy and they brought death and despair. I was awoken by Edgar.

"My lord, we have heard screams and the sound of wolves."

I was out of my bed in an instant. "Where?"

He pointed north to the land to the east of the Hart Burn. "Towards the farm of Alan of Aldborough."

Even as I was dressing I remembered that Alan had come to us with his family the previous year. He was a young farmer whose family had been either killed or enslaved by the Scots. He and his wife had four children. I prayed that they were safe and cursed that he had not come within my walls as some other families had. "Have five archers and four men at arms readied." Harold was dressed already. "Bring your bow."

I did not dress in mail but a leather byrnie with my surcoat on top. The cloak I wrapped around me would keep out some of the cold. I took a spear and strapped on my sword. Aiden was already there with the horses. We left by the north gate. "Keep a good watch for farmers seeking refuge but keep the gates closed until you see them. With wolves about I would not invite danger into my castle." Ethelred and Alf were at the gates of the town. I paused to speak with them. "There are wolves. We go to fetch in the farmers. Keep a close watch. My men say they have crossed the river."

"We will, my lord and we will keep torches burning. Wolves cannot abide fire!"

The ground was mercifully frozen but it was slippery and we had to travel slowly. I was relieved when I saw Alan of Aldborough and his family trudging towards us and the safety of the castle. "Thank God you are safe. We thought that the wolves had had you."

"No, my lord, we were woken by the noise of them but they were to the west of us. They were close to the Ox Bridge over the beck."

I wracked my brain to think who lived there. I remembered it was a small hamlet of four farms who eked out a livelihood by the old stream. Oswald was the head of the families. He was one of the original farmers of the manor and had lived there since William the Bastard had scoured the north. He was as old as my father had been. I spurred Scout on.

We saw lights flickering in the distance. Fire was the only foe the wolves feared. Some of Oswald's family lived still. I held my spear like a lance. It was more accurate than trying a throw. As we crossed the frozen beck and climbed up the other side it was a scene from hell which we saw before us. It was a pack of twenty wolves. Three men were fending them off with flaming brands but there were six who were carrying off the dead and dying already. Our duty was to the handful who lived. I needed issue no orders. All of the men I had with me knew what we had to do. I leaned forward and charged Scout at the centre of the baying, growling, howling pack. A large she-wolf turned and leapt at Scout. Scout was a brave mount and did not flinch. It gave me a steady platform. I punched forward with my spear as though it was a lance and the spearhead plunged into the chest of the beast. Even then its savage jaws tried to clamp on Scout's neck and I hurled the spear and dying wolf to the side. Drawing my sword, I swung it down on to the neck of the next wolf which was preparing to launch itself at Edgar. It took the animal's head in one scything motion.

My archers, aided by Aiden and Harold had done the damage. Ten of the wolves lay dead and the rest fled.

"Edgar, get after the wolves who took the bodies. Bring the bodies back. We would have a Christian burial for them."

I dismounted as my men left. Edward son of Oswald strode over to me and dropped to his knee. "Thank you, Baron. We would have all died had you not come."

"Where is your father?"

He pointed to the middle of the family. They had protected his dead body with their living ones. His throat had been torn out. "He died with a sword in his hand. When was younger he had been a warrior and he had kept his old sword. There is a wolf out there who knows that my father fought to the end." He shook his head. "It was the young that they took."

I put my hand on his arm. "My men will fetch back their bodies." Waving my arm around the hamlet I said, "You cannot stay here. Have your families bring what they can carry and you shall spend Christmas in the castle. I want no more deaths."

By the time my men returned with the bodies of the children and the young women who had been taken we had all that they could carry. The wolves had not had enough time to do much damage to the bodies but the six were a tragic sight and the mothers and the fathers fell upon the bodies weeping. My men looked away. It was too much to bear. They had lost friends in war but these were children and should have grown up. I said the words I did not want to say but which I knew I must. "The ground is too hard to dig a grave, Edward son of Oswald."

He looked up from his dead daughter's body. "I know my lord but we cannot leave them for the rats and the foxes."

"We will build a pyre and when daylight finally comes we will collect the ashes and put them in an urn. Father Peter will bury them in the church at Norton. Your father and his grandchildren will rest together close by my father."

They could see it was the only way. We built a pyre in the centre of the huts and placed Oswald's body with his sword on his chest and then the bodies of the others. Piling kindling and wood on the top the fathers of the dead threw their burning brands on the bodies and we watched them burn. The sword would mark their ashes.

When the flames had died and the bodies no longer recognisable as human we loaded the dead wolves on to the horses, put the ashes in a pot and carried Oswald's sword to be interred with his ashes. We wearily trudged the mile back to the castle. We reached there on a cold and misty Christmas morning. Father Peter had told us that when the baby Jesus had been born then wise men brought gifts and the shepherds, lambs. We brought the survivors of Oswald's families and dead wolves. It was a reminder of what a harsh world we lived in.

Adela proved to be a tower of strength. When Alan of Aldborough had come into the castle and she knew what we were about she had rearranged how my men slept and curtained off a corner of their hall for the refugees. Our broth would not be for our Christmas feast it would be the sustenance which gave hope to the shocked survivors. As the morning drew on more families came from the east. The sounds of the howling wolves had drawn them in. While Adela and John son of Leofric saw to the domestic arrangements my men skinned the wolves. In many ways although we had lost children the wolves provided a lifeline for the rest of us. The wolf skins made the best cloaks and fur. The meat meant that all of us, including those in the town, would eat well. We would devour those who had meant to devour us. As Father Peter might have said, "It is God's will."

By the time the food was ready I was exhausted. I had worked so hard that day that I felt not the cold. It was crowded in the two halls we used to eat but no one minded. The presence of so many bodies made us warm for the first time in a long time. Edward, Adela and myself made sure that all of our refugees were fed first. We left Wulfric presiding over the telling of tales and the singing of songs and wearily headed to my hall for our own feast. There were just the five of us around my table and I felt guilty about the crowded hall we had just left. I began to rise and Edward asked, "Where are you going, my lord?"

"We have much room here and they are so crowded down there."

You are right, my lord, but I tell you to sit, Baron. You have done more for them than they might have expected and none of them would thank you for bringing them here where they would have to watch what they did and said or what their children touched. Wulfric is a good man and he will care for them."

Adela put her hand on mine. "He is right, my lord. You have done what Christ would have wanted. You have provided shelter for those without one. This is their stable. You can do no more. Let us enjoy this Christmas here in your castle and be thankful for what we have."

I smiled, "And I am thankful to you Adela. I know not what we would have done without you and John organising what you did."

We had a pleasant time despite the presence of the wolves and the biting cold. Edward showed what a sense of humour he had by telling us tales of his youth and his early campaigns. I suspect there were some risky parts he omitted for the sake of Adela but he kept us amused. Then John totally surprised us by singing. He had a beautiful voice. He sang in Latin and although neither Edward nor Harold understood the words it did not matter. It was such a beautiful sound and it echoed through the castle. The Christmas of the wolf winter ended better than it had begun. Sadly, our troubles did not end that night.

As the weather showed no signs of abating Adela and my men worked with Alf and Ethelred to accommodate all of the refugee families. The willows and hurdles were covered to provide shelters. I went with Edward and his brothers to take their families ashes to be buried. I had loaned them horses and we gathered the pot and the sword and rode to Norton. Father Peter was distraught at the deaths. He, of course, had known Oswald all of his life, having grown up around Norton. Athelstan and Osric joined us as we placed the urn in a niche in the church. When the weather warmed the land, they would be interred beneath a stone along with the sword which rested against the wall of our church.

As we left the church I said, "I will have William the Mason carve a stone for them. When we return to my castle tell him the names of those who died and they will be remembered."

The brothers left and Harold and I as I spoke with my steward and castellan. "We heard the wolves but we did not suffer any losses."

I sighed. They were good men but they thought little of the life beyond their walls. "Have you visited Wulfestun? Have you seen those who live to the west of you?" They hung their heads. "Then Harold and I will visit. Prepare to have those within your walls who cannot survive beyond."

"But Alfraed we have little enough food as it is and with the water frozen we cannot grind at the mill."

"Then tighten your belts. We all survive this wolf winter not just those lucky enough to be behind Norton's walls!" There was an edge in my voice which I did not intend. It was my fault. Osric and Athelstan were too old to rule the manor for me. When the spring came then I would have to make other arrangements. They both looked embarrassed.

Osric said, "We have let you down, Alfraed. Better we had died with our lord."

I softened my voice. "No, it is my fault. You two should be enjoying the twilight of your lives and not worrying about the problems of those who would be strangers to you. Do this until the spring. Then I can make changes."

"We will not let you down again. We swear."

It was sad that two old men who had helped to bring me up were almost begging to seek my approval. I felt ashamed. "You never have."

I rode north to Wulfestun. Thomas Two Toes and his family lived there. They had fought off Scots before now. After the last raid, we had helped them build a wall and ditches around their hamlet. I was relieved to see a shut gate when we reached there. He and his two sons, Edgar and Tom came out to greet us.

"I was worried about you when we heard the wolves. They killed Oswald of the Ox Bridge and some of his grandchildren."

Like Father Peter, Thomas Two Toes had known Oswald all of his life. "He was a good man. We heard the wolves."

"You can always shelter in Norton."

"I know, my lord, but we are well provided with wood and we eat well."

I smiled. Aiden had told me that Thomas and his sons hunted both rabbits and deer. I should have been offended at such poaching but it did not hurt me. The King might not be very happy but as he rarely visited I would turn a blind eye. "Good but do not let pride and a stiff neck keep you from the safety of Norton. I have buried one of the oldest men in the manor this morning; I would not bury a second."

"Do not worry my lord I was not born to end up in a wolf's belly." He was a tower of strength and always had been. So long as he lived in Wulfestun then the approach to Norton from the west was protected.

The other three farmsteads felt the same. They were closer to Norton, less than a mile away and I knew that they could reach the safety of the walls should danger threaten. We headed back as darkness loomed from the east. The road home had not become any easier and the two of us struggled to move at more than the pace of a snail. The days should have been getting longer but it seemed that darkness and the night ruled my land. The long nights stopped what little sun there was from warming the air. The snow and the ice were here to stay. I felt a great sense of relief when the gates of my castle were slammed behind me.

Chapter 16

Looking back, years later, I am still amazed at how long the snow and the ice lay. Each day we looked for a break in the weather and a little warmth but none came. We eked out our provisions and killed more of our cattle as they succumbed. The husks and the dried grass had kept our animals going longer than we would have possibly hoped. There were little enough scraps for the pigs but they survived. When spring finally came then we would have larger herds and flocks. I just prayed that we would survive to see another spring. Aiden managed to cut holes in the ice and hunt for the fish who dwelt beneath its icy shell. Every mouthful meant we were closer to surviving.

The wolves came again a month after Christmas. The days were a little longer and we were more prepared. When Aiden and his fish hunters returned from the river they noticed, in the fresh snow, the prints of wolves. They had come scouting. Each day Aiden used a different part of the river. On this day, he had been at the bend in the river two miles to the south of the Hart Burn.

"There were the tracks of just four wolves. This is the time of year when they have cubs. They will risk the wrath of men for they have young to feed."

"Why did they not attack? You found their tracks and they were recent. Why did they return to their pack?"

"These wolves came from the north, my lord. I am guessing that they have finished hunting in the hills and there is little left for them. These are not the same ones as came across the river. Their scouts will have been searching for new hunting grounds. Close by the prints we saw where Wulfstan's men had been chopping trees. The wolves picked up their scent for they had relieved themselves there."

I summoned Edward and Dick. "Have your men rest today. We go hunting wolves tonight. Harold, ride to Wulfstan and warn him and his people of the presence of wolves."

Since the winter had started we had learned to protect ourselves from the cold better. The wolf fur I used went beneath my cloak and I had boots lined with rabbit fur. My mittens kept my hands warm and I wore a linen mask across my face. We did not look warrior like but we were better protected. The others took bows but I was happier with my spear. Aiden led us. It was the only choice. Had I led we would have blundered into them and they would have escaped.

As we left the castle at dusk there was a wind coming from the west. Aiden led us north. We headed towards the Durham road. If the wolves had come down from the hills then they would see the security of the forests which were to the north west of us. We were down wind of the animals we hunted and they would not smell us. We were reliant upon the senses of Aiden and Scout. Both would warn us of the presence of wolves. Wulfestun was just two miles to the east when we entered the forest. We walked our horses. Wulfstan and his men were waiting close to the Hart Burn. Our plan was simple; catch them between us and kill them.

We cut their trail half a mile in and found that they were heading south west. It was a large pack. Aiden marked the tree where we crossed the trail so that we could back track and find the cubs. The tracks we followed were only adults. The threat needed elimination. Once we found the trail we mounted and I followed Aiden. It was such a large pack that even I could follow it. After a mile or so the forest petered out. We passed a farmstead and we halted there. I had visited this six days ago and Carl and his family had been fine. Now there was no smell of smoke and the door of the hut was open. When we found the bones, we knew what had happened. The wolves had found this family first when they were scouting. The dismembered, inedible parts of his animals lay discarded amongst the human bones. The easy meal had encouraged them. I had thought Carl was safe for he was close to both Norton and the Hart Burn. I had been wrong. I should have forced the family to safety. Now we knew why the wolves had chosen this route. There were no humans to stop them. There was just one farm between us and Wulfstan now and I prayed that it had been evacuated.

When we reached it there was smoke and, although the door was closed the farmer, Robert of Trimdon had taken his family to safety. Suddenly Scout snorted and Aiden looked around. The wolves were close and my mount had smelled them. We saw that the tracks spread out. They were circling. As we were less than a mile from the two homes of Old Tom and Wulfstan we knew that they were following the smell of the humans. Old Tom and his son did not keep animals. I could not see the wolves hunting them. They would head for the smell of Wulfstan's pigs and sheep.

164

I waved my hand to the left and the right. My men spread out to emulate the circle of the wolves. When we heard a shout in the distance and saw the flare of a torch we knew that the wolves had struck. All need for silence was gone and we spurred our horses on. We could hear the wolves as they howled and snarled at the defenders of the hall. The wolves had the advantage of a moonless night and dark coats. Wulfstan had had torches prepared and we could see them but a man cannot hold a torch and fight effectively. The best he can hope for is to keep the wolves at bay and there was a large pack.

The memory of Carl and his family put steel in arm and anger in my heart. I pulled back my arm and punched into the spine of the young male which had failed to hear my approach. I twisted and pulled to remove the head of the spear. A second wolf launched itself at Scout. I jerked my reins around and stabbed with the spear. I caught the old wolf on the side but the weight of his body knocked me from my saddle and I fell to the ground. He was not dead, though dying, and his teeth sought my throat. I pushed my left hand under his throat to push his jaws up and I sought my dagger. He was a powerful animal and his claws scratched at me as he did all that he could to kill me. I was beginning to fear he would win. His teeth were less than a hand span from my face when I found the dagger. I brought it around and rammed it through the wolf's eye and into his skull. I pushed his dead body from me and, drawing my sword, stood. It was over. Between Wulfstan's men and mine, we had slain all but three who ran north.

Wulfstan and Edward ran to my side, "Are you injured?"

In the light of Wulfstan's torch, I saw that I was covered in blood. I smiled, "It is the wolf's blood. He was a tough one. He took some killing. Did you lose any?"

Wulfstan shook his head. "No, but your arrival was timely. I learned that you cannot fight and wield a torch. Old Tom?"

"They went nowhere near him but they killed Carl and his family."

"I should have brought him in."

"We have learned our lesson. Tomorrow we hunt the pack. Aiden marked the tree. Now let us divide up the carcasses. We eat well again, at least for a while."

It seemed that we were in bed for moments only and then we had to head out again. I rested Scout and took another of our palfreys. As we left amid a sleet storm I wondered if the weather was improving. It was not; the sleet soon turned to snow again! We found the tree and Aiden saw the trail. The sleet and snow had made it a little hard to follow but when we did find it we made up the time. There were occasional patches of blood in the wet snow. One of the wolves had been injured. We found a large puddle close to the rocks where the pack had sheltered with their cubs. They had left. We found their trail heading towards the north-west. They were heading for the high ground beyond Durham.

Perhaps we were complacent for we failed to see the wounded wolf who waited at the small mound of rocks above the trail we were following. He leapt at my scout as he passed beneath him. He knocked Aiden from his horse. My falconer must have been winded for he lay there inertly. I threw my spear as the wolf's jaws opened, ready to bite. Although I hit the beast it was only in the haunches. It merely slowed down the movement of the mouth towards Aiden's throat. Miraculously Aiden opened his eyes and pushed his hands towards the wolf's throat as I had done the previous night. The wolf clamped his teeth around Aiden's left hand. I had drawn my sword and I leaned forward in the saddle to slice down across the back to the wolf's neck. As soon as my blade ripped through the spine it became still. I leapt from my horse and threw the carcass to one side.

Wulfric joined and held Aiden's hand in his. He sighed, "The hand can be saved but the little finger has been lost." I saw that the little finger had been severed while the others showed teeth marks. In the driving sleet, there was no chance of a fire and so Wulfric wrapped the hand in a piece of cloth. "My lord, I should take him back and heal this. If not, he may lose all of his fingers."

Aiden shook his head, "I will continue the hunt!"

"You will do as your lord commands. Take him home."

I led the rest of our men north. The trail was unerring. It kept going north east and I took a chance. I spurred on the horses. I would have to risk the pack moving from their course for we needed to catch them. If not, they would return next year. The sleet was in our faces and I knew that they would not know of our approach. Their sense of smell was not as keen in winter. Although we kept going the pack was elusively always too far ahead of us. As night approached I knew we would have to give up the chase. The wounded wolf had bought the time to save the pack. It was the way of the wolf. We turned around and headed home. We were soaked to the skin and frozen by the time we reached Stockton. We felt we had failed for Aiden had been hurt and we had not caught the wolves.

While the men went to fill their empty bellies, I sought out Aiden. Adela and Wulfric were with him. "We have saved the other fingers of the hand, my lord but I am not certain if they will function as they once did."

"I am sorry you were hurt, Aiden."

He shrugged, "It was my own fault but I want to thank you, lord. But for your quick thinking I would be dead. I owe you my life. I was ever your man but now I will be your man unto death."

I smiled. He meant every word. "You just get well. I am happy with all that you do."

"And the pack?"

"It escaped but I think they will find easier hunting grounds in the future."

The sleet was a false sign of a change in the weather. The winds and blizzards returned and we had to clear the bailey and the town of snow again. However, the slight rise in the temperature meant that the ice on the river melted a little and became thin where it remained. One of our boundaries was secure once more.

As Candlemas came and went I began to fear for my people. Illness spread throughout the town. Wulfric was our only healer and he was just someone who could repair bodies injured by war. Faren had some remedies which helped some of those with the coughing sickness but a few of the old died. When I became distraught Adela explained that it was inevitable that the old would succumb in such a harsh winter. I took comfort from that. What I should have realised was that if we were suffering then there would be others in a far worse condition than my manor. We had plenty of cattle and we had prepared for this winter.

I had just woken and was eating my frugal meal of porridge when I was summoned to the tower. I knew that my meal would not have been disturbed if it were not urgent. I ran. It was Roger of Lincoln who had sent for me. "It is Norton, my lord. They have lit the beacon."

We had put a brazier at the top of the tower we had built and it was there to summon help. "Rouse the men! We ride when we are armed."

This would be the first opportunity I had had to try out Alf's new armour. As Harold helped to dress me I realised that I had not worn any armour since we had been at Hexham. Although it felt heavier than my old armour it was not uncomfortable. The new coif incorporated into the byrnie and the ring of mail around my forehead meant that I did not need to wear my helmet until I was actually going into combat; I had protection. I left six men at arms to guard my castle and sent a rider to warn Wulfstan. He could watch over my manor. I rode Scout for I wanted speed and not a warhorse.

We left Aiden in the castle. He wanted to be with us but Wulfric forbade it as did Adela. We rode quickly. As we neared the manor I saw smoke billowing from the walls. They were under attack. The walls were surrounded. Even as I donned my helmet I wondered where this warband had come from. I saw neither banners nor horses. It might not have knights but there were far greater numbers than my handful of warriors.

"Form line!" My men knew what that entailed. With lances in one line my archers would cover us with their arrows.

I lowered my lance and we galloped towards them. The ones at the back turned to face the new threat. There was no armour on many of them but they all wielded axes and old swords. Some even had shields. I pulled my arm back and punched forward to spear the axe wielding savage before me. I flicked my hand to the side and the weight of his body slid it from the lance. Two men clambered towards me from the ditch. I jabbed at one and hit him in the middle of his head and as the second swung his axe I pulled back on the reins so that Scout rose and clattered him in the head. The dead warrior slid from my lance and I edged Scout forward. I stood in my stirrups and stabbed at the back of a warrior trying to scale the walls. As he fell back he took the lance with him. I drew my sword as two men came at me. Although I swiped one man across the face, ripping it in two, the second swung his sword at my side. He hit my mail and Alf's fine work held. I stabbed him in the eye and pushed until the sword came out through the back.

Although we had been outnumbered the force of our attack had thinned them somewhat. Dick and his archers now released arrows at all those who had reached the top of the walls. Osric and his men despatched the rest. As the warband fled I shouted, "Wulfric, Edward, after them. Archers, stay with me." I looked around and saw that Harold had survived. I no longer had to keep turning around to see if he was there. He had become an extension of me. He protected me from all attacks from behind.

As my archers went amongst the warband killing those that survived I went to one warrior who had fallen from the walls. I could see from the unnatural way he lay that his back was broken and he would have to be put from his misery but I needed answers to my questions. I put my sword to his throat, "Your back is broken and you will take many hours to die. You are in pain and that pain will become worse. I will end it now if you answer my questions." I spoke in Saxon for he did not look Norman or Norse. If he had not answered then I would have assumed he was a Scot.

"Ask what you will for the pain is unbearable."

"Where are you from?"

"South of the New Castle."

"Then who leads you? Which lord?"

"No lord. We were starving. The Scots attacked the New Castle and then crossed the frozen Tyne. They stole our cattle and animals. When our families began to starve we asked our lord for food but he said he had none. He said he had given our cattle to you and we came to reclaim them. "

I nodded, "And you came because you wished to feed your families."

He tried to nod but he could not move, "A real man cannot stand by while his bairns die of hunger and cold."

"I know. Go to God."

I slit his throat with my sword. Osric and Athelstan had joined us. Osric shook his head, "I am beginning to think that gaining cattle is more trouble than it is worth. It invites thieves."

"This was a poisonous seed planted by the treacherous William of Morpeth. It is as well we prepared our people well and provided food for them. Did you lose any men?"

"Our men at arms were all on watch and they died raising the alarm. Had they not done so then we would be dead."

I could not wait for spring. "I will base Edward and half of my men at arms here. Edward can be the lord of Norton."

I looked in their faces for resentment but all that I saw was relief. "That is a wise decision, Alfraed." Osric clapped me on my back, "You speak true and do not spare feelings. It is what your father would have done. Edward is a good man and will make a fine lord of Norton. We will do all that we can to aid him."

I went inside with them while my archers collected the bodies and made a pyre of them. There was little to be had from their emaciated bodies. Their weapons could be melted down and Alf could make ploughshares. We had been very fortunate and I knew it. Had these men been led by knights then there might have been a different outcome. My men at arms returned sometime later.

Edward dismounted, "They fled rather than fight my lord. They were bandits."

I shook my head, "There were men with starving families. William of Morpeth sent them here to reclaim the cattle."

"Truly? Then we should go and teach him a lesson in manners."

"There is little point. He will deny it and the men who could have gainsaid him are dead." I put my arm around his shoulders, "Edward I wish you to be lord of Norton and be based here."

"But Osric and Athelstan…"

"Are both happy about it. Choose six of the men at arms and six of the archers. Wulfric and Dick will be with me but you may choose your own. You know them as well as I."

He nodded his acceptance, "We will come and get my war gear tomorrow."

"I charge you with defending Norton. I know you have few men with which to do so but you have a soldier's eye for defence. I know you can make this plum hard to pick. When I am summoned by the King for service you, as will Wulfstan, shall be with me."

"Aye my lord." He paused, "Thank you for the chance, my lord. Until I was hired by you in Northallerton I was doomed to wander the land hiring out my sword. I now have a home and it is thanks to you."

As we knew it would the winter eventually ended. We had escaped remarkably well. We had lost farmers and a few warriors but having had the raid by the desperate men we knew that others had fared worse. Our animals, too, had survived. We put them out to pasture as soon as we could and were gratified when they put on weight and showed signs that they had young. When Olaf and his ship headed up the river then we knew that winter was finally over. We had survived. We had not beaten winter but we had shown him that he could not defeat us.

Chapter 17

The winter ended and the green land was slowly revealed as the snows melted and the frost ceased. Adela had the slaves and the servants begin to clean out the castle and the halls. Our extra guests had long since returned to their farms and the castle seemed emptier. This was exacerbated by the fact that Edward and half of my men now lived in Norton. I found I had more space in my own home now. I could sit and think without being disturbed.

As it was coming up to Easter and all that it entailed I sat with John and went through the finances of the manor. It was coming up to the annual collection of taxes. My position as defender to the valley would mean nothing to the officials who would travel from York to scrutinise my accounts.

"You are doing well my lord. There is a healthy surplus. The extra cattle and gold were unexpected and we can pay whatever taxes are demanded of us."

"Can we afford more men at arms?"

He frowned. He was a clerk and not a soldier, "It would be better if a knight came to serve you. It would incur less expense."

I sighed, "I have told you before, John, knights are rare in these parts. We are the poorer end of the country. If I could induce a young landless knight to serve then I would. So, answer me, can we afford more men at arms?"

"Aye my lord, we can."

I smiled, "Good, then we shall hire some and can we make improvements to the castle and the town?

He brightened a little, "The castle? Aye my lord. What have you in mind?"

"We need a stable block. The animals did provide some warmth this winter but I fear the smell in the summer is a poor trade."

"We could do that quite easily. We can fit one between the keep and the northern wall. You said the town, my lord; what improvements did you plan?"

"The roads in the town were deadly this winter and now they are a quagmire. I would have stones laid. We need a stone jetty. The wooden piles are unsatisfactory. And we need a church."

"I can see the need for a church, my lord, but that is expensive. If we built one then we would not be able to do the other things you wish."

I knew he was right, "We need the improvements. They will encourage more people to come to live here and we will make more from taxes."

"The town burghers should incur some of those costs, my lord." He hesitated, "Perhaps a council?"

"Perhaps. But in terms of the costs, I can use some of the monies from the sessions to pay for civic improvements."

"They are yours by right, my lord but it would be a source of revenue."

"Good. Have notices prepared. We will have our first session of the year seven days after Easter. I will speak with Alf and Ethelred and see if they would wish to form a council."

As I was preparing to leave Adela entered. "You are going out, my lord?"

"Yes, my lady. I go to Stockton to speak with the people there."

"I hoped that we could resume our weekly circuits of the town together now that winter has released his icy grip."

"Of course, but I warn you this may be boring for I will be speaking business with my tradesmen."

"A walk with you, my lord, is never boring." She smiled, "And it is almost Easter."

I donned a cloak for there was still a chill wind blowing from the east. I spoke with every man who had a trade in the town and suggested the formation of a council. Ethelred was the only one who was suspicious. He had done well from the growth of the town and had become rich. I think he worried about having to spend some of his money. We arranged to hold the first meeting the day before the sessions in my hall. There was nowhere large enough in the town. I saw the wisdom in John's suggestion.

The next day I had Harold prepare Scout for I needed to visit Norton and my farms. John would accompany me with his wax tablet. The King's tax man would want to extract every coin he could from my farmers and they needed to be prepared. Once again, Adela approached me. "I would deem it an honour, my lord, if I could accompany you."

"This will not be like a pleasant stroll around my town, Adela, this will be a long ride. You would be all day in the saddle."

"I have been cooped up here for over six months my lord. I would see something of the world even if it is only Norton. It was my home once."

After we had visited Wulfstan we headed east and, Norton. I was pleased I had brought her for she was lively company and remarked on many things I had taken for granted. She saw ways that the farmers might improve their fields and their homes. John scribbled away and nodded at her ideas. The first thing we did was to visit the church and Father Peter. We had decisions to make.

"Father Peter, the last winter was so severe that we could not come to church as often as we would have liked. I believe we need a church in Stockton."

"You are right, my lord, but I cannot be in two places at once."

"No, we need a priest too."

He nodded, "I will write to the Abbot at Guisborough. There may be one of the lay brothers there who wishes to become a priest. It will take time to build a church."

"It will indeed."

We stayed too long at Adela's former home. I enjoyed talking with Edward, Osric and Athelstan. My father's warriors were more content now that Edward was there to manage the defence of the manor. I saw that he and his men had worked to improve the defences of the village which had grown beyond the walls of the hall. The damage from the attack had been repaired and the walls were solid once more. It was getting towards dark when we headed south.

As we rode back I was silent. Adela asked, "What bothers you, my lord?"

"I am thinking about those hungry men we killed in the winter. They were only doing what any man would do. They were trying to feed their families."

"We must have laws, my lord."

"I know, John, but that did not make what we did right."

Adela leaned over and put her hand on mine."

"You think too much, my lord. It was the lord of their manor who was at fault. You cannot be responsible for everyone."

"I know."

To clear my mind of such dark thoughts and guilt I threw myself into the manor. When we held the first council meeting John and I helped Alf and the others create a set of rules. Ethelred was the stumbling block for many ideas the others on the council had. Eventually, I used my authority. "Ethelred, you are now a wealthy man." He smiled and nodded. "That wealth has come, largely because I allow you to operate a ferry on my river." I emphasised the word river. "The King's authority to me extends along the length of the Tees. If I choose to award the ferry to another man then what would you do for income? Rely on your tanner? Perhaps I should tax the exports of hides?"

"My lord, this is unfair! I am an honest man. Is it a sin to try to make money?"

"No, but it is a sin not to use that money for good. I am going to have a church built in the town. I could ask for a tithe from every burgher in the town and the church and the King would approve. However, if I am willing to pay for the church then I would expect you, Ethelred the rich, to improve other aspects of the town."

He subsided a little, "My lord, it sounds as though you are threatening my livelihood."

I laughed, "Of course I am!"

Alf and the others all joined in the laughter at Ethelred's expense. The smith smiled, "I will explain it to him over a jug of ale my lord. He cannot see beyond his tight purse strings. We are all more than happy to pay for civic improvements. We will all benefit in the long run. But, my lord, if I could suggest a fair when you hold the next sessions. There will be many strangers in the town and we can all profit." He nudged Ethelred in his ribs, "Especially those who operate the ferry."

It was Ethelred's turn to laugh. "I had forgotten the sessions. Forgive me, lord. Alf is right; I must take the broader view and think of others."

Ethelred would never change. He would always think of himself first but his enterprise was good for trade and that meant we all profited.

The sessions and the fair went well and I even managed to hire three more men at arms and two archers. They had come to the sessions with a claim against the smith of Hartness and they stayed to serve me. William the Mason and John worked on the plans for the new church which would be built at the western end of the town on a rising piece of land. It was a clever piece of planning for it meant that when the people in the town looked west they would see both the church and the castle. In the summer, we would be framed against the sunset and be a physical reminder of the power of God and the King.

When the tax man arrived, we were all prepared to pay our due but that was not the most important aspect of his visit. He brought a missive from Robert of Gloucester. The normally officious official was almost humble when he went through my books. I left him with John while I read the letter. I read it twice to make sure that I had understood it properly. The tax collector, Roger of Ripon, looked at me when I put down the letter.

"It is grave news is it not, my lord?"

I nodded, "It is." John and Adela had questions written all over their faces. I held the letter up. "The lords north of the Eden have risen in revolt. There is a threat to the King's authority. We are summoned to war."

I sent riders to all of my knights and ordered them to Stockton. This would be the first time I met my new knight, the lord of Normanby, Sir Guiscard d'Abbeville. I would have visited with him before had it not been for the wolf winter. Edward and Wulfstan rode over directly. I showed them the orders. "Wulfstan, I will not leave the valley undefended. I wish you to stay. I will leave four of my men at arms to help you."

I saw the relief on his face. His third child had been born during the coldest part of the winter. His second son, Thomas, would be a hardy warrior when he grew. Aiden's hand had healed and he had not lost the use of his other fingers as we had feared. He wore the fur of the wolf which had taken his finger as a reminder of how close he came to death. As he said to me, "I wear death on my back; it is fitting that the dead wolf should protect me still."

When the other four knights arrived, I discovered that they had suffered badly during the harsh winter. The wolves had decimated their flocks and outlying farms. All were keen for war as that meant profits. Success breeds success. The castle was full on that last night before we left for war and we ate well. Adela sat on my right-hand side. During the meal, she leaned over and asked, "How long will you be away?"

I shrugged. "It could be as it was when we went north and over in a few days or it could be like the Welsh campaign and last weeks. Why?"

"I wondered if you might be back by Midsummer's Eve."

I smiled as I remembered my promise. "If I am not back then you can send me a message with your answer."

"I can give you the answer now."

I shook my head, "I said you had a year to think and I will not go back on my word. Who knows what may happen. I may be wounded and disfigured so that you may not even want me."

She shook her head violently, "Do not say that but it would matter not. It is the man beneath the skin that I would wed."

We were both aware of the sudden silence which had descended. When I looked around the table I saw a sea of smiles.

When we left the next morning for the gathering at Carlisle, we showed that we had learned our lessons. We had more rounceys, sumpters and palfreys to carry all of our war gear and tents. The wolf winter had given us time to make leather and linen tents. The surplus of cattle hides had proved useful. It was also the first time I left feeling sad as I saw a tearful Adela waving from the north gate. She and John would have to run the Manor while we were away. It was also the first time that the people of Stockton came to wave us off. I was touched. These were my folk and they were showing it.

We each had a squire and I put them in charge of the destrier and our weapons. Wulfric commanded as he had before, the men at arms and they followed the squires. Dick and the archers rode ahead. We were slowed by the crossbowmen and those archers who had no horses but it could not be helped. Not all the lords were as well off as Edward, Richard and myself.

I used the first leg of the journey to the castle at Barnard to get to know Guiscard d'Abbeville. He was Norman and the manor of Normanby was his reward for bravery during the border wars against Anjou. After his first winter, he was wondering if it had been a mistake to accept the title.

"You cannot upset the King, my friend, and Normanby is a fine manor."

"But you cannot grow wheat there!"

"Have your farmers tried?"

"I was told..."

"Do not listen to those who say you cannot. Try and then you will know. And if you cannot grow wheat then rye and oats can be grown. Trade for wheat. Our river teems with salmon. Encourage fishermen. Your land has iron in the hills. Trade that."

He nodded as though considering the ideas. After a short while he ventured, "I am told that you are not Norman. You are a Saxon brought up in the Eastern Empire."

"Half Saxon but I feel English rather than anything else. It is in my blood."

"My blood is in the heart of Normandy. I had thought to go to Italy with my cousins the Hautevilles."

"They have done well over there."

"After that winter I wondered if I should not have gone with my heart."

"You will grow to love this land. Believe me."

He smiled, "The main reason I chose to come was because of the Empress."

"You met Empress Matilda?" I felt my heart race a little. I had managed to put her from my mind and replace her with Adela but the mere mention of her name brought her face to mind.

He nodded, "She spoke highly of you as did her Swabian bodyguards. They told me you were a good knight and I could do worse than emulate you. She also said that you spoke highly of this valley."

"That was kind of them."

He waved a hand at the other knights. "They too echoed the sentiments. I will be proud to follow your banner."

When the Earl had sent me the letter he had told me that I was entitled to my own banner for the conroi. We still had the blue background with blue stars but the centre of one of the stars was now yellow. It would show my men where I was. Edward and Wulfstan still had the two blue stars on their smaller banner. While we rode they remained furled.

The lord of the castle at Barnard had already left for the muster but we were expected and we ate well. With his conroi gone there was accommodation aplenty. The next section of the journey took us over the high West Moors and we spent the night at Appleby Castle. The longest and most arduous journey was the last march to Carlisle. It was long and over a rugged descending terrain. I felt sorry for those on foot and I saw their lords looking enviously at our mounted riders.

The Earl of Gloucester had gathered a mighty host at Carlisle Castle. I had thought my own castle had a good aspect but the one at Carlisle was protected on one side by the River Eden and on the other by the River Caldew. An attacker could only approach from the west. I could see why the Scots had failed to take it in their recent raids. The Earl of Chester, Ranulf du Bessin had been Lord of Carlisle but he had to give up that title and he was now with the King in Normandy. Sir Hugh Bacon had been appointed the Lord of Carlisle and it was he who greeted us when we arrived just before dusk.

"The Earl is north of the river scouting for the enemy. He will return shortly. I am afraid that you will have to use the outer bailey for your men. The castle is a little cramped with the retinue of the Earl."

I smiled at Sir Hugh, he was not much older than I was. "Do not worry; we slept comfortably for the past two nights. It will do us no harm to prepare for the campaign."

We discovered, as we struggled to find an uninhabited corner of the bailey, that we were the last to arrive. The majority of the conroi were from the west and Cumberland. We would be fielding over a hundred and twenty knights and we had five hundred men at arms. It was a force almost as big as the one with which we had invaded Wales. My newly elevated status meant that I was invited to dine with the Earl and the other leaders of conroi when he returned. There were six conroi although I led the smallest conroi with just five knights. I looked at the faces of the knights with whom I would be fighting and I saw men who looked much like my knights. Few were older than the Earl and most were of an age with me. Each one looked as though they knew their business. I saw none of the sly sideways glances I had witnessed in Worms. They were not here for political reasons. They were here to punish rebels.

The Earl stood and raised his goblet. "Welcome, now that we are assembled I intend to strike quickly at these rebels. We crossed the Eden this morning and we saw the enemy host gathering just north of here. They are just twenty miles away. They are led by William of Dunbar. He has shown his allegiance by having a yellow lion on his banner. He sides with Scotland."

I almost asked if this made them rebels or Scots. It was a fine distinction. The Solway marked the border. Many knights held manors on both sides of the border. Then I thought better. I did not wish to appear foolish. Sir Hugh asked another question which was on my mind. "My lord what of the east? Are there not rebels there?"

He nodded, "Last year Sir Alfraed and I visited the Gospatric family. They swore fealty but I fear that they are playing a dangerous game. With lands on both sides of the border, they are vying to become more powerful. The Bishop of Durham has returned to the Palatinate to organise the defence there. It is why I summoned Sir Alfraed. It may be that we have to divide our forces and Sir Alfraed's knights have shown before that they can deal with the Gospatric family. We will go to the Bishop's aid when we have dealt with these traitors."

I felt my anxiety levels rise as he mentioned rebels in the east. I had left just a handful of men to guard my lands and the river. I hoped that the Earl knew his business. What did a Bishop know of fighting?

"We will advance on the morrow towards the Solway. The enemy has more men than we do but not as many knights. Nor are they as disciplined. Some of the knights may be Norman but most of the men they lead are the savages who fought the Romans. They are fierce and they are wild but they are no match for the men at arms you lead. We will guard our flanks with our archers protected by half of our men at arms. They will be the rocks upon which the enemy will waste their efforts. They will fight dismounted. We will use two lines to break their defence. I will lead the knights myself. Sir Hugh will lead the men at arms. With God's help, we will drive them back into the Solway and the heads of the rebels will adorn the walls of this fine castle."

The clatter of hands on the table and the cheers told the Earl of Gloucester that the force he would lead were ready for the fight.

It was a glorious host which headed north the next day. The enemy, our scouts informed us, had marched to Gretna where they awaited us. They appeared confident that the river and the land would protect them. Their lack of aggression encouraged us for they outnumbered us so greatly that they should have attacked. The Earl did not bother to parley. He offered no quarter. They had rebelled against the King and had we not held Carlisle then they would have swept south. My men at arms had been chosen to guard the archers, also led by Dick, on our left flank. The rebels had fewer horses. These they had placed upon their right flank. If they charged it would be against my men at arms and archers.

My knights and squires were to the left of the Earl and his household knights. Star was keen to get into action and he stamped and snorted impatiently. The Earl's herald lowered his banner twice and that was the signal for us to begin to move. The rebels had neither prepared pits nor laid traps but they had archers arrayed before them. As we moved forwards, at the trot, I prayed that Star would be spared the attention of the archers. My father had told me how, at Hastings, the housecarls had tried to get at the Norman horses. A knight who fell from his mount would not last long on the battlefield. We had left my banner with Wulfric and my conroi would follow my gonfanon. That now had a yellow centre to one of the stars.

As we began to canter I noticed that the bows the rebels were using were the short bows rather than the long bows Dick and my archers used. They had neither the range nor the penetration of our longer bows. When we were a hundred and odd paces from their front rank they pulled back on them; they were ready to release. The Earl lowered his lance as a signal to charge. I pulled my shield tighter to my body and I rested my lance on my cantle. I glanced at Harold; this was his first charge in the front rank. I prayed he would not suffer Alan's fate. The arrows flew. I tightened my shield close to my body and tucked in my head. Three arrows pinged off my helmet and two off my shield. I was pleased that they had aimed at me. They would have been better to have aimed at Star. I remained unhurt and we were now travelling so quickly that we would be terrifying the archers who faced us. It was then that I concentrated on the man I would kill. It was not an archer, they would flee. Behind them was a line of spearmen. Their shields were not as big as ours and they had no armour. My lance was longer and I could gain extra length when I punched forward.

The archers fled as I pulled back my lance and punched at the red-bearded warrior who stood before me. As my lance sank into his chest I felt his spear as it grazed my legs. The mail did its job. It turned the head. Star was a powerful beast and he kept going even with the speared man on the lance. I lowered the end and the body slid off. Star crashed into the shield and the man in the second rank. He crumpled beneath Star's hooves and I punched forward with the lance at the warrior in the third rank. This warrior managed to bring his shield up but Star's momentum and my punch drove the lance up under his chin and into his head. The lance broke and I threw it to the ground. Drawing my sword, I saw that I was amongst the rear ranks. These had not expected to fight yet. I could see fear in their eyes. As my sword came clear of my scabbard I pulled back on my reins and Star reared. It enabled me to stand in my stirrups and bring my sword down on the swordsman to my right. Even though he tried to parry my blow the edge shattered his blade and split his head in two.

With no one before me I glanced around and saw that my knights were still with me although we were no longer knee to knee. Harold was fighting two men and I jerked Star's head around and swung my sword across the man to his shield side. The sword tore across his back. Harold wheeled his own horse around and stabbed the second warrior in the chest. We had broken their lines and their army was split into three. Their knights were charging our left flank. They were trying to do as we did and charge our foot.

I yelled, "Stockton!" loudly and when my knights looked at me I pointed to the rebel charge. I led my handful of knights and squires obliquely across the field. The Earl had not seen the danger and he and the men at arms were surrounding and slaughtering the rebel foot. If our left flank was destroyed then all would be in vain. I had to take my tiny conroi to the aid of our foot.

We had the advantage that no one was loosing arrows at us and we were unseen. The rebel knights were focussed on the archers and men at arms standing before them. Dick and my archers released flight after flight. Standing behind the men at arms meant that they could keep releasing longer than the rebels had. They were better archers and they brought down horses as well as men. Wulfric had a hedgehog of spears. Unlike the rebel spearmen, Wulfric had the second and third rank presenting their spears over the shoulders of the front rank. It was a solid line of iron which they would have to breach.

I smiled as I heard my sergeant at arms yell, "Stand fast!"

We were not knee to knee but we did not need to be. We were approaching the knights on their shield side. As the rebels struck Wulfric and his men we hit the left side of the charging knights. I stood in the stirrups and brought my sword around the back of the end knight. He wore mail but the length of my sword struck his back. The links could not hold such a blow and they severed. Star had kept going and my blade ripped through his gambeson and into his back. All that kept him in his saddle was the cantles on his saddle.

The knights were in a quandary. They were desperately trying to face us but their cumbersome lances got in the way. They could not turn without striking their fellow knights. When Dick's archers attacked from the other side those who could fled but those closest to my knights yelled, "Quarter!"

"Yield and drop your weapons and we shall give you quarter!"

Ten rebels surrendered to us. Our warhorses were too exhausted to charge again and so, after disarming the knights, we watched as the men at arms charged north after the fleeing rebel army. It was mainly my knights, men at arms and archers who were closest and they began to cheer. We had won and we had captured knights. We would all be richer.

"Sergeant at arms, collect the weapons of these knights and guard them. Come, Harold, we will find the Earl."

Robert, Earl of Gloucester, was in the middle of the field surveying the dead. As I approached I took off my helm. "My lord, we have captured ten knights and driven off the rest."

He took off his own helmet and grasped my forearm. "Well done, Alfraed. That was nobly done. I did not see the charge until it was too late and then I saw you and your conroi. You did well."

"It was my men at arms and archers who held them, my lord. We were just lucky."

"I believe, Alfraed, that you seem able to make your own luck."

"The field is ours."

"Aye, it is. Have you their leader?"

"I do not know but I doubt it. None of them looked to have the standard of William of Dunbar."

"I fear you are right. He will have fled across the Solway."

"Do we pursue?"

"My father would not be happy if I incurred the wrath of the King of Scotland. Until he has finished with the Angevin we are only to keep our borders safe." We trotted back to the prisoners and he glanced over to the disconsolate knights standing beside their horses. "You will all have fine ransoms."

I nodded, "That will please my new lords. They are all keen to equip more knights and employ more men at arms."

"Take your men and prisoners back to Carlisle Castle. Announce our victory. Perhaps, when we have questioned the prisoners we will discover the extent of this rebellion."

Chapter 18

The knights who had surrendered must have wondered at the wisdom of their decision as we took them back to Carlisle. The ransom we would ask might ruin their manors. I did not know how I would react in such a situation. We discovered that all of them had manors in England. Most had a manor in Scotland too. That alone meant we could ask for larger ransoms. As they had surrendered to my conroi we would all share in the profits. Sir Guiscard was particularly ebullient. "If it is always this way I shall soon be a rich knight."

Sir Richard shook his head, "Sometimes we are lucky and at others, we fight and go home poorer than before. When we sent back the raiders from the valley we gained naught."

I nodded, "It is a gamble but you all fought well and we lost no one this time. That to me is almost payment enough."

Edward laughed, "That is going too far, Baron! We want the ransoms!" They all cheered and banged their shields with their swords. Everyone was in a good mood.

By the time we had passed through the gates of the castle we had discovered the names and manors of our prisoners. Wulfric and Edgar led the prisoners away to our tents. Harold had just taken Star away when Edgar sought me out. "My lord, one of the prisoners is asking for a quiet word in private with you."

I was intrigued, "Bring him over and then keep watch on us from a discreet distance."

He was one of the younger knights. He looked to be no more than eighteen years old. In helmets and with a ventail all knights look the same but bareheaded, as he was now he looked like a youth, little older than Alan had been before he had been killed. "Thank you for speaking with me Baron. Could we go where my comrades will not see us?"

"No tricks. I am not a patient man." I led him through the gates of the inner bailey and Edgar followed. "Now then, I would like to eat and drink so be swift."

"I am Guy of Gisburn. My estates are hard by the river close to Skipton. It is a small and poor manor for it is mainly upland."

"Is this to ask for a smaller ransom? If so then your words are wasted. You have English estates and you are a rebel. The Earl could have you executed. If it is not worth a ransom then you might pay with your head."

He shook his head and hurried on, "No, this has nothing to do with a smaller ransom." He paused, "I would like you to forego the ransom," I opened my mouth and he said, "Baron, let me speak, I would have you forego the ransom in exchange for information."

"Information?"

"Information which the Earl of Gloucester and the King would find useful."

"And of course, you will not give us the information unless we agree to your terms." I pushed my coif from my head. I was still hot from the battle. I needed a cool head. "This information which you think is so valuable may not be valuable to the Earl. Besides you are my prisoner. Why should it matter to me?"

It was his turn to smile, "Because, my lord, your reputation precedes you. Everyone knows of your nobility and honour. If you give your word then you will keep it and you are the Earl of Gloucester's man. When we saw your banner on the field our hearts sank. We hoped you would have protected your valley still."

There was something in his words which arrested my attention. Why should I need to protect my valley? The Bishop of Durham was guarding my northern borders. I waved Edgar forward, "Guard Sir Guy here. Find somewhere close by the Great Hall. I must find the Earl." I pointed to Sir Guy. "You are playing a dangerous game, my friend. I may be honourable but I will gut you like a deer if I discover you are playing me false."

I found Harold and had him saddle Scout. "I will get my horse, my lord."

"No Harold, I go to meet the Earl. I will be safe. You did well today. How was it charging in the front rank?"

"Not as frightening as I thought, my lord, but I suspect it would be different charging other knights."

"You are right but I will be happy for you to face barbarians until you are more accomplished."

I headed back towards the battlefield. I found the Earl and his household knights prodding more prisoners towards the castle. These were the foot and the men at arms. They would not be ransomed but they would be put to work in one of the Earl's castles on the Welsh Marches.

Their days of fighting were ended and their lives of servitude were about to begin. They were alive and, I dare say, they believed that where there was life there was hope. I pulled Scout around to ride next to the Earl.

"You have something to tell me, Alfraed?"

I knew that I could trust his knights and I did not lower my voice. "One of the prisoners says he has information which you would find useful and if I forego the ransom he will tell us."

"And what do you think? I value you your judgement."

"He only has estates in England and it is a poor manor. I believe he may have information but he plays a dangerous game for if he betrays his betters then it may go ill for him."

"You think he means to betray others?"

"He asked to speak with me out of sight of his fellow captives."

"Then we will speak with him and then decide what to do. Bring him to my quarters in the castle."

Once we returned to the castle I left Scout in the outer bailey and walked through the gates to find Edgar and my prisoner, "Thank you, Edgar, I will take him now."

I led the young knight to the Earl's room. Edgar had ensured that this was not an assassination attempt and that there were no weapons on the knight. I had not been particularly worried. I believe that the Earl and I could have dealt with him even if he had tried anything underhand.

The Earl was waiting. He gestured for me to take a seat next to him. We let Sir Guy stand. "Well, Sir Guy, what is this information you have which you think is so valuable?"

"Do I have your word that there will be no ransom if I tell you."

Robert of Gloucester roared, "Do not presume to bargain with me! Give me the information and I will decide if it is valuable or not. You are a rebel and your life hangs in the balance, never mind your ransom. Your estates are in England. Remember that. I am the King's representative here. Tell me what you know or be prepared to pay with your life."

I could see that he was shaken. "I am sorry, my lord, it is just that I have a wife and a young family..."

"Then you should have thought of that before you gambled on this ill-fated rebellion."

He nodded and bit his lip. Taking a deep breath, he said. "I was told that if I did not join the rebellion then I would lose my lands when the north rebelled and the King of Northumbria was created."

Robert nodded, "With Gospatric as the first king." He waved an impatient hand at the knight. "Go on for your information so far is not worth a silver coin. The rebellion has failed and William of Dunbar has fled north."

"My lord, he is not the leader of the rebellion." He sighed. "This attack was to draw you west so that Durham could be taken. We hoped that we could inflict a major defeat upon you and that Durham could be taken easily."

I sat up in my chair. "But the Bishop of Durham returns to the palatinate, how could Gospatric hope to take it?"

There was silence. Robert growled, "Boy, do not test my patience."

"Bishop Flambard will be held as hostage for the Dean Albemarle is part of the conspiracy and William of Morpeth is heading for Durham with his knights."

That all made perfect sense to me. We could never assault Durham and each day it was held would weaken the power of the King in the north. If the Dean was party to the conspiracy then the mighty bastion in the north could fall without a blow being struck. Only our routing of the western rebels had given us a chance.

"Tell me Guy of Gisburn, when did William of Morpeth leave for Durham?"

He looked at me, "As soon as word came that you had left Stockton, my lord." This was devastating news.

The Earl stood, "You stay here. Alfraed, come with me." Once outside he said, "I believe him. Now, what do we do?"

"They are in Durham and cannot possibly know what occurred here yet. The survivors fled north not east. If I take my conroi then I can reach Durham by the morning."

"What good does that do? How can you assault the castle with your hundred men?"

I had a plan already but it was a little vague. "My lord, if you force march the army then you can reach Durham by tomorrow evening. Lay siege to it and I will gain you entrance."

He smiled, "I will bring the army. The constable here will hold your hostages until they can be ransomed. I will keep our young friend with me as much for his own safety as for yours. Now tell me your plan or is it still fermenting in that fertile Greek mind of yours?"

"No, my lord, I have the plan. There are two parts; first I must gain access to the castle and then I must enable my men to do two things: secure the bridge gate and the main gate."

As I told him my plan I saw him nodding. "It has a chance of success but it is risky."

"Life is a risk, my lord. I hope to give you and the rest of the army a chance to take the castle. If you do so then my people will be safe."

Shaking his head, he said, "You worry too much about your people. They are there to serve you."

"That is not what I was taught by my father and it is hard to undo that belief. Not that I wish to."

I left the castle and sought my knights and squires. "We are leaving tonight. I believe that Durham has been taken through treachery. We ride tonight. I am going to get us inside the castle. We must capture the bridge and the gate and hold them for the Earl."

The new knight, the Baron of Normanby shook his head, "I have heard that the castle is one of the mightiest in the land with just one bridge across the river. It is impossible."

Sir Richard laughed, "It will be difficult but if the Baron says it can be done then it will be."

"And the captives?"

The Earl has promised that the Constable will watch them until we return. Edward, have them taken to him. Prepare the men. If they have food ready they should eat it. We will be travelling quickly and we have no chance to eat on the way. Harold, fetch Dick and Aiden."

While I hurriedly ate I began to refine my plan in my head. There were clearly a number of parts I had to complete and in a set order. When Aiden and Dick arrived the four of us sat and I explained my ideas and asked what they thought. Dick and the archers would have the hardest part. He grinned, "Aye, my lord. I believe we could do that. When we lived in the forest we used many such ruses did we not, Harold?"

"Yes, my lord."

I smiled. If they believed we could do it then that was half the battle. "First we see the abbot of the monastery. Harold, come with me. Dick, make sure that all is ready. It is growing late and I would leave as soon as I return. Have those of the retinue without horses stay here and guard the warhorses. They can follow with the Earl tomorrow. We will not be hampered by men on foot. Speed is of the essence."

It was coming on to dusk as we left the rest of the army. The men were surprised for the knights were all with the Earl holding a war council. We had seventy five miles to travel and it would take all night. I wanted to be south of Durham Castle by dawn. The men would be able to rest during the day for what I had planned needed the cover of night to succeed. We travelled along the old Roman Road which ran south of the wall. Although we were passing through the land ruled by the Gospatric family I had to assume that all the knights and the rebels would be within Durham. They would want as large an army as they could muster. We had to be quick for I knew that they would be waiting to hear of the success or failure of their attack in the west. Some might have escaped and be heading east even as we were. We had to beat them there. It was the gamble I made as we passed the burnt-out shell of Hexham. We had destroyed that last year. Corbridge was still held and we were challenged as we crossed the river but no arrow or bolt came our way. We rested the horses each hour to make sure they were not exhausted although we travelled light. Our armour was on the small sumpters for we travelled with as little weight as was possible.

The Castle and the Cathedral had been built on a large loop in the river. It was like an elongated O. At the southern end, on the side of the cathedral, there were trees and woods which abutted the river. My small force would wait there. As we had travelled over I had explained my plan to my knights. They helped to refine it. The biggest problem lay in the fact that I might be recognised. While we waited for dawn we shaved my beard. It would disguise me, as would the monk's habit I adopted. I could not take my sword but I did have two sharp daggers and they would have to do. Beneath my habit I would wear a leather byrnie for protection. Aiden and Harold donned their habits too. I had thought to take Sir Richard's son for he spoke Latin but Harold and Aiden had other skills which I needed.

I pointed to the small postern gate on the south-west corner of the wall close to the Cathedral. We could see the shadows of the guards as they patrolled the walls above it. "Watch for us there tomorrow in the late afternoon or early evening. Stay alert and watch for a signal."

As I turned to leave Edward said, "What if you are captured?"

"Then many men will die assaulting these mighty walls. Remember Edward, do not let knights head south on the road. I fear that William of Morpeth may wish to wreak revenge upon my manor. This is one of the main reasons I chose this as our way into the castle. It controls the road and gives us access to the gate."

Dick nodded, "Do not worry, my lord. I will have archers watching the road. None shall pass."

The three of us were barefoot and we walked around the bend in the river towards the stone bridge which the bishop had built across the river. We were walking over rough ground and the harsh winter had broken many of the stones so that, by the time dawn broke and we were closer to the bridge, our feet were cut and bleeding. It would aid the illusion that we were pilgrims who had come a long way. We made our way to the top of the low hill which was opposite the bridge and we waited under a large elm tree for the road to Durham to become busy. I knew that they would be watchful but Durham was a busy place and with the extra garrison it would require more food than it had stored. I counted on busy traffic across the bridge and through the gate. We watched dawn as it broke in the east.

We rested but did not sleep. Hidden from the road we could hear the carts and the people as they headed for the castle. At first a trickle, it became a throng as the morning progressed. We joined after a pair of carts had passed. We would walk in between the two of them. The man leading the horse of the first cart turned and said, "Good morning, father."

I made the sign of the cross and blessed him in Latin. "Good morning, my son. This road is busy. I had thought it to be quiet."

"It normally is but the castle has many visitors." He pointed at my bleeding feet. "You look to have travelled far."

"We are here on pilgrimage to see Saint Cuthbert's bones."

"He was a great man. Many who have been to see them have had miraculous cures." He and his son who accompanied him spent the last mile or so to the bridge telling us stories of the cures. The result was that we did not even have to tell our story to the sentries at the bridge. They waved us across with the carts. I could have brought my sword! Once over the bridge, the road wound up to the walls of the bailey. Our carter friend halted his cart. "We will rest the horses here, father, and carry our goods up to the castle."

"We can help, my son."

The carter shook his head, "No father, for you are on God's work and making a pilgrimage."

We trudged up the hill. I saw that an attacker would have to endure arrows, stones and spears all the way to the main gate. We passed the stalls and the booths selling food and other necessities. It was already busy and I could see why the carter had left his horse at the foot of the hill. He would have struggled to find the space for the horse and the cart. There was a throng of people in Durham.

This time we were stopped at the main gate into the castle proper. There were four men at arms and they crossed their poleaxes before us. I had my cowl over my head to help with my disguise and I peered up from beneath the dark recess but I did not recognise them.

"What is your business, father?"

"We have travelled from Mount Grace to pay homage to St Cuthbert and seek his help." I held out my hand and took Aiden's maimed one. "Our brother here was attacked by a wolf in the winter and he cannot use his fingers. We believe that St Cuthbert can heal him."

"Aye, we had problems with wolves too, father." He shook his head, "What a shame to lose a hand when so young. Pass, father, but expect to be challenged." He leaned in, "There are enemies aplenty. If you are stopped then say that Roger of Rothbury allowed you to pass."

"Thank you, my son," I made the sign of the cross, "God will reward your kindness."

We entered the castle and crossed the green towards the Cathedral. It would not do to study the keep too much and we would have time enough for that later on. There were more stalls and booths close to the cathedral. Pilgrims often looked to purchase something after they had visited the cathedral and the saint's shrine. St Cuthbert must have been a mighty man to have so many bones. Every booth offered us a digit of the saint or a lock of his hair. As soon as we said we were Carthusians we were ignored. That order shunned wealth of any description. We were considered as the lowest of the low for we had no coins.

The Cathedral doors were open. Inside there were worshippers who had prostrated themselves on the floor of the mighty Cathedral. Although I had visited Durham many times I had yet to visit the interior. A lay brother approached us and spoke in Latin. He asked our business. When I said we were Carthusians he too became disinterested. Had we been Benedictines or Cistercians then he would have seen the potential for a donation. I waved a hand, excitedly in the direction of the crypt and we headed towards the other pilgrims who were there. As we approached I saw that many of them were knights. I pulled my hood further forward, grateful for the Stygian gloom. It would not do to be recognised here.

We waited patiently for spaces to appear. The four knights who turned almost knocked us over. When they saw our habits, they apologised. "Sorry, father we did not see you."

"There is no need to apologise my son, God forgives all in this holy place. Go with God."

As I made the sign of the cross they bowed and scurried off. We knelt by the crypt for some time to show our penitence. After a suitable time had elapsed we walked back into the light of the Palace Green. There was a stall selling small cakes with a cross in the middle. The smell made me hungry. Surprisingly the stall holder approached us and bowed with an offering in his hand, "Father, some knights came out and said to give the three barefoot monks food." He handed us two of the cakes.

I shook my head, "We have no coins or wealth, my son. We are Carthusians, a poor order."

"The knights paid. They said you had blessed them."

As we took the cakes and headed for a quiet corner of the green I wondered what they would think when they faced my sword? We sat well away from anyone else and slowly ate our cakes. We needed to become part of the Cathedral so that no one noticed us. I was studying the defences. I could see the postern gate and its two sentries. I believed we could easily dispose of those. The gate into the keep was a larger problem. It was guarded by one knight and six men at arms. No one was getting through. I had already seen that the gate from the town and the bridge was heavily guarded too. My men could take the bridge but they would never be able to take the barbican. It would be up to Dick and my archers. I looked carefully at the gate into the keep. There looked to be an entrance at the level of the green and then two more which led, from the first floor to the ramparts. That gave me hope. We could use the ramparts to gain entrance to the gatehouse in the keep. With that secure we had a chance.

As the afternoon wore on I became worried that we would be noticed. The stalls and the booths departed leaving us conspicuous on the green. I led my two companions back into the Cathedral. It was almost empty now. The priest who had approached us before frowned as we entered. "We close the doors when it becomes dark brother."

I nodded and smiled. "Brother Aiden's hand showed signs of improvement after we visited the relics. Show him, Brother Aiden." Aiden waggled one finger. "When we arrived, he could move none of them. This is a miracle. Allow us to stay within until dark, brother. God works in mysterious ways."

I saw the priest already adding to the story so that the miracle of St Cuthbert could continue. Miracles such as this, especially to a maimed priest, would bring even more pilgrims to the crypt and that meant more money.

"Of course, brother. Praise God!"

We prostrated ourselves next to the tomb. When the priest had departed to the doors we rose. Once it became dark then we could begin our real work.

Chapter 19

"I am sorry brothers but we must close the doors." The priest leaned in and said quietly, "There are many unsavoury soldiers in the castle and they are not averse to taking our plate and our candlesticks."

We had managed to last until almost dark but now the priest was ejecting us."I understand and the Saint is helping Brother Aiden. He can feel more in one of his other fingers. We shall return tomorrow. With the help of Saint Cuthbert and God he shall be cured."

"Have you somewhere to sleep?" Since the apparent miracle the priest had become friendlier.

"We are a poor order and used to hardship. We will sleep on the green."

He shook his head, "No, I insist that you come to the chapter house and share our food. Then you can sleep within our walls."

I shook my head, "We will share your food but we must endure hardship. In our own cells, we sleep in hair shirts. A night on the grass will seem like luxury to us and we need to endure pain as our lord did. We will share your food but we must abide by our rules."

He nodded sympathetically. I daresay he was wondering why anyone would endure such rigorous rules. It is strange the way that fate intervenes. The priest had changed completely since we had first met him and now we would have somewhere to wait while the sentries were set for the night. I had not planned this and yet it was working out better than I could have hoped.

It was dark when we bade farewell to the priests in the chapter house. The gruel we had eaten had filled a hole. We slipped along the side of the cathedral keeping to the shadows. We had found, when we had watched in daylight, a storeroom behind the Cathedral. It looked to contain the stones and the tools the masons were using to build the Cathedral. Although the main work was done they had the intricate carving to finish. It was a large empty room and we could use it later. There were now three guards there. Two were on the walls and one was by the postern gate itself. I frowned. This had not been in my plan. We were far enough away to be able to talk without being heard.

As we watched we saw a knight leave the gate and walk across the green. He approached the sentry at the gate and spoke to him and then ascended the stairs. He continued his walk back around to the far stairs and descended. I guessed he did this periodically. We had to act before he returned.

"Harold, Aiden, could you get on the walls and take out the two sentries?"

They looked and nodded. Harold said, "We would need a distraction."

"I can provide that. Watch for my approach and I will speak with the guard by the postern gate." They both flitted like shadows across the green. The wall which surrounded the castle, the Cathedral and the green was a large one and they had guards at the gates only. The nature of the defences of the castle meant that it was believed to be impossible to assault the walls. The river and the high bluffs would stop almost every type of attack. When I saw their shadows vanish from view I walked towards the gate. As I went I slipped my dagger into my right hand. The guard at the gate was suspicious and he called up to his two comrades.

"Ralph, someone approaches."

One of the figures on the wall, illuminated by the brand he held threw the brand down and shouted, "See who it is."

As I approached the sentry held the torch to get a better view of me. I saw the relief on his face when he saw my habit. "You cannot approach the gate, father."

"I thought to bathe my feet in the river, my son. I hoped that Saint Cuthbert's good would extend there." I had the attention of the two men on the walls and I saw the shadows as they slipped along.

The guard with the torch lowered it and his gaze as I lifted one foot. "They are a mess, father, but we cannot let you out. It is more than our lives are worth. Sir William would have our eyes. He can be a cruel master."

In one motion I drew my dagger, grabbed his helmet and plunged my dagger into his throat. The two sentries above were already oozing their lives away. Harold and Aiden had been silent assassins. I took the torch and went to the postern gate. I waved it and then closed the gate. I took the helmet and weapons from the dead man and, after opening the gate again, rolled his body down the slope. I discarded the monk's habit revealing my leather byrnie beneath. I donned the helmet and grabbed the spear. If anyone looked they would see three guards still. Aiden and

Harold were now disrobed and dressed as guards. I threw the brand up to Harold. All had to appear as normal as possible.

It was strangely quiet. I hoped that Dick and the archers would be able to make it across the river. It was not moving swiftly but, even so, it would not be easy. When the door opened to reveal a bedraggled Captain of archers I was relieved. I pointed to the mason's store. "You can prepare over there."

He grinned as he handed me two bow staves and quivers, "I wondered if you would have managed it, my lord. I should have had more faith."

I gestured at the cathedral, "This is the place for faith, Dick."

As my twelve dripping archers scurried past me I knew that we had now set things in motion and we could not halt them. Even now Edward would be leading the rest of my men to take the bridge gate. Although it would not be easy they would be attacking when the sentries least expected it. I hoped that the Earl had managed to bring the army or this could be the end to the conroi of Baron Alfraed of Norton. If anything went wrong at this point then all fifteen of us would die and our heads would adorn the spikes on the gate.

I climbed the stairs to join Aiden and Harold now dressed in the dead guards' clothes. I gave them the bow staves and they started to string them."Can you see anything?"

Aiden pointed to the east. "I can see the first thin line of dawn my lord. It will not be long."

"Remember we wait until the guards go to the walls and then we enter the keep."

"Aye my lord." Harold hesitated, "Are you certain they will do that. Will they not just stay in the keep?"

"That depends upon the Earl. If the rebels see the banners of our army outside then they will have to defend the walls. We have cast the bones let us see how they fall. It may be that I have to come up with another strategy." I looked towards the gate to the keep. I could see the guards moving now that it was a little lighter. "Keep watch over there and listen for the sound of our attack. I will find Dick."

The archers all had their bows strung. "Have the door ajar and you will hear the sound of the alarm bell. When you hear it then rush to the walls as though you are the guards. With luck they will not notice where you come from. We will try to take the gatehouse from the upper level of the walls."

"We will my lord. Do you think Edward and the knights will succeed?"

"I trust them. If any can take the bridge and hold it then I believe we have a chance."

I walked back across the increasingly lighter green. Suddenly I heard the clamour of battle in the distance. My men had attacked the bridge gate. A few moments later the alarm bell in the keep sounded. Aiden and Harold strung their bows. We looked over to the gate of the keep. It opened and knights and men at arms rushed into Palace Green and raced to the ramparts.

"Now!" I drew my sword and ran along the ramparts to the keep gate. I knew there had to be a way in from the walls as I had seen the knight disappear during the night watch. My two men followed me. A handful of men emerged from the gatehouse and moved along the walls. They were led by a knight and as we ran towards him he shouted, "Where are you going you fool? Get back to your post."

I knew that he would soon notice my archers flooding across the green to join us and I had to distract him. "My lord, the gate is under attack!" I pointed with my left hand and he turned. I ran him through and my archers sent their arrows to clear the walls of those who followed him. Their bodies fell to the ground. There was so much noise that their death cries went unnoticed. I felt naked without a shield but it could not be helped. I took my dagger and held it in my left hand.

They had left the door to the keep gatehouse open and I raced through it. There were four men at arms within. They looked in surprise at my arrival. I struck while they were still stunned. I stabbed one and ripped my dagger across the throat of a second. As they reached for their weapons I lunged forward. My sword caught one and the other shouted, "Treachery! Treachery!" Aiden's arrow ended his shout and I finished off the last defender.

"Harold, get down and close the gate." As he went I pointed to the door leading to the other side of the gate house. "Bar that door, Aiden."

I found a shield and, with that on my arm felt more secure. When Dick and my archers began to arrive in the tower I sent them down to help Harold. Aiden barred the other door so that the gate tower was now secure. I ran down the stairs, I heard the clatter of sword on sword and arrived just in time to see four men at arms coming from the interior of the keep. As Dick and his archers loosed their arrows the entrance was cleared.

"Dick, have four of your archers hold the gate until we have found the Bishop. Harold, grab a shield!" The gate was now as secure as it could be. Most of the defenders were now on the castle walls or in the towers at the main gate and along the wall.

If we could hold the keep then the men on the walls might be forced to surrender to the Earl. All I had were Aiden, Harold and twelve archers. It was hardly an army. I just hoped that the majority of the garrison were on the walls. I led my men up the stairs. They were designed to aid the defender but, thankfully, there were none who were coming down. We emerged on the first floor. I could hear raised voices coming from the Great Hall. I moved, silently, towards it. The rest of my men followed Harold behind me. We had three of us with swords and one of those was Aiden; he was no swordsman. The odds were not in our favour,

I listened, mainly to gauge numbers. They were Norman voices. "Give it up William of Morpeth. You have gambled and lost."

I heard Sir William's voice. "We have lost nothing. They have captured the bridge and that is all. So long as we hold the keep we can laugh away a siege. We are well prepared."

I heard the voice which I assumed was Bishop Flambard's, "If that is Robert of Caen outside then the siege will not be a long one. Surrender to me now and I will give you terms."

I heard a blow and a clatter as someone was knocked over, "There are my terms, Bishop. You are our hostage and the Earl of Gloucester will not risk your life!"

I had heard enough. I heard other movement in the hall but it did not suggest large numbers.

I waved my archers to move beyond us and then I leapt into the room. The Bishop of Durham lay on the ground being tended to by a pair of priests. Sir William and three of his knights were in the middle of the room and there were four men at arms. We had surprise on our side and I used it. I hurled myself towards them swinging my sword as I did so. I took one knight by surprise. He was still drawing his sword as I sliced down and across his neck. It was not a good sword I had taken but it hacked into his neck and he fell dead at my feet. I threw the sword at one of the men at arms who came at me with his spear levelled. He ducked and I dropped to my knees to pick up the sword the knight had been drawing. As I did so I felt a sharp pain in my shoulder. I flung my shield around and knocked the blade of William of Morpeth to the side.

I saw blood on his blade and knew I had been struck. "I will end now what Odo should have done. You may be a fine knight when wearing armour but that piece of leather will not lengthen your life."

I concentrated on what I would do and I ignored his words. I swung at his head. He had picked up his shield and he parried my blow. When he hacked at my shield I found I had no power in my arm. I was pushed back. As I stumbled backwards I saw that my archers' bows were of little use in such a confined space and they had to use their swords and daggers.

Seeing my weakness, William of Morpeth swung again at my shield. I anticipated it. I could not take many such blows and I spun around so that his blade missed me completely. I brought my sword around and hit his back. It did not sever the mail but it hurt him. Before he could turn I threw myself at his back and he tumbled to the ground. Out of the corner of my eye, I saw a man at arms hurl himself and his pole axe toward me. As I rolled away I saw Dick stab the man at arms but my movement allowed Sir William to leap to his feet and flee towards the tower of the keep, I ran after him. I could feel the blood as it trickled down my back. That in a way was reassuring for it was not gushing. I heard steps on the stairs behind me and saw that Harold and Aiden were following. Aiden had blood flowing from a scalp wound but he was grinning and I knew it was not life threatening.

As I stepped out into the light I had to react quickly as one of the tower sentries lunged at me. His sword slid across my middle. The leather prevented it slicing into me. I hacked down with my own sword and lunged at him with my shield held up. He tumbled over and cracked his head on the stone of the tower. I just managed to bring my shield up as a crossbowman sent a bolt in my direction. It pierced the shield. I ran at him before he could reload and I ran him through. Dick and the archers joined me. Ignoring everyone else I made for Sir William. I would leave them to deal with the rest of those who manned the tower.

Despite his wounding of me he was afraid. I could see it in his eyes. This had to end quickly. If I died then my men might lose heart and we would be defeated. If the Earl did not take Durham then my people might be in danger. My father's words came into my head, *'They are your people. You must protect them.'*

I rushed at him. I had no armour and a poor helmet. I could afford to take no blows. All that I had was the speed of my borrowed blade. As he slashed wildly at me I feinted towards his head with my sword and even as he brought his shield around I switched my attack and jabbed forward. His shield parried nothing and the tip of my sword sank into surcoat, mail, gambeson and then the unmistakable softness of flesh. Although I did not penetrate far it was a shock and he stepped back. I was becoming weaker and I knew it. I punched with my shield. Although it hurt me he parried weakly and I was able to bring my sword around at head height. He was so disorientated that he had no idea where the blow was coming from. As he tripped backwards, the edge of my sword took him in the neck and, as he flung his arms outwards, his head flew one way and his body the other. Sir William of Morpeth, traitor and rebel died at Durham.

As I sank to my knees I yelled, "Get their standard down! Dick, rain death upon their walls!"

I lay in a widening pool of blood. I knew that my handful of archers would use every arrow to clear the walls. I had done all that I could. Now it was down to Edward and the Earl of Gloucester.

Harold ran over to me and ripped the surcoat from Sir William. He jammed it beneath my byrnie. "My lord! You are wounded."

I smiled, "Just stop the bleeding. When Wulfric arrives, he will heal me." I could feel myself becoming woozy. I leaned on Harold and pulled myself towards the battlements. I could see that Dick and his archers, although few in number were raining death upon the defenders. There was no protection from them. The walls were being relentlessly cleared and that allowed the attackers to scale the walls. The Earl of Gloucester and his army had already forced the men at arms from some parts of the ramparts. We were forcing them back. I wondered if I would survive until the end of the battle. I could no longer hold onto Harold and I felt myself slipping down the stone.

I heard cheers and saw the smiles on my men's faces.

I heard Dick shout, "We have won! My lord, they are surrendering!"

I smiled, we had won. I had gambled and won. At least our army had won; as for myself then that was in the hands of God. I closed my eyes and I saw my father smiling at me. He held out his hand to grasp it. I tried to reach up but I could not. Suddenly I heard Wulfric's voice, "My lord! Come back to us!" I opened my eyes and saw a bloodied Edward looking at me with deep concern. "Sir Edward, grasp his hand I am losing him."

I felt myself slipping into a deep sleep. It was comfortable. It was like sinking into a hot bath. I closed my eyes again. Why should I fight this warm feeling which was washing over me?

Suddenly I felt a sharp pain in my back and when I opened my eyes I was staring at the stone floor of the tower of Durham Keep. I could hear voices but I could see nothing. "Hold him still! Bring fire! I must staunch the bleeding or we shall lose our lord."

I wondered who they were speaking of as I slipped slowly into a deep sleep. There was nothing to fight. This was meant to be. Suddenly I heard the voice of Adela. *'Come back to me! Alfraed! Come back!'*

I opened my eyes and I was looking at a ceiling. The stone floor of the keep had been there when I closed my eyes and now it was a ceiling. It was plainly decorated but it was a ceiling. Where was the sky? A face loomed into view. It was the Earl of Gloucester. He smiled, "You have come back. We thought we had lost you." He grasped my arm. "You have saved the north for your liege lord. Well done Baron Alfraed!"

I saw my knights gathered behind him and the priest I had spoken to was wiping his bloodied hands on a cloth. "You were near to death for a while my lord. I have stitched your back but you will not be fighting for some time."

The Earl clapped him on the back, "Do not worry priest, thanks to the efforts of the Baron and his men the north will be safe for some time."

My back felt numb and I felt sleepy. I suspect I had been given some potion to make me sleep and to ease my pain. "And the rebels?"

"The heads of their leaders adorn the walls. Some of their men escaped across the river." He smiled, "Some left the postern gate unguarded and they fled through there. I will lead my men north to gather tribute from the dead rebels' lands. Your conroi will wait here until you are fit to travel. Then you can go home, Baron Alfraed. You have, indeed, earned the title 'Defender of the Valley.' You will be rewarded."

Epilogue

Adela and I were married soon after Midsummer Day. As I had lain in the bed in Durham I realised that I had come closer to death than at any time in my life. The thought of dying without heirs and, even worse, without giving Adela the chance of some happiness prompted me to honour my promise. We were able to make it a fine celebration for we had the ransoms from the rebels and our share of the tribute from the Earl's northern foray. He was generous. We were able to hire more men at arms and to arm and mount them.

William the Mason had begun a small church in Stockton. Bishop Flambard was so grateful to me for saving him that he consecrated the church himself and provided the priest, an earnest young man called Father Absalom. Although the church roof had yet to be raised the weather was so clement that we married in the half-finished edifice. Adela and Faren had it decorated with sweet-smelling flowers so that our roof was a fragrant lattice of fragrant summer flowers.

My knights attended with their families. All of them were now rich and that enabled them to be well attended. Their retinues were enlarged and their manors better defended. I knew that even if trouble came whilst I was recovering then the valley would be in safe hands. I had a most pleasant summer as I slowly recovered and learned how to love Adela.

When King Henry returned from Normandy in the autumn I received a message to tell me that he would be visiting the northern barons to thank those who had been loyal and to punish those who had not. Adela, now with child, enjoyed the opportunity to spend some of my gold on fine plates and furniture for the visit of the King. Stockton itself was transformed. The council of guilds had paved the main streets so that it would not be a quagmire in winter. The towers on the gates of the town had been rebuilt to make them sturdier and more imposing.

We watched as the King and his retinue were ferried across the river. The King, the Earl and his bodyguard came first. King Henry was genuinely pleased to see me. "My son has told me of your work over the last year. I know that you have striven to overcome great odds. Know that I appreciate it. I grant you permission to create a manor at Hartburn and to tax the ships which use your river. This is now a bastion. You have shown that you can defend this land."

"Thank you, my liege, and this is the Lady Adela, my wife."

The King kissed her hand. "She is as lovely as my son told me. Soon you will be a father." He looked a little sad, "Since my son died I have felt a hole in my heart. You will soon be filling your heart with your child."

"I hope so."

"The Empress sends her regards and reminds you that you are still a knight of her order."

I touched the medallion I always wore. "And Edward and I are still her men."

The ferry bumped into the harbour wall and knights disembarked. The King held his hand out, "This is my nephew, Stephen of Blois."

As I went to greet the knight who smiled at me I realised that I knew him. It was the knight I had seen in Normandy; it was the knight with red shield. I smiled and shook his hand. If he would play a game of deceit then so would I. That day I met the man I would fight for the rest of our lives. I met the man who tried to steal the throne of England from Matilda, the man who made civil war and shattered the peace of England. I would not enjoy peace for long. I was a Marcher Lord and I would have to fight to save my land, my manor, my people and my Empress.

The End

Glossary

Battle- a formation in war (a modern battalion)

Cadge- the frame upon which hunting birds are carried (by a codger- hence the phrase old codger being the old man who carries the frame)

Conroi- A group of knights fighting together

Demesne- estate

Destrier- war horse

Fess- a horizontal line in heraldry

Gambeson- a padded tunic worn underneath mail. When worn by an archer they came to the waist. It was more of a quilted jacket but I have used the term freely

Gonfanon- A standard used in Medieval times (Also known as a Gonfalon in Italy)

Hartness- the manor which became Hartlepool

Maredudd ap Bleddyn- King of Powys

Mêlée- a medieval fight between knights

Musselmen- Muslims

Palfrey- a riding horse

Pyx- a box containing a holy relic (Shakespeare's Pax from Henry V)

Surcoat- a tunic worn over mail or armour

Sumpter- packhorse

Tagmata- Byzantine cavalry

Ventail – a piece of mail which covered the neck and the lower face.

Wulfestun- Wolviston (Durham)

Historical note

The book is set during one of the most turbulent and complicated times in British history. Henry I of England and Normandy's eldest son William died. The King named his daughter, Empress Matilda as his heir. However, her husband, the Emperor of the Holy Roman Empire died and she remarried. Her new husband was Geoffrey of Anjou and she had children by him. (The future Henry II of England and Normandy- The Lion in Winter!)

When the King died the Empress was in Normandy and the nephew of Henry sailed for England where he was crowned king. A number of events happened then which showed how the politics of the period worked. King David of Scotland who was related to both Stephen and Matilda declared his support for Matilda. In reality, this was an attempt to grab power and he used the Norman knights of Cumbria and Northumbria to take over that part of England and invade Yorkshire. Stephen came north to defeat him- King David, having lost the Battle of the Standard fled north of the Tees.

The Scots were taking advantage of a power vacuum on their borders. They did, according to chroniclers of the time behave particularly badly.

"an execrable army, more atrocious than the pagans, neither fearing God nor regarding man, spread desolation over the whole province and slaughtered everywhere people of either sex, of every age and rank, destroying, pillaging and burning towns, churches and houses"

"Then (horrible to relate) they carried off, like so much booty, the noble matrons and chaste virgins, together with other women. These naked, fettered, herded together; by whips and thongs they drove before them, goading them with their spears and other weapons. This took place in other wars, but in this to a far greater extent."

"For the sick on their couches, women pregnant and in childbed, infants in the womb, innocents at the breast, or on the mother's knee, with the mothers themselves, decrepit old men and worn-out old women, and persons debilitated from whatever cause, wherever they met with them, they put to the edge of the sword, and transfixed with their spears; and by how much more horrible a death they could dispatch them, so much the more did they rejoice."

Robert of Hexham

Meanwhile Matilda's half brother, Robert of Gloucester (one of William's bastards) declared for Matilda and a civil war ensued. The war went on until Stephen died and was called the anarchy because everyone was looking out for themselves. There were no sides as such. Allies could become enemies overnight. Murder, ambush and assassination became the order of the day. The only warriors who could be relied upon were the household knights of a lord- his oathsworn. The feudal system, which had been an ordered pyramid, was thrown into confusion by the civil war. Lords created their own conroi, or groups of knights and men at arms. Successful lords would ensure that they had a mixture of knights, archers and foot soldiers. The idea of knights at this time always fighting on horseback is not necessarily true. There were many examples of knights dismounting to fight on foot and, frequently, this proved to be successful.

The word Fitz shows that the owner of the name is an illegitimate son of a knight. As such they would not necessarily inherit when their father died. There were many such knights. William himself was illegitimate. Robert of Gloucester was also known as Robert of Caen and Robert Fitzroy.

Ridley, the father of my hero, was in three earlier books. There were two regiments of Varangians: one was English in character and one Scandinavian. As the bodyguards of the Emperor they were able to reap rich rewards for their service.

The Normans were formidable fighters. The conquest of England happened after a single battle. They conquered southern Italy and Sicily with a handful of knights. Strongbow, a Norman mercenary took a small mercenary force and dominated Ireland so much that as soon as a force of Normans, led by the King landed, all defence on the island crumbled. In one of Strongbow's battles a force of 100 knights defeated 4000 Irish warriors!

Ranulf Flambard was the controversial Bishop of Durham who was imprisoned in the tower by Henry for supporting his brother. Although reinstated the Bishop was viewed with suspicion by the King and did not enjoy as much power as either his predecessors or his successors. Hartness (Hartlepool) was given to the De Brus family by Henry and the family played a power game siding with Henry and David depending upon what they had to gain. They were also given land around Guisborough in North Yorkshire.

Squires were not always the sons of nobles. Often, they were lowly born and would never aspire to knighthood. It was not only the king who could make knights. Lords had that power too. Normally a man would become a knight at the age of 21. Young landless knights would often leave home to find a master to serve in the hope of treasure or loot. The idea of chivalry was some way away. The Norman knight wanted land, riches and power. Knights would have a palfrey or ordinary riding horse and a destrier or war horse. Squires would ride either a palfrey, if they had a thoughtful knight or a rouncy (pack horse). The squires carried all of the knight's war gear on the pack horses. Sometimes a knight would have a number of squires serving him. One of the squire's tasks was to have a spare horse in case the knight's destrier fell in battle. Another way for a knight to make money was to capture an enemy and ransom him. This even happened to Richard 1st of England who was captured in Austria and held to ransom.

At this time, a penny was a valuable coin and often payment would be taken by 'nicking' pieces off it. Totally round copper and silver coins were not the norm in 12th Century Europe. Each local ruler would make his own small coins. The whole country was run like a pyramid with the King at the top. He took from those below him in the form of taxes and service and it cascaded down. There was a great deal of corruption as well as anarchy. The idea of a central army did not exist. King Henry had his household knights and would call upon his nobles to supply knights and men at arms when he needed to go to war. The expense for that army would be borne by the noble.

The border between England and Scotland has always been a prickly one from the time of the Romans onward. Before that time the border was along the line of Glasgow to Edinburgh. The creation of an artificial frontier, Hadrian's Wall, created an area of dispute for the people living on either side of it. William the Conqueror had the novel idea of slaughtering everyone who lived between the Tees and the Tyne/Tweed in an attempt to resolve the problem. It did not work and lords on both sides of the borders, as well as the monarchs, used the dispute to switch sides as it suited them.

The manors I write about were around at the time the book is set. For a brief time, a De Brus was lord of Normanby it changed hands a number of times until it came under the control of the Percy family. This is a work of fiction but I have based events on the ones which occurred in the twelfth century.

I can find no evidence for a castle in Norton although it was second in importance only to Durham and I assume that there must have been a defensive structure of some kind there. I suspect it was a wooden structure built to the north of the present church. The church in Norton is Norman but it is not my church. Stockton Castle was pulled down in the Civil War of the 17th Century. It was put up in the early fourteenth century. My castle is obviously earlier. As Stockton became a manor in the 11th century and the river crossing was important I am guessing that there would have been a castle there. There may have been an earlier castle on the site of Stockton Castle but until they pull down the hotel and shopping centre built on the site it is difficult to know for sure. The simple tower with a curtain wall was typical of late Norman castles. The river crossing was so important that I have to believe that there would have been some defensive structure there before the 1300s. The manor of Stockton was created in 1138. To avoid confusion in the later civil war I have moved it forward by a few years.

Vikings continued to raid the rivers and isolated villages of England for centuries. There are recoded raids as late as the sixteenth century along the coast south of the Fylde. These were to the huge raids of the ninth and tenth centuries but were pirates keen for slaves and treasure. The Barbary Pirates also raided the southern coast. Alfred's navy had been a temporary measure to deal with the Danish threat. A Royal Navy would have to wait until Henry VIII.

The Welsh did take advantage of the death of the master of Chester and rampaged through Cheshire. King Henry and his knights defeated them although King Henry was wounded by an arrow. The King's punishment was the surrender of 10,000 cattle. The Welsh did not attack England again until King Henry was dead!

Matilda was married to the Emperor of the Holy Roman Emperor, Henry, in 1116 when she was 14. They had no children and the marriage was not a happy one. When William Adelin died in the White Ship disaster then Henry had no choice but to name his daughter as his heir however, by that time she had been married to Geoffrey Count of Anjou, Fulk's son and King Henry was suspicious of his former enemy's heir. His vacillation caused the civil war which was known as the Anarchy. However, those events are several books away. Stephen and Matilda are just cousins: soon they will become enemies.

In the high middle ages, there was a hierarchy of hawks. At this time, there was not. A baron was supposed to have a bustard which is not even a hawk. Some think it was a corruption of buzzard or was a generic name for a hawk of indeterminate type. Aiden finds hawks' eggs and raises them. The cadge was the square frame on which the hawks were carried and it was normally carried by a man called a codger. Hence the English slang for old codger; a retainer who was too old for anything else. It might also be the derivation of cadge (ask for) a lift- more English slang.

Gospatric was a real character. His father had been Earl of Northumberland but was replaced by William the Conqueror. He was granted lands in Scotland, around Dunbar. Once the Conqueror was dead he managed to gain lands in England around the borders. He was killed at the Battle of the Standard fighting for the Scots. I had used this as the basis for his treachery. He was succeeded by his son, Gospatric, but the family confirmed their Scottish loyalties. His other sons are, as far as I know my own invention although I daresay if he was anything like the other lords and knights he would have been spreading his largess around to all and sundry!

The incident with Bishop Flambard being held captive is pure fiction. However, he died in 1128 and there was a great deal of unrest while King Henry was away in Normandy. The Gospatric family did show their true colours when the Scottish king tried to take advantage of the internal strife between Stephen and Matilda and invade England. A leopard does not change his spots. The land between the Tees and the Scottish Lowlands was always fiercely contested by Scotland, England and those who lived there.

Hartburn is a small village just outside Stockton. My American readers may be interested to know that the Washington family of your first President lived there and were lords of the manor from the fourteenth century onwards. In the sixteenth century, they had it taken from them and it was replaced by the manor of Wessington, which became Washington. Had they not moved then your president might live in Hartburn DC!

Books used in the research:
The Varangian Guard- 988-1453 Raffael D'Amato

Saxon Viking and Norman- Terence Wise
The Walls of Constantinople AD 324-1453-Stephen Turnbull
Byzantine Armies- 886-1118- Ian Heath
The Age of Charlemagne-David Nicolle
The Normans- David Nicolle
Norman Knight AD 950-1204- Christopher Gravett
The Norman Conquest of the North- William A Kappelle
The Knight in History- Francis Gies
The Norman Achievement- Richard F Cassady

Griff Hosker April 2015

Other Books by Griff Hosker

If you enjoyed reading this book, then why not read another one by the author?

Ancient History

The Sword of Cartimandua Series
(Germania and Britannia 50 A.D. – 128 A.D.)
Ulpius Felix- Roman Warrior (prequel)
The Sword of Cartimandua
The Horse Warriors
Invasion Caledonia
Roman Retreat
Revolt of the Red Witch
Druid's Gold
Trajan's Hunters
The Last Frontier
Hero of Rome
Roman Hawk
Roman Treachery
Roman Wall
Roman Courage

The Wolf Warrior series
(Britain in the late 6th Century)
Saxon Dawn
Saxon Revenge
Saxon England
Saxon Blood
Saxon Slayer
Saxon Slaughter
Saxon Bane
Saxon Fall: Rise of the Warlord
Saxon Throne
Saxon Sword

Medieval History

The Dragon Heart Series
Viking Slave
Viking Warrior
Viking Jarl
Viking Kingdom
Viking Wolf
Viking War
Viking Sword
Viking Wrath
Viking Raid
Viking Legend
Viking Vengeance
Viking Dragon
Viking Treasure
Viking Enemy
Viking Witch
Viking Blood
Viking Weregeld
Viking Storm
Viking Warband
Viking Shadow
Viking Legacy
Viking Clan
Viking Bravery

The Norman Genesis Series
Hrolf the Viking
Horseman
The Battle for a Home
Revenge of the Franks
The Land of the Northmen
Ragnvald Hrolfsson
Brothers in Blood
Lord of Rouen
Drekar in the Seine
Duke of Normandy
The Duke and the King

New World Series
Blood on the Blade
Across the Seas
The Savage Wilderness
The Bear and the Wolf

The Vengeance Trail

The Reconquista Chronicles
Castilian Knight
El Campeador
The Lord of Valencia

The Aelfraed Series
(Britain and Byzantium 1050 A.D. - 1085 A.D.)
Housecarl
Outlaw
Varangian

**The Anarchy Series England
1120-1180**
English Knight
Knight of the Empress
Northern Knight
Baron of the North
Earl
King Henry's Champion
The King is Dead
Warlord of the North
Enemy at the Gate
The Fallen Crown
Warlord's War
Kingmaker
Henry II
Crusader
The Welsh Marches
Irish War
Poisonous Plots

Knight of the Empress

The Princes' Revolt
Earl Marshal

Border Knight
1182-1300
Sword for Hire
Return of the Knight
Baron's War
Magna Carta
Welsh Wars
Henry III
The Bloody Border
Baron's Crusade
Sentinel of the North
War in the West

Sir John Hawkwood Series
France and Italy 1339- 1387
Crécy: The Age of the Archer
Man At Arms (January 2021)

Lord Edward's Archer
Lord Edward's Archer
King in Waiting
An Archer's Crusade

Struggle for a Crown
1360- 1485
Blood on the Crown
To Murder A King
The Throne
King Henry IV
The Road to Agincourt
St Crispin's Day

Tales from the Sword

Modern History

The Napoleonic Horseman Series
Chasseur à Cheval
Napoleon's Guard
British Light Dragoon
Soldier Spy
1808: The Road to Coruña
Talavera
The Lines of Torres Vedras
Bloody Badajoz
The Road to France

The Lucky Jack American Civil War series
Rebel Raiders
Confederate Rangers
The Road to Gettysburg

The British Ace Series
1914
1915 Fokker Scourge
1916 Angels over the Somme
1917 Eagles Fall
1918 We will remember them
From Arctic Snow to Desert Sand
Wings over Persia

Combined Operations series
1940-1945
Commando
Raider
Behind Enemy Lines
Dieppe
Toehold in Europe
Sword Beach
Breakout
The Battle for Antwerp
King Tiger
Beyond the Rhine
Korea
Korean Winter

Other Books
Great Granny's Ghost (Aimed at 9-14-year-old young people)

For more information on all of the books then please visit the author's web site at www.griffhosker.com where there is a link to contact him or visit his Facebook page: GriffHosker at Sword Books

Made in the USA
Columbia, SC
24 March 2021